She Knew
He Was Going to Kiss Her
before He Even
Lowered His Lips to Hers. . . .

She waited expectantly, filled with anticipation. His skin was a healthy golden-tan and the small scar above his eye was nearly covered with a lock of hair falling across it. She focused on the scar as he brought his head down to hers. When his lips touched the coolness of her own, she forgot the scar, the tan and her protests. She was conscious only of the gently insistent pressure of his lips on hers.

Putting his hands around her back, he drew her closer as his kisses deepened. Kate knew he was pulling her into the whirlpool of emotions she had tried so hard to avoid; she felt heady with the excitement of the moment and immensely secure at being so close to him. The increasing fervor of his kisses fueled her own desire, but lacing through that growing longing was a trembling feeling of panic. She was standing on the edge of something very vast, and she knew she had never been there before.

ROMANCE LOVERS DELIGHT

Purchase any book for $2.95
plus $1.50 shipping & handling for each book.

___ **ROYAL SUITE** by Marsha Alexander. Fabulous success threatens the passion of new love.

___ **MOMENTS TO SHARE** by Diana Morgan. Her ambition might destroy the only man she ever loved.

___ **ROMAN CANDLES** by Sofi O'Bryan. In the splendor of the Eternal City she found a daring and dangerous lover.

___ **TRADE SECRETS** by Diana Morgan. Passion and power steam the windows amidst the world of publishing.

___ **AFTERGLOW** by Jordana Daniels. She had but one choice to make — glamorous romance or success.

___ **A TASTE OF WINE** by Vanessa Pryor. In lush vineyards, she took her first intoxicating sip of love.

___ **ON WINGS OF SONG** by Martha Brewster. In the glory days of opera, their voices mingled in passionate melody.

___ **A PROMISE IN THE WIND** by Perdita Shepherd. A peasant beauty captured by a ruling enemy, desired by a noble love.

___ **WHISPERS OF DESTINY** by Jenifer Dalton. While love bloomed in her heart, the seeds of war grew in her homeland.

___ **SUNRISE TEMPTATION** by Lynn Le Mon. Her defiant heart battled between the power of wealth and the pursuit of passion.

___ **WATERS OF EDEN** by Katherine Kent. She tasted the fruits of passion that grew wild in a lover's paradise.

___ **ARABESQUE** by Rae Butler. Two defiant hearts, one impossible love dared to challenge the might of a nation.

Send check or money order (no cash or CODs) to:
PARADISE PRESS
8551 SUNRISE BLVD. #302   PLANTATION, FL 33322

Name _____

Address _____

City_____ State_____ ZIP_____

FOR LOVE ALONE

Candice Adams

Paradise Press, Inc.

Plantation, Florida

EXCLUSIVE DISTRIBUTION BY
PARADISE PRESS, INC.

ISBN #1-57657-233-1

Printed in the U.S.A.

*Dedicated to
Denise Marcil,
with Appreciation*

FOR LOVE
ALONE

Chapter 1

"The noble Brutus hath told you Caesar was ambitious. If it were so, it was a grievous fault . . ." The words ran through Kate's mind as she walked down the hall beside the executive vice president of Amalacorp. She was ambitious. She wanted this job, and the more she saw of the Amalacorp offices and listened to Frank Moyer describing some of the projects his company was in the process of constructing, the more she wanted it.

"The structures and foundations sections are on the next floor up," Frank explained as they stopped at the end of the onyx-tiled corridor by the elevators. As he pushed the button, the distinguished-looking man with silver-gray hair continued encouragingly, "I'll take you up to Burke Walter's office now. He's anxious to meet you."

Kate smiled. "I'm looking forward to meeting him." She hoped the lie sounded convincing. From what she had heard of the president of Amalacorp Engineering, he was not the sort of man anyone actually wanted to meet. "Cold," "calculating" and "a real son of a bitch" were some of the milder epithets she had heard used to describe him. Personally, she didn't care if he was King Kong, she wanted the job of manager of projects, and he was the one who would make the final decision on hiring.

She and Frank stepped off the elevator on the top floor of the 45-story structure. "Burke's expecting us," Frank told the secretary in the spacious outer office as he walked past her toward the closed door. Kate followed.

Behind the door lay an even larger room with a wall of windows that looked out over downtown Dallas. Kate noticed the sweeping view only briefly before she focused on the man rising from behind the massive desk. He was balding, and had intense dark eyes that held her in a hard gaze. Burke Walters looked like a police interrogator inspecting a criminal, Kate thought as she flashed him a confident smile and they shook hands.

"Ms. Justin. I've been looking forward to meeting you. Sit down, please." He gestured toward the leather chairs in front of his desk. While she and Frank complied, he continued, "I guess Frank has shown you most of our little operation by now."

The "little operation" he spoke of was one of the largest civil engineering firms in the country. Kate was well aware that Burke Walters knew Amalacorp was twice the size of the company where she now worked.

"It's quite impressive, Mr. Walters," she said politely. Her instinct told her too much enthusiasm would not be well-received.

"Well, tell us a little bit about yourself," he said briskly as he paced slowly back and forth behind his desk. "I've heard what an excellent job you're doing for Higgins, Powers and Barnes. How many people are under you there, and what capacity are they in?"

"I supervise the drafting and pipeline sections," she replied. "That is a total of twenty-five people."

"I see." He walked as far as the window across a cantaloupe-colored carpet and gazed down to the street below as if he had just become aware that it was there.

Kate waited for the next question. The questions were purely a formality, of course. Amalacorp had not invited her from Kansas City to make such elementary inquiries. She was certain they had compiled a dossier on her that covered everything Burke was asking. Kate knew what Burke Walters really wanted was to see how she responded to his questions and to judge for himself the type of person she was, and probably also how eager she was to have the job.

Turning, he continued, "Where did you get your master's?"

"At Harvard," she answered simply.

"Oh, yes," he murmured, as if the answer to that question had occurred to him after he had asked it. "Then you worked for Grannon for a while, didn't you?" He didn't wait for her to answer before continuing, "At the risk of asking a question I'm sure you've heard a hundred times before, how did you get into the field of engineering?"

Kate *had* heard the question often. It was odd that after all those times she didn't have a pat answer, she thought fleetingly. "Science and math were always my strong points, so naturally I was interested in pursuing a course of study that would use them," she began. "Since I've always been more intrigued by the practical application of principles than by purely theoretical work, engineering appealed to me." With a smile, she added, "I suppose, also, I'm the type of person who likes to see results from my work. A bridge, a dam, a marina—those are tangible evidence that the science works. Engineering offers a constant challenge." She could hear the crisp, cool assurance in her words. She had learned to project a confidence she didn't feel

during her senior year of college, when she had re-
hearsed for her first interviews for engineering jobs.
But secretly she wondered if her assured answer had
been wasted on Burke Walters; perhaps he had really
been asking, "What's a nice girl like you doing in a field
like this?"

"I see," Burke said casually. "You mentioned engineering is a challenging field. Do you thrive on challenges?"

That was a tricky question, Kate thought. He was
really asking her to impart something of her personality
and explain to him the force that drove her. "To a
certain extent, I do. I couldn't work in a field that didn't
constantly demand me to keep pace with improvements
and progress. I suppose to that extent I thrive on
challenge." She concluded with a softening smile, "But
I don't look for complications when a simple solution
will do." Kate felt more sure of herself now, calmer and
more in control. Burke Walters had an unreadable
face, but a glance at Frank convinced her he was
pleased with her presentation of herself.

Burke looked down at a sheet of paper in front of
him. From where Kate sat it looked blank, but it must
have provided him with some inspiration, for he looked
up again and continued in a clipped tone, "You have
been with Higgins, Powers and Barnes for five years
now. I'm curious why you wish to leave that company."

Kate hesitated only an instant. He was asking about
company loyalty, she decided quickly. She put one
hand over the other in her lap and hoped the gesture
did not betray her nervousness. Careful, she warned
herself, she had to convince Burke Walters why she
wanted out of her present company without saying
anything derogatory about it. Well, she reminded herself, she had not expected the questions to be easy, and
she would be off the rack before long. "I enjoy the
work I do now, but I feel somewhat limited as to how
far I can advance. As you know, it's a small firm, and
the projects we undertake are not on such a large scale,

or as varied, as those Amalacorp builds." She looked at him to gauge whether she had said enough or if he expected her to add more.

"You spoke of advancement. You will be in a position of responsibility if you come to work here. Where will you expect to be in five years?"

For a moment she felt panic. She should have known he would ask her that question, but she had not fully considered it beforehand, and no answer came immediately to mind. If she told him she expected to be a company vice president she would look awfully pushy, but that was the next logical place she could go. If she *didn't* tell him she expected to be a company vice president, it might appear that she lacked drive and was going to coast from here on out. The thoughts flashed through her mind in confusion, but her carefully-modulated voice betrayed none of her inner turmoil.

"The position requires learning a great deal about the company and its employees. I realize it would take time, possibly more than a year, to become thoroughly acquainted with all facets of the company. In addition, as manager of projects I would constantly find myself in new situations and with new things to learn." She hadn't given a real answer to his question, but she had bought enough time to think it out, and now she knew what to say. "Frankly, I think where I might be in five years time at Amalacorp would depend on both myself and the company. I can foresee advancement to a higher level if the company is pleased with my performance and if I become thoroughly familiar with all aspects of the industry. However, even without a promotion, I think the changing nature of the work would provide a constant challenge." There was an art to fence-sitting, Kate mused as she turned her hands over in her lap. She hoped she had provided Burke Walters with the answer he wanted—the one that would make a difference in whether or not she got the job. She fervently hoped this ordeal would be over soon. If it went on much longer, both Frank and Burke were sure to realize that beneath her composed façade was a woman whose stomach was tied in knots.

"I see." Burke looked toward Frank. "Is there anything else we need to know?" he asked.

"I can't think of anything."

"Do you have any questions about Amalacorp, Ms. Justin?" Burke Walters asked; he had stopped behind the desk again with his eyes fixed on her. They swept over her conservative navy linen suit and navy and white striped blouse.

"No, I think Mr. Moyer has answered most of my questions," Kate replied. The interview was over; Kate knew to ask anything further would only annoy Burke Walters. He had seen what he wanted to see, and she suspected he had already made a decision. She wished she knew what it was, but his hooded eyes revealed nothing; she wondered if the other two contenders for the position had felt as curious as she did right now.

"It was good of you to come," Burke said, formally concluding the meeting as Kate and Frank stood. "I hope you enjoy the rest of your stay in Dallas."

"I'm sure I will." Smiles were exchanged as Frank ushered her out into the hall. They both stood word-lessly waiting for the elevator.

When the doors had closed and the secretary was left safely behind, Frank smiled at her. "You're doing great," he encouraged. "After lunch we'll meet the other vice presidents and I'll show you the rest of the building."

"Sounds good."

"In the meantime let's stop by and see the office you'll have if you come on board with Amalacorp."

She knew that was a tactful way of saying, "if Amalacorp decides to hire you." If she got the job, the raise in salary would be impressive and she would supervise twice the number of people she now super-vised. Those were attractive prospects, but they weren't her real reason for wanting the job so badly.

Even if she were promoted to a higher position with Higgins, Powers and Barnes, it wasn't a large enough firm to match the dazzling prospects Amalacorp offered. The more she saw of the large office building that housed Amalacorp, the more aware she was of the responsibility she would have and the respect she could command. And she wanted it. She and Caesar were a pair.

The doors to the elevator slid open, and Kate and Frank stepped out into another long hall, walking past Renaissance paintings hung beneath soft track-lights to a door at the other end of the hall. Kate walked through the secretary's office to a door marked "Foundations, Manager of Projects," and stepped inside, while Frank held the door open for her. Her eyes wandered from the wine-red expanse of carpeting to the pearl-gray walls accented at the floor and ceiling with patina-rich oak moldings. The plush carpeting gave beneath her tall heels as she crossed to the desk. She ran her hand lightly over the rich grain of the leather chair and gazed down at a faint reflection of herself in the top of the polished oak desk.

"This office also has a view of the city," Frank commented from the window. "Of course, we're only on the thirty-fourth floor, so it doesn't have the panorama Burke has. Still, it's not bad."

"The view is nice," she agreed as she glanced toward the window. But her eyes roved back immediately to a small conference table with six beige-colored chairs in one corner of the room. In another corner dark wooden bookcases displayed company reports in austere black bindings. As far as she was concerned, a brick wall would do just as well for a view; she was far more interested in the contents of those books and the things that would go on inside this office than she was in what went on in the world outside.

Frank started toward the door. "If you'll excuse me, I have to make a phone call. There's a lounge through the door behind you. I'll be back in a few minutes and we can go to lunch."

As he left, her eyes swept the room again, lingering on the walls that gleamed like damp mollusk shells. Around the large room hung colorful aerial pictures of projects Amalacorp had built. A large picture showed an azure-blue lake impounded behind a dam Kate was certain Amalacorp had constructed.

Kate turned and walked into the lounge. The small room, carpeted in a pile the color of a newly unfurled leaf, was furnished with chairs upholstered in a diamond-pattern of white against forest-green. The walls were hung with Impressionist-style paintings.

Someone in the company was a real art-lover, she reflected as she walked through the lounge into the rest room. Over a china pedestal lavatory, complete with brass fixtures, was an oval mirror. Kate stopped in front of it and surveyed her reflection.

She tried to look at herself as Burke Walters might have, and imagine what he had seen. The woman she scrutinized had black hair that fell in soft curls to her shoulders. Her face was oval-shaped and her skin was creamy, with two dashes of rose highlighting her cheekbones. Her lips were full, and dewy with the cinnamon gloss she had brushed over them this morning. And her eyes, set under delicately-arched black brows, were a deep violet.

Kate had never been vain, but she was honest enough to acknowledge that she was attractive. Sometimes she wished she were less so. She had often wondered if she would have to keep proving herself over and over again if she were more ordinary-looking. Now she wondered if her looks would work for or against her in landing the job she wanted so badly. She knew decisions on hiring were often based on irrelevant factors. The other candidates for the job were as qualified as she. The final selection would be based on someone's personal preference.

She plucked a speck of lint from the lapel of her tailored jacket, brushed a lock of hair back from her face, and returned to the office just as Frank entered. "Ready for lunch?" he asked cheerfully.

"Yes." She smiled at him as they started out the door. Frank was in her camp, she knew that, but she wondered if one of the other vice presidents was pulling just as hard for his own particular favorite. She hoped Frank would give her a few clues about how matters stood over lunch.

Kate was not disappointed. While they were seated over chef salads in a crowded restaurant that was redolent of cedar and airy with hanging ferns, he leaned forward with a confident look. "I think things are going well for you."

"Do you?" she murmured, and waited for him to continue.

"Robert Harris was here last week, but between the two of us, I think he's out of the running." He glanced around and lowered his voice. "He has something of a drinking problem," he confided. "He got a glowing report from his present company—*too* glowing, so we did a little more checking. I'm sure he's out of the game."

"I see." She added vinegar and oil to her salad and listened with the same outward calm as if he were discussing the weather instead of her future.

Frank's silver eyebrows lowered slightly in a frown. "I won't kid you about the other man. Oliver Sebastian is a damn good engineer, and he has a lot of experience. He's personable too, and Burke likes that in someone who'll be dealing with so many different people. Of course, that's an asset you have too. I think what it comes down to is whether Burke will want a person with more actual experience or someone with an advanced degree from one of the top schools in the country. The fact that you studied at Harvard will make a difference. Oliver doesn't have a master's, and Burke likes to see initials after his people's names. Of course," he concluded as he applied himself to his food, "I'm merely speculating."

"I understand." Admittedly, it wasn't as good as having him leak the news she was a shoo-in, but at least she knew she was no longer in competition with two people. "I really appreciate all you've done for me, Frank. I know you've pushed hard for me and I want to thank you, whichever way the decision goes."

"I'm doing it because I think you would be a real addition to our company," he replied.

"I'm flattered you think so." She was as sincere as she knew he was. Kate had met Frank Moyer at a concrete symposium five years ago, just after she had left Grannon for Higgins, Powers and Barnes. At the time he had occupied the position with Amalacorp that she now aspired to. They had seen each other afterward at other professional conventions, but it was at an American Society of Civil Engineers' seminar that they had really become friends. Kate and Frank had both been presenting papers, and he had been impressed both by the report she had delivered and the way she had handled the questions from skeptics.

Frank was a big supporter of ASCE. He believed a professional organization was the only way for a young engineer to learn about the field and grow. He had been pleased with Kate's interest in it. When he had run for an office in the organization, she had worked for his election among her colleagues. It had seemed only natural when the position in Amalacorp became vacant that Frank had suggested her name and called her to find out if she was interested.

The waitress arrived with their check. Frank put some money on the small tray and they stood. "Well, I guess we'd better get back."

She picked up her straw clutch-purse and stepped out into the brisk March afternoon. The city streets were crowded with lunchtime pedestrians as they threaded their way back to Amalacorp's steel and glass building.

Frank turned to her as they crossed the vast lobby of travertine marble. "I feel sure the final decision will be made this Friday, so I think you can expect a call on Monday." They moved into the crowded elevator and conversation between them ceased as the cubicle started upward.

Chapter 2

Kate was in her office Monday when the phone rang. It was not the first call of the day, but somehow she knew before she picked up the receiver that it was the one she had been waiting for. She was right. The call was from Frank Moyer; his message was short and indescribably sweet: "You got the job, kid. Congratulations!"

"I did? I mean, you're absolutely sure?"

"Well, your name is on a dozen forms now, so I hope I'm right. I'd sure as hell hate to have to sign all those papers over again."

"Thank you!"

He laughed easily. "Whoa now. I rooted for you, but I wasn't the one who did the final selecting. I'm glad you got it though, I think you'll enjoy working with Amalacorp."

"I know I will." She was smiling exultantly as she twisted the telephone cord between her fingers. Over the past week she had vacillated between feeling confident that she would land the job and feeling a dread certainty that she would not. She had tried to focus her mind on other things, but her stomach had fluttered nervously all week as she waited for the news. Now she knew, and she was jubilant.

"Listen," Frank said, "I have a long distance call on the other line, but I'll get back to you. Congratulations again."

"Thanks, Frank."

She hung up and sank back in her brown suede chair. For the past week she had maintained a deliberate calm—outwardly. Inwardly, she had been far from the composed woman she had presented to her co-workers each day. Her smile broadened as she wondered what they would have thought if they had realized she was pacing her apartment restlessly at night.

Kate glanced at her watch. Her mother would be out with a real estate client now, or Kate would have called her to relay the happy news. But she knew Agatha always went out with clients in the morning. Kate was so engrossed in her thoughts that she jumped when the buzzer on her desk sounded and her secretary informed her, "Mr. Vollmer would like to see you in his office, Ms. Justin."

"Okay, Dotty." Kate glanced at the report on her desk. Ross probably wanted to talk about it, she decided as she pushed her chair back and stood. Carrying the thick volume with her, she started down the hall to his office.

He greeted her by lifting his glasses up just above his eyes and holding them there while he surveyed her. "Well," he demanded peremptorily, "what have you heard?"

"I got the job," she announced, making no effort to suppress her beam of triumph.

He motioned to a chair and she sat down while he lowered the horn-rims back into place and pushed aside a stack of papers on a desk that was piled with reports, books and errant scraps of paper. "So you beat out the other two boys and landed the job?" he said with a note of pride. "Congratulations."

"Thank you." At his mention of the other two men, Kate knew a fleeting moment of guilt as she remembered that her elation was at their expense. She smoothed her hands across her beige jersey dress; she wondered if they had been informed yet.

"We're going to miss you," Ross continued. He took his glasses off and laid them on the desk atop the clutter. "But Amalacorp can offer you challenges that you'll never find here. Everybody knows you love a challenge," he continued with a grin. "You're something of a scrapper, Kate."

She laughed easily. "You make me sound like an old dog fighting over a bonè."

"You know what I mean. Some of our engineers are content to put in their eight hours a day, go home and forget work completely until the next day. But you've never been like that. I've seen you drag home volumes of reports. Of course," he added with a wry smile, "I don't know that you actually read them. Maybe it was all for show."

"I didn't read a single one of them," she returned solemnly.

"Humph. The hell you didn't," he snorted. "Well, I always knew you were on your way up. I was telling one of our new men just the other day that the only way to get ahead these days is to be willing to relocate where the jobs are. There are big promotions overseas for someone who's willing to work in godforsaken places."

Kate knew. She had moved four times in just under two years pursuing such promotions in the States. It had paid off, she reflected, although at times she had wondered if she had condemned herself to a permanent nomadic life.

"When's your last day?" Ross asked. He tilted the chair forward and searched for his glasses with his hands.

"I was hoping I could make it a week from this Friday."

Ross frowned. "That soon? Well, I'll tell Carney." He paused. "I'm not promising anything, and certainly we couldn't match the salary they can give, but I could talk to Carney about increasing your responsibility—"

She shook her head with a smile. "Thanks, Ross. It's nice of you to ask, but I really think I'm ready to move on."

"Yeah," he said matter-of-factly. "All right, we might as well make you earn your money while you're here. Did you bring the Panama report with you? There are a couple of things in it that will definitely have to go."

While Ross talked, Kate's mind was not entirely on his words. She was savoring her happy triumph; winning the job with Amalacorp was an achievement for any engineer.

Burke Walters had asked her why she had become an engineer. Her answer, that she liked practical applications of science, was true as far as it went, but her reasons actually went much deeper. She had been attracted to engineering mainly because it was a stable field in an uncertain world. And it paid well.

After her father died, Kate had watched her mother struggle to make ends meet. She had been young at the time, but the memory remained vivid. It had developed in her a fierce desire to insulate herself from the financial difficulties her mother had faced. Engineering provided Kate the challenges she thrived on, and it also paid—paid well enough to block out the insecurities of her earlier years.

Kate had forgotten how much there was to learn when one went to work for a new company. During the first week with Amalacorp, she was made aware of it again. She was introduced to the fifty people who worked in her section and she set about learning their names, trying to associate each name with a person, and memorizing that person's function in the company. In addition to those in her own section, Kate met other people in the company she would be working with frequently—the vice presidents and the managers of projects of the other sections.

Aside from meeting people, there was also the process of familiarizing herself with the projects Amalacorp had under construction and the ones they were currently bidding on. The steady stream of correspondence that came across her desk required Kate to keep updated on all the projects and their changing status.

It was demanding, but Kate had expected that. In fact, she had wanted it. After the predictable pace of her old job, she found Amalacorp exhilarating. She wondered if every new executive felt as happy as she did in a new job.

Kate was considering that thought as she stood looking out the window from her office. Everything in her life was falling nicely into place. She had found an apartment to sublet that was going to go condominium, and she would be moving in this weekend. In addition, Duane Rodgers, one of the vice presidents, was giving a party Friday night, and she would be able to indulge her passion for shopping for pretty clothes finding something to wear to it.

This was Thursday of her first week at work. Tonight she would go to Neiman Marcus and pick out something special to wear to the Rodgers' party. Of course, it could not be anything *too* daring, but at least she could select a more interesting color than the neutral colors she almost always wore to work. And she could choose a style with more flair than her usual uniform of tailored suits. Admittedly, the clothes she wore to work were less than exciting, but they helped create an image of a dignified, competent professional. Kate knew that image counted heavily in her line of work.

That evening she walked down to the Neiman store in downtown Dallas. There were only a few customers on the floor that sold women's formal clothes. Kate browsed slowly through a rack of long gowns; the silks, crepe de chines and velvets were feathery in her hands. They were far from her usual clothes. These gowns had chic and the promise of evenings by the ocean with a man in a tux, or an intimate dinner over candlelight. Kate could see a host of women she knew wearing any one of these lavender, cream or black gowns with slits and plunges, but she was not sure she could visualize herself in any of them.

"May I help you?"

Kate looked up at a plump, smiling saleswoman. "I'm looking for a long dress, but I haven't seen anything I want to try on yet," she replied.

The woman looked concerned. "These are the latest we have. They're very nice gowns." She selected a deep blue chiffon and pulled it from the rack. "With your coloring, something like this would look *smashing.*"

"I'm afraid that's a little too revealing," Kate said. "Do you have something that doesn't take such a definite plunge?" The party would consist mainly of company personnel, Kate was certain.

The saleslady glanced at the neckline and then at Kate's street clothes, an eggshell-white jacket with a dull-burgundy plaid skirt. She led the way to another rack of clothes.

"These are not as revealing." She paused before she continued sincerely, "Actually, I think they're a little matronly for you. But this is a charming little dress that certainly doesn't show too much." She took a red gown from the rack. It had a high neck and was covered with sequins down to the waist.

"I don't know, red is rather dramatic," Kate said as she touched the fabric.

"Try it on," the woman insisted.

Kate did, despite her reservations. She couldn't resist seeing herself in it. Regarding herself in the mirror, she noted that the dress clung to her figure, revealing every curve. She looked smart and worldly,

Kate reflected as she viewed herself, turning from side to side. She swept back her hair on one side and studied the effect.

"How are you doing?" The saleswoman peered into the dressing room. "Oh, my word! That's perfect for you."

Kate let her hair drop. Suddenly she felt a little foolish. She had been with Amalacorp such a short time; she really could not appear at a party in this gown. It accented far too much of her willowy form, and the dress definitely moved when she did. "I'm afraid the color is a little too loud. Let me look some more."

The woman looked at her in disbelief. "Suit yourself, but that one is stunning." She left.

Kate took the red gown off and hung it carefully on the hanger. If she didn't have an image to maintain, this would be a smashing gown, Kate admitted. But she had to be careful of the clothes she wore, along with the depth of her smile to her co-workers and the way she presented herself to the world. The clothes she wore might be boringly conservative, but they made a statement about herself; they proclaimed she was a no-nonsense person. No-nonsense people didn't wear red sequinned gowns.

Kate walked back onto the floor and looked through several more dresses before she took a jade satin one and a blue-violet silk to the dressing room. The saleslady returned to assist her into the gowns. "These are lovely too," she said noncommittally. "More regal-looking."

The jade fit snugly, molding itself across Kate's breasts and down to her waist before following the curve of her hip downward and falling straight from there. It was a seductive dress. "I don't think this will do," Kate said regretfully.

The saleswoman was mute as she unzipped the gown and held out the blue-violet silk for Kate. It had a wide belt of the same color that emphasized her small waist and drifted to the floor in soft folds. The color was almost the same shade as Kate's magnificent eyes, and the cut looked graceful and elegant, but definitely not playful or daring. "I'll take this one," Kate decided after pushing aside a wistful hankering for the red gown. The saleslady nodded in acquiescence.

As Kate dressed for the party Friday evening, it occurred to her that it had been a long time since she had attended such an affair alone. In Kansas City, Joe had always escorted her to parties and to an occasional cotillion or coming-out ball.

She paused in the act of blow-drying her damp hair and reflected that Joe had not called her since she had moved to Dallas, nor had she called him.

In many ways, Kate realized, her moving away from Kansas City had released them both from a rut. When they had started seeing each other over a year ago, they had had some wonderful times together. The problem was that it gradually became apparent to Kate that theirs was not a romance, even though they enjoyed one another's companionship. In fact, they had fallen into a relationship of convenience.

For a long time Kate had accepted it for what it was; she had even wanted their dates to stay light and without commitment. But in the past three months she had begun to chafe under the loose bindings that held her to Joe. Although it was understood that both of them could date others, the truth remained that no man would ask her while she was seeing Joe. Everyone she knew had come to regard them as a pair.

Kate flipped the hairdryer on again and began to brush the long, silky strands as the warm air rushed through them. She was going to be more careful about any entanglements she got into in the future. She didn't want another staid relationship. Not that she expected a great passion, she was past that stage. What would be ideal for her was someone warm and sensible who understood that she was dedicated to her job; someone who would let go when the spark went out of their friendship.

She turned off the dryer and set it on the dresser, then added a few electric curlers to give her hair extra bounce. It really didn't matter if she dated or not. She was busy right now learning her job, and she would just go with the flow for a while. If she met someone interesting, fine; if not, that was okay too. After all, she had her career, and that was more important to her than any man could be.

A glance at the lighted alarm clock pushed all thought of men from Kate's mind. It was half an hour later than she had thought it was. She pulled her blue-violet gown from the closet and hastily slipped into it. Then she released her hair from the electric rollers and combed through the curls that tumbled down to brush against her shoulders. Leaning forward toward the mirror, she checked to make sure the silvery-blue eye shadow she had brushed lightly across each lid had not strayed outside its boundaries. She made certain her rose-mauve lipstick was applied evenly before picking up her silver clutch-purse and starting for the door.

Chapter 3

In the crowded room around Kate men were dressed in formal evening wear, with black ties worn against snowy white shirts. The women were not confined to such a rigid mode. They wore Oscar de la Renta jackets of black velvet embroidered in turquoise and rose, Bill Blass cranberry confections of taffeta and ruffles, and ivory chemises that Kate recognized as Anne Klein. Dom Perignon flowed freely, delivered by waiters moving among the guests with trays, while a table at one end of the long room was loaded with caviar, pâté de fois gras and hors d'oeuvre of every description.

Kate stood near one side of the room. Beside her, a small group of men were speculating about the stock market and probing each other for inside tips, while on the other side several women discussed a benefit being planned for their social sorority. She took a sip of her drink and blocked both conversations out of her mind as she looked around the room. There had been a man who had caught her attention briefly when she had entered. She wasn't sure she would recognize him if she saw him again; all that she had really registered was that he was tall. That, and a certain bearing to his manner, as if he were not a man who would stand in the shadow of another.

Kate studied the liquor in her glass with a smile. Really, did she think she was Cinderella at a ball? It was impossible to tell anything about a man simply from seeing him once, and from across the distance of a large room at that.

"What's the joke?"

Kate looked up to see Letty Rodgers, Duane's wife and the hostess of the party, smiling at her.

"I'm daydreaming."

"Ah, it must have been pleasant; tell me, I have a prurient interest in such things."

Kate laughed. "There was nothing lascivious about my thoughts. Sorry to disappoint you."

Letty drew a long cigarette from a gold case. As if on cue, her husband materialized at her side to light it. "Have you been keeping count of how many people ask you if you like Dallas?" Duane teased Kate.

"I quit counting at five hundred."

He glanced around the room. "Where's that English guy? I'll introduce him to you and you can ask him how *he* likes Dallas."

"Is he the tall man?" Letty asked. "I wondered who he was. Over there," she indicated to Kate with an inclination of her head.

Kate looked toward a man with dark hair burnished with golden tints. His chiseled features were accented by a slight cleft in his chin and a mouth that dipped in a sensuous curve that was not quite a smile. He was talking to a man from Amalacorp whose name Kate could not recall.

"You're not matchmaking, are you, dear?" Duane prodded Letty gently. "I expect Kate gets more than her share of that."

"I'm just pointing him out," she said virtuously, and added, "He is handsome."

He certainly was; Kate had to agree. She thought he was the man she had noticed when she had first entered the room, but she wasn't sure. After all, the men were all dressed almost identically.

"Did you learn any good stock-market tips from these guys?" Duane changed the subject, motioning to the circle beside them.

"I wasn't listening," she confessed.

Letty exhaled a puff of smoke and watched her husband edge into the Dow-Jones group. "My husband, the entrepreneur. When he talks, nobody listens."

Kate smiled. In the corner she saw Burke Walters talking to Frank Moyer. Poor Frank. To her it looked as if Burke was talking business and Frank was being put on the spot. Kate suspected Burke's only purpose in being here was to discuss business with someone from the office he had not had a chance to see that day. She didn't think Burke would come to a party for companionship; he hardly seemed like a social creature.

"If you'll excuse me," Letty said, touching Kate's arm, "I need to make sure we're not running out of anything at the refreshment table. I think the caterers are all in the kitchen, drunk."

Kate was soon drawn into another conversation with a tall, red-haired man named Myron, who displayed an unconcealed interest in her. Behind Myron, moving easily among the crowd, Kate caught occasional glimpses of another tall man. He was the Englishman; she had decided he was definitely the one who had caught her eye as soon as she had entered the room. Kate smiled at something her companion said and forced her eyes back to Myron. Staring at a man across a room was simply not done, she told herself, no matter how compelling he might be.

Half an hour later Kate gently extricated herself from Myron's soliloquy on himself and started across the crowded room. She glanced toward the far corner, and for a moment her eyes met and held the tall Englishman's. He looked urbane and charming, holding a glass of wine in one hand while the other arm rested casually on the back of a chair. As she watched, his mouth tilted up slightly in a smile that she knew was directed at her alone. She smiled back and then directed her attention to the two men who had joined her.

"And this is Kate," Duane said as he introduced an amiable-looking man with thick glasses. "Kate, I'd like you to meet Edward Masoner. He twisted my arm for an introduction," Duane tattled.

Edward beamed at Kate. "I'm afraid it's true."

"I'm flattered," she murmured, and directed her attention toward Edward, trying to push aside thoughts of the other man who had so captured her imagination.

As Kate listened politely to Edward, she still looked now and then at the other man. It was odd, she mused, she didn't know a single thing about the stranger, and yet she knew instinctively that she liked him. Someone had said he was English, but presumably he now lived in Dallas. She was interested in knowing more about him.

Kate finally drifted away from Edward. It was while she was standing by herself in a corner, enjoying the solitude, that she heard someone say, "I'd like you to meet Kate Justin. She's new to Dallas. Kate, this is Ian Nigel."

Kate looked up with an automatic smile to see Frank Moyer and the tall Englishman. Her smile softened and became less impersonal as she looked into a pair of blue-gray eyes set in a handsome face.

"If you'll excuse me," Frank continued, glancing over his shoulder, "there's someone over there I'd like to talk to." He turned and was lost in the crowd. Kate's eyes moved from Frank back to Ian Nigel.

"So you're new in town," he began conversationally, and then broke off with a self-deprecating smile. "I guess that's not a terribly original way to begin a conversation, especially to a woman who has been beseiged by men ever since she stepped into the room."

He *had* noticed her from the very beginning, Kate noted with a secret triumph. And his nicely-couched compliment was far more intriguing than the overt flattery she had been subjected to so far this evening. She wondered if he knew that she had been continuously aware of him since she had entered the room. Kate said casually, "I don't mind getting to know someone by going through the time-honored questions like where I'm from and what I do. After all, those statements surely wouldn't have become so established if they weren't useful."

His face lit in a smile that revealed even white teeth. "I think that must be true," he agreed. "I want you to know I had a splendid follow-up to my lead question. I was prepared with the equally suave, 'Haven't I seen you somewhere before?' After I'd exhausted those conversational gems, I have a pocket reference book that I carry to all parties. It's full of witticisms and ice-breakers."

"I don't think it will be necessary to refer to it," she responded lightly. Kate didn't believe this tall specimen of masculine perfection needed to speak at all to impress her. Just the sight of his broad shoulders, deep brown hair with golden highlights, finely-chiseled face and devilish blue-gray eyes would surely be enough to send any full-blooded female into his arms. Who cared if he could talk? But she was glad he could, she reflected; she liked the resonant sound of his voice and the precise English accent.

A particularly raucous burst of laughter near them broke into their conversation for a moment. Ian Nigel waited until it subsided before he suggested, "Would you like to go for a walk outside? It's really quite pleasant in the garden, and a bit quieter since it lacks the Greek chorus."

Kate smiled. "Love it," she replied promptly.

They threaded their way through the crowded room

and stepped out the back door onto a balcony. The fresh air felt good. The colonial-style building was surrounded by large elm trees. Beneath the trees, azaleas grew in pretty abundance, the flowers visible even at night because of soft lights placed under the bushes. Ian took her hand lightly and they started down the stone steps that led from the balcony into the garden.

Although there was a briskness to the April night, it wasn't uncomfortable. Kate stepped off the bottom riser onto a pathway that crunched under her shoes. Pecan hulls, she suspected. As they walked into the stand of elms, Kate realized it was considerably darker there than she had anticipated. The tall trees shaded the bushes and shut out the soft light of the moon, leaving only the lights under the bushes for illumination.

"Since I know you're new to Dallas, where are you from?" Ian asked as he put his hand more firmly under her arm to help her over the uneven path.

"I just moved here from Kansas City," Kate replied. "In fact," she continued, "I'm still in the process of moving. I've been living in a hotel, but I'm going to move into my new apartment tomorrow." She picked up the hem of her skirt as she stepped over a particularly rooty area. Ian's arm came around her waist to steady her. She had surely had a bit too much wine, Kate told herself, otherwise the mere feel of his arm on her would not send such tremors of excitement pulsing through her. "I shouldn't have worn such high heels," she offered apologetically.

"Believe me, I don't mind," he replied.

He stated the words as if they were the simple truth and not in a predatory or leering way. For a moment Kate was tempted to lean even closer to him or feign that she had lost her balance altogether. She banished that thought as completely unworthy of her. She was a sophisticated woman, not an adolescent, even though being with this man did seem to rekindle some of the breathless fires of earlier years. "Did you just move to Dallas?" she asked, putting the conversation onto a more rational footing.

"No, I'm just passing through on my way back to London. I've been in Los Angeles for the last week."

Separated by an ocean, she thought with a suppressed sigh. She felt a pang of regret. She was sorry that she would not be seeing more of Ian Nigel. There was much about him that she found appealing. It wasn't just his looks either, although they were certainly easy on the eyes. What struck her more was the unstudied air of confidence he had. He must be successful, she decided, at whatever he did. She plucked a flower and brought it to her nose. Around her the bushes were rich in blooms of white and pink and lilac.

Perhaps it was simply the romantic setting that made her think of Ian Nigel as such a special person and so different from any man she had met in a long time, Kate told herself. She would do well to continue to discuss purely impersonal matters with him. "The only adjustment I'm having moving to Dallas is with my cat," she offered lightly. "He hasn't shown any interest in his food of late; he's most unhappy about the move from Kansas City, where he was courting the Angora next door. He's snubbed me for the last two days."

"What a pity. I daresay I'm fortunate not to have any animals, after all. After spending a day in meetings with surly board members and facing London traffic, I don't think I would be in the mood to argue with a cat."

Kate nodded as they followed the curve in the path that wound around out of the garden and sloped down toward a large rectangle of glistening water that was the swimming pool. So he was on a corporate board. That confirmed her opinion that he was a man of some importance. She was just about to ask him what company he was with when she felt him put his hand beneath her elbow to guide her down the grassy slope to the pool.

She knew his hand was there for support, to keep her

from tripping in her stiletto heels, but she liked the strong touch of it all the same. The quiet April breeze stirred across the water and ruffled their reflections as they reached the side of the pool and started walking slowly around it.

"This is almost like being in the country," he said. "It's so quiet that it's hard to believe we're close to a city the size of Dallas."

"Yes, it's peaceful." The wind stirred through the water again, lapping it gently against the sides of the pool and tossing Kate's hair back away from her face. She looked up to see Ian Nigel looking down at her. Perhaps it was the balmy night air and the beauty of the setting around them that made her feel a little shiver of excitement, but she thought it was mostly Ian Nigel's presence. If he lived in Dallas, Kate would have had no qualms about showing her interest in him, but there was little point in doing so when he would be leaving for London soon. As attractive as he was, she wasn't going to be a temporary fling for him. No, she must remain distant. "What do you do?" she asked in a tone that was meant to sound impersonal but somehow came out rather coy.

"I'm with Denham company."

Denham company. Amalacorp was building a dam for them in the Cotswolds in England. It had not even occurred to her that he might work for a firm her company did business with. She casually disengaged her arm from his hand under the pretense of pushing back a lock of hair, and then moved half a step away from him. "I work for Amalacorp," she said in a friendly voice. "What do you do at Denham?"

There was a barely perceptible pause before he replied, "I'm chairman of the board."

For a moment she was without words. Then she said slowly, "My, that's an important position."

He was a business associate. That put a greater distance between them than the thousands of miles that separated Dallas from London. The fact that he was chairman of the board was merely icing on the cake. She had not really expected to see Ian Nigel again anyway, but the fact that she couldn't was somehow disturbing. He was a man she would not have minded knowing better.

Chapter 4

The Sandpiper Apartments were just down the road
from the Highland Village complex. Kate thought one
name made as much sense as the other, since the closest
real sandpiper must be frolicking near the gulf waters
250 miles from landlocked Dallas. It was hard to
imagine where the nearest highlands were. Certainly it
was some distance, since Dallas was set in the midst of a
great plain.

Kate thought the Sandpiper was perfect in a surre-
alistic way. The carefully-manicured lawns surrounding
the complex were such a deep emerald-green that the
grass didn't look quite real. Immediately inside the high
stone wall that surrounded the Sandpiper, past the
guard's small security station, was a wide circle with
white flowers planted in the center and a border of
purple phlox. The apartment buildings themselves were
clean, unpainted redwoods that had aged to a mellow,
old-barn gray. They stretched out in a neat row with
shade trees planted around them.

The little streets and parking areas of the complex

also had names. Kate smiled as she read them—Heron
Boulevard and Seagull Lane. She wondered if the
person who had named the complex and its streets had
labored under the misconception that it was near the
ocean. But then, Kate reflected as she drove toward her
own apartment, there was something so calm and
orderly about the tiny world inside these walls, that it
was almost possible to believe it was near the ocean. It
was a village that could well have an identical twin in
Galveston or Des Moines. There too, affluent tenants
would be persuaded to believe they might see a real
sandpiper at any time or hear the swell of the ocean.
Illusions were big business.

Kate parked her burgundy Seville in her space and
picked up the sack of groceries from the seat beside
her. Later she could return to the store and buy a
complete stock of staples. This trip had been for the
essentials of cold cuts and bread. Letting herself in the
front door, she stepped into the small entryway. A
parquet tile stretched out the length of the hall that led
to the kitchen. Two doors opened off either side. The
first room on the left was a living room, with cool blue
shag carpeting and matching draperies. It flowed into
the dining room, minimally separated by a built-in
bookcase that jutted out between the two rooms. The
dining room led into the kitchen. It was a cheery room
with gleaming white counters and avocado appliances.
A pastel-flowered wallpaper in avocado and pale pink
gave a fresh, cheerful feel to the room. Along the back
wall a sliding glass door led out to the patio.

On the right side of the hall was a study paneled in a
dark pine, with a fireplace of brick that stretched across
one side of the room. Next to it, across from the dining
room, was a large half-bath with beige tiles and gleaming fixtures.

Beside the bathroom, in the hall, a flight of steps led
to the second floor. Kate put the food in the kitchen
and walked up the steps. A small landing had a
bedroom on either side and a large bathroom in the

middle. She walked into the larger of the two bedrooms and sat on the queen-sized bed, slipping off her shoes as she looked around. The walls of minty, spring green were a pleasant reminder of the gown she had worn to her high school prom.

She lifted her feet off the floor and stretched out on the bed. What had ever happened to that dress? she wondered idly. Her mother must have given it away. "Saving just leads to accumulating things that will have to be thrown out eventually," Agatha had once said practically.

As Kate looked around the room at the unpacked boxes, she was inclined to agree with her mother. What was she going to do with all these things that she had moved from Kansas City? She must have more half-stubs from tickets than any other person living. If torn tickets ever appreciated in value, she was rich. But she had always kept them, and oddly enough, remembered most of the events and even who her date had been. She still had most of her childhood toys that she had salvaged when her mother had ruthlessly put them out for the Salvation Army. Kate smiled as she thought of some of the toys she had saved. What in the world did she need with a one-eyed teddy bear and a hairless doll? Never mind, she would find a place for them. They were old friends and they had come with her this far.

Certainly they had come a long way from Tiffin, Ohio, she reflected as she rolled over on the bed. So had she. Burke Walters had asked her why she had decided to become an engineer. A lot of men had asked her that question. A woman in this field was rare. Although little boys played with erector sets and delighted parents marked them for the career early, it didn't happen so easily for little girls. At least it hadn't for her.

Originally, she had considered a career in modeling. She was pretty; everyone told her so. Sometimes strangers came up to her in stores and said it, and men watched her covertly from across lunch counters. She was a cheerleader and a homecoming queen and she was only seventeen. She was young enough to break into modeling. Many people had told her she had the face of a cover girl, so why not become one?

She had approachd her mother with the idea a few weeks before graduation. "I'd like to go into modeling," she inserted into the conversation casually between the beef stew and the dessert.

Her mother glanced up at her curiously. "Really? What brought this on?"

"I've been thinking about it for a long time. I know I've already been accepted at State, but I don't see any point wasting money going there if I have no intention of working in a field that requires a degree." Kate tasted her strawberry shortcake during the ensuing silence. It was hard to read her mother sometimes, but experience had taught Kate that she was most dangerous when she was quietest. Kate readied her arguments.

"Modeling would certainly be glamorous," her mother conceded.

Kate felt herself relaxing. "Yes, and the money is terrific," she noted.

"I've heard that it is." Agatha looked thoughtful. "Modeling might be a very good thing. You're certainly pretty enough. There's only one thing about it that bothers me." She paused. "Well, never mind." She turned her attention back to her plate.

"What? What is it that bothers you?" Kate urged.

"What worries me is that models become—I don't want to use the word 'has beens,' but I can't think of any other way to put it. I mean, by the time they're thirty, they're old." She glanced at Kate's dessert. "You'd certainly have to give up sweets, and you'd have to drop about ten pounds."

Kate looked down at her figure. "I'm not fat!"

"No, but models photograph heavier than they are." Agatha took a bite of her own dessert. "I tell you what would concern me if I were you. I'd want to have something I could always fall back on. If anything happened when you were forty and you lost all of your savings and had to start over, what would you do then? I was twenty-eight when your father died, and I certainly wish I'd had a profession to fall back on."

Kate pondered her mother's words for a moment. It was hard to worry about something going wrong when she was forty. Forty was too remote, too removed from her seventeen-year-old life. But it was her mother's words about how tight things had been after her father's death that had really jolted Kate. Even at six she could remember being worried when her mother had to pass up certain things at the grocery store because she didn't have enough money to buy them. Money was important. Kate already knew that nothing moved without it. "What do you suggest?" she asked her mother.

"I don't know. It seems to me that to really get ahead a woman needs to be in the same tough fields men have been succeeding in for years. Nurses are always limited by the fact they're in a woman's field and the pay is held down accordingly. Teachers are the same way. I'd look toward something where there is a shortage of people and the pay is good."

"What about engineering?" Kate suggested.

Her mother looked at her in surprise. "I didn't know you had any interest in it."

"I've always been good in math and science and there's a shortage of engineers now. My physics teacher said so." Kate repeated almost everything she knew about the field in that one sentence, but she managed to look well-informed to her mother.

Agatha gave a slow smile of approval. "If I had a vote, it would be for engineering. That sounds a whole lot better to me than modeling. After all, Kate, you are bright as well as pretty, and engineering would provide a mental stimulation that modeling wouldn't."

The decision had not been made that day, but the

idea had taken strong root in Kate's mind. When her high school counselor had asked her what she intended to study in college, Kate had told her proudly that she was going to be an engineer. The counselor had looked at her askance. "There aren't many women in that area of study," she cautioned.

When Kate relayed those words to her mother, Agatha's reply was, "It's small-thinking people like Mrs. Dougherty who have kept progress at bay in this town. If she had any talent herself, she wouldn't be stuck in the same high school she's been in for the last twenty-five years giving ill-considered advice to students."

Kate stared at her mother. She had never heard Agatha speak in such disparaging terms about any teacher or school official.

Agatha laughed lightly. "Sorry, Kate. I shouldn't have said that. But when I first started selling real estate, a lot of people raised their eyebrows at me. All I know is that I was able to provide you with a kind of life that you could never have had if I had stayed a secretary. Right now we wouldn't even be discussing sending you to college, because there wouldn't be money for it. If you want something in this world, you have to go out and take it yourself, and to hell with what people say." She leaned over and kissed Kate lightly on the cheek. "I'm proud of you, hon. I don't want to push you and I don't want to hold you back. I just want you to know that there's a tough world out there."

Kate rolled over on the bed and opened her eyes. Where would she be today if she had pursued the idea of becoming a model? Even if she had succeeded in that competitive field, she would be nearing the end of her working life now. As it was, she was just beginning to soar. And her mother had been right about the mental challenge—she could never have found fulfillment as a mere fashion-plate.

She pushed herself up off the bed. Later, after she

had unpacked and put some things away, she could think about resting. In the meantime there was a lot to do. Saturday was already half over, and she had little to show for her effort.

An hour later Kate was in the kitchen putting away utensils when the doorbell sounded. She wiped her hands on her jeans and straightened her pink and white knit top before padding barefoot down the hall to the front door. "Who is it?"

"It's Jessica Holmes. You met me yesterday when you were putting your name on the mailbox."

Kate opened the door and greeted her visitor with a smile. Jessica was an attractive blonde with a fragile, almost doll-like quality to her. Pretty green eyes were set beneath long dark lashes and her skin was a glowing cream color. She wore a red velour top and white cotton slacks that revealed a trim, petite figure.

"Come in," Kate invited.

"Am I interrupting?" Jessica's voice was definitely a Dallas drawl, but with a certain sophistication.

"No, I'm just putting a few things away." Kate led the way to the living room and motioned toward the off-white sectional sofa while she took a seat in a blue and white patterned armchair.

Jessica glanced around the room at the boxes stacked in the corners and behind the furniture. "I feel sorry for you; I know what you're going through. I've lived in these apartments over a year, and I still haven't unpacked everything yet."

"I'm going to sort through and throw a lot of this away. Saving things is one of my bad habits," Kate noted. "I'd offer you a Coke or a cup of coffee, but I don't have any groceries yet."

"I understand. I won't keep you from your work long. I just wanted to drop over and let you know that I'm only two doors down. If you need anything until you get to the store, I'll be glad to loan you a cup of sugar."

"Thanks. I don't think I'll have to bother you."

Jessica continued with an artless smile. "That was sort of an excuse to visit you anyway. There aren't many single women in this complex, so I was anxious to get to know you better."

Kate was pleased with that declaration. She had known few women in Kansas City and she found she missed the companionship of her own sex. She would especially like to have this pleasant woman for a friend. Jessica had a self-confidence and style that Kate admired. "What sort of people live here?" she asked.

"There are a few older, retired couples and a lot of single men." She paused before continuing candidly. "At the price of these units, not many single women can afford them unless daddy's paying the bill."

"Oh." Of course, Kate had encountered this situation before. She was isolated from women primarily because few were her financial peers. Secretaries couldn't afford to live where she did, buy the kind of clothes she wore, or eat at the restaurants she frequented. Money had its charms, but for a single woman it could also have its drawbacks. "What kind of work do you do?" Kate asked.

"I'm the Lifestyle editor for the Dallas paper. You can translate that 'Women's' or 'Society,'" she offered with a self-deprecating laugh. "What do you do?"

"I'm an engineer, but I work primarily as a manager."

Jessica's eyes widened in surprise. "Really? What a great field to be in."

"It has its advantages," Kate agreed casually.

"One of them is that you're not trapped by stereotypes," Jessica observed as she leaned back on the sofa. She added with a smile, "Roles are my current area of interest. We're doing a series of articles about women's jobs in historically male-dominated areas. The focus is on how such women have no role models and have to create their own images."

Kate considered that thoughtfully. "I suppose I can create my own image," she agreed slowly.

"You're lucky."

Kate shook her head with a smile. "It sounds easier than it is. As one of the few women in my profession, I'm constantly on stage. Men watch me to see how I handle myself and what mistakes I make. Being under such steady observation doesn't make for much relaxation," she concluded. "So tell me about your job. It sounds glamorous."

Jessica reached down to pet Kate's cat as he wandered through, exploring his new domain. "I go to a lot of fashion shows and parties," she said, as if it were a fact of little interest. "I also spend a good deal of time at my desk reviewing my assistant editors' work."

Kate listened with interest. Parties and fashion shows. She could just picture the dainty Jessica sitting at an afternoon tea in the lush garden of some philanthropic matron. Jessica's world sounded as if it were full of designer clothes, beautiful people and the good life. That was certainly far removed from Kate's own life. She had had few enough glimpses of anyone in the corporate structure leading exciting lives. She wanted to get to know Jessica better. It would be nice to be friends with someone whose everyday world revolved around such interesting people as Jessica must know.

Chapter 5

Sometimes when Kate woke up in the morning, her dreams were so vivid it took her a moment to realize they were not real. Two days after the Rodgers' party, she awoke thinking of her mother hugging her father and fondly watching him go to work with briefcase in hand. That was one of Kate's more frequent dreams of her father. All she'd ever really noticed about him were his laughing blue eyes. She could vaguely recall that he used to tease her, but she could never remember anything he had said, only that he'd made her giggle and that she had repeated the conversations to her grandmother later.

Robert Justin had seemed old and strong and wise to his six-year-old daughter; it was hard to realize that when he died he had been younger than she was now. Kate pulled the covers up closer against her as if to protect herself from a chill that was not there. She always thought of her father as having died, rarely did she attach the word "killed"—even in her thoughts.

But he had been killed, shot by a robber who had

broken into the tiny insurance and real estate office for
the $123 petty cash resting in the metal box in the
bottom drawer of his desk. To Kate, the pitiful amount
of money the robber had taken had further demeaned
her father's death; not that anything could have made it
acceptable. She still recalled how she had taken her
bank book out of her jewelry box with the dancing
ballerina on top and carefully read the amount she had
on deposit. She had $204 in her own account, more
than enough to have bought her father's life. Kate had
felt an unspoken guilt that she had not been able to do
so.

Kate became slowly aware that she was gazing at the
mint curtains in her bedroom. The sun was stealing in
past the loose weave of the fabric to scatter dappled
patterns of gold across the carpet. She watched as the
curtains shifted slightly and the patterns changed.

It was Sunday morning and she was in her new
apartment. She rubbed a hand across her eyes and lay
back on the bed. Odd that she had dreamed of her
father, Kate considered, since she rarely did anymore.
She lay quietly for a moment trying to recall another
piece of her dream; there had been something about it
she wanted to remember.

Then a fragment came back to her. She had been
dancing in a man's arms. He was tall and handsome,
she was sure, although she could not see his face. All
that she could feel was the steady pressure of his arm
around her waist. Kate opened her eyes as the truth
dawned on her. She had dreamed of Ian Nigel.

She had not seen him since the Rodgers' party two
nights ago, nor did she expect to see him again. It was
odd how much he had dominated her thoughts since
she had met him. There was a simple explanation, of
course; she was in a new town and she was lonely.
Under those circumstances it was not illogical that she
would believe herself attracted to an appealing
stranger. The important thing for her to remember was
that he was only a passing interest. A woman could

really become confused if she began to put too much emphasis on a chance meeting with a man. Kate had seen it happen to other women. The one thing in her favor was that she would not be seeing Ian Nigel again.

She closed her eyes again. She really didn't have time for Ian in her life now, even if he had lived in Dallas, she reflected. She would be busy establishing herself in her new position for the next few months. New beginnings required complete concentration, and she intended to give that singleminded attention to Amala-corp.

Kate snuggled further down beneath the covers. The clarity of her thoughts subsided into the hazy thinking of half-sleep. She was at the Rodgers' party again, and she saw herself and Ian Nigel walking beside the pool. She could see the tall trees and azaleas in the background.

Then the scene shifted imperceptibly. Kate and Ian were no longer at a party; they were alone by the side of the pool and he was dressed in a pair of swimming trunks instead of the tux he had been wearing only a minute ago. Kate became aware that she was clad in the most abbreviated of bikinis. It was a deep red color, and sparkling across the scanty top with sequins.

For a moment Ian smiled at her, a smile that held promise, and a suggestion of things to come. Then he dove into the water and she followed. Beneath the moonlight the water was cool and laced with dark patches. Kate barely noticed its coldness on her skin; she was too busy trying to keep pace with the swimmer who was going the length of the pool ahead of her. She swam with strong, deliberate strokes, but she was not fast enough to reach Ian's side. He moved further and further ahead out into a vast length of shadowy pool and Kate followed relentlessly, moving her body as rapidly as she could through the water and feeling the cool liquid resistance of it. He was almost out of sight and she was struggling breathlessly to gain on him when he turned and swam back to her. He caught her up in his arms and swung her around as if she weighed no more than a child. Her happy laughter blended with his, and she knew unbounded delight at being so near him. She could see the dampness of his skin and little glistening droplets of water caught by the moonlight. When he set her down, she stretched out a finger and touched a drop; it disappeared beneath her finger.

Ian put a hand under her chin and raised her face to his. For a moment Kate gazed steadily into his eyes. They were clear to her even in the uncertain light. She could read tenderness in them along with an unmistakable flicker of desire. He bent his head toward her as she raised her lips to meet his. Their mouths joined in a slow exploratory kiss. Kate felt the wetness of his lips and experienced the feel of his strongly-muscled chest against her own. He wrapped his arms around her and pulled her even closer against him. Their kiss deepened and his tongue swept lightly over hers before returning for a more satisfying encounter.

There were kisses and then there were *kisses*. Kate thought this one definitely belonged in the latter category. Her whole body was becoming involved in the exchange as the water lapped gently around them. She moved her hands unconsciously up and down his smooth back while his hands tightened on her hips and drew her closer against him. She was close enough to feel the lines of his body and she derived a sensual satisfaction from the knowledge that Ian's body responded to hers as intensely as hers did to him.

Suddenly, illogically, she and Ian were both naked in the pool. Kate could not recall when they had removed their clothes, but she didn't care. The cold water brushed against her, but she was barely aware of it. Every part of her was far more interested in the man who was drawing her with maddening slowness out of the water and up onto a sandy beach that had materialized where the concrete patio around the pool had been before. Kate wanted to rush headlong onto the sand and throw herself down onto it, pulling Ian down beside her, but they continued at the same slow-motion speed.

Time jumped again, and Kate was lying with him on the beach. A soft breeze blew past them and fanned the dark palm trees above. The rhythm of the water flowing gently against the shore made a soothing background music, but it was Ian's deep breathing and the sounds of satisfaction coming from deep in his throat that were the real symphony. His lips took hers with new intensity and moved roughly across them. His hands slipped in and out of the valleys of her body and up and down the peaks. With every new inch of skin he touched, Kate felt he had somehow marked it as his, and she reveled in that thought.

She could feel his legs moving against hers and then their bodies slid together in the final embrace. New emotions and sensations swirled through her body. She was aware of the tickle of his hair on her smooth breasts, and the intentness of his movements. And she was conscious of more subtle exchanges. His mouth on hers was almost imperceptibly more demanding, and she could feel controlled passion in every muscle of his body.

Her own body was not so restricted. She was reaching out and grabbing for pleasure as if she were a starving person allowed into a banquet hall. Her lips clung to his and her fingernails bit sharply into the golden flesh of his back. Then his body and hers became indistinguishable in her mind. Hands stroked and caressed and bodies moved seductively. She could not even assign responsibility for the small cries sounding around her. All that Kate knew for certain was that she had a wild and unnamed desire for something only Ian could give her. He had aroused her to fullblown longings, and she waited breathlessly for their fulfillment.

Even though she was anticipating fulfillment, when it came she was surprised by the intensity of the moment. It grew and expanded, threatening to choke off all of her breath. The ache of joy felt as boundless as the ocean, and she was drowning in the glory of their passion as wave fell over wave somewhere deep inside her.

Kate was acutely aware of the tingling of her body when she shifted slightly. She reached out a hand to feel the hard lines of Ian's body, but all she touched was air. In confusion, she blinked her eyes open to look. She saw no beach, no water and no Ian. Instead, she realized she was in her bedroom. She had been dreaming.

For a moment she lay quietly, still experiencing a small sense of the wonder her dream had created. Then thoughts came tumbling in, pushing aside the fantasy and making her acutely aware of the present. What had possessed her to have such a sensual dream about a man she hardly knew? She had not entertained such thoughts about any man for longer than she could remember. And she did not recall ever dreaming about a man in the terms she had just imagined Ian.

She was almost glad she would not be seeing Ian again. Could she have looked at him in perfect casualness and revealed nothing of the images that had flowed through her mind today? Really, it would have been embarrassing for him to have any inkling of what she had dreamed about him. She felt a warm flush flow into her cheeks at the memory of her sleep-induced fantasy. Of course, Ian would never know of her dream, but it was better that she not be around a man who affected her as strongly as Ian Nigel had. She would be far better off directing her attention to something like her work than letting her fantasies build around someone she could never have.

Chapter 6

Kate returned from a five-day trip to Denver, Colorado, where she had been supervising the construction of a pipeline, to find Jessica complaining of her cat. Jessica had volunteered to care for Cuddles in Kate's absence, but the arrangement had proved less than an ideal honeymoon.

"Cuddles is the most uncuddly cat I've ever met," she tattled, as she helped Kate take her suitcases out of the taxi.

"I know," Kate sighed. "He was such an adorable kitten, I just don't know where he went wrong." Kate inserted her key into the door and flung it open. "He hasn't attacked the doberman next door yet, has he?"

Jessica followed her up the stairs to the bedroom. "No. No direct attacks, just a very snotty outlook on life. He was interested in me when he heard the can opener and thought I was opening a can of cat food, and that was the extent of our friendship."

"It's a stage he's going through," Kate assured her as

she set her suitcase down on the flowered bedspread. "I'm sure he'll outgrow it."

Jessica looked disbelieving as she changed the subject. "I've been meaning to ask you if I could send someone over to interview you."

Kate looked at her curiously. "What for?"

"For the series I told you about on women who are successful in male-dominated areas."

Kate nodded. "I suppose I could make time for an interview."

"Good. I'll have Belinda call you to set up a date and time." Jessica sat down on the bed. "Where are you going to be traveling to next?"

"England," Kate replied. She kept her back to Jessica as she continued hanging up clothes. She would be in London; that was where Ian Nigel had told her he lived. It would be so simple to pick up the phone while she was in London and call him. But she wouldn't, of course, because it wasn't sensible to start anything with him. As long as Amalacorp was contracting to do work with his company, it wasn't expedient for her to see him socially. That was something Kate knew she would have to remind herself of again when she was in London. She was certain the temptation to see Ian once she was there was going to be great.

Kate was in the office only three days, and most of that time was spent reviewing material about the job sites she would be visiting in Europe. The first one was a small generating station in northern Italy, then she was stopping to inspect a bridge that was under construction in Spain. But the final project was the one she was most anxious to see. It was a dam in the Cotswolds that Denham company was having constructed as a source of power for some of their downstream industrial plants.

Frank Moyer stopped in her office late Wednesday afternoon while she was putting some papers into her attaché case. She greeted him with a smile. "I glanced at the report on the tunnel work in Argentina and sent it up to your office with my recommendations."

"Good." He crossed to the chair across from her and sat down. "I talked to Ian Nigel on the phone today, and mentioned that you would be in England. If you're not too busy, I'd like for you to call him; he likes to stay abreast of what's going on at the project. Fill him in on any details about the work that he's not clear on. His company has never built a dam this size or as expensive as this, and he's taking a big personal interest in it."

"I see," she murmured, recalling suddenly the intimate dream she had had of Ian and feeling even now a surge of longing at the memory. She kept her thoughts about Ian Nigel concealed as she asked briskly, "Denham has a man at the site, don't they?"

"Oh, sure," Frank agreed, "but Ian likes to get his information from several sources. He's a bit like Burke, you know—doesn't exactly trust anyone."

Kate had not seen that side of him at the party, but naturally he would be skeptical. Anyone who had become chairman of the board at his age would have a finely-developed sense of suspicion; people who survived and prospered always did. "Isn't Mr. Nigel rather young to be a chairman of the board of a company the size of Denham? From what I've read, it's quite large and has holdings in diversified areas. He doesn't even look like he's forty years old."

"He's thirty-seven or thirty-eight," Frank replied. "His father was the last chairman, but I don't think Ian slid in on his name and shares alone. He's a pretty shrewd man. Damned shrewd," he added thoughtfully as he rose. "I'll see you when you get back from your trip. Have a good time."

Kate watched Frank leave and then sat for a moment staring down at her desk, a small smile playing on her lips. So she would be seeing Ian Nigel again after all, she reflected.

The secretary's voice on the intercom brought Kate back to the present. "Ms. Hines, the journalist from the *Record*, is here to see you."

"Thank you. Send her in." Kate smoothed her dusty-rose linen jacket and looked up with a smile as the door to her office opened and Belinda Hines stepped through the door. Kate rose and stretched forward a hand to introduce herself to the elegant black woman.

Belinda Hines settled down to her task with notebook in hand. "Could you begin by telling me what your position is within the company?" she asked with crisp efficiency.

"I'm in charge of the foundations section," Kate replied. "Basically, there are three main sections that deal with the engineering facet of the company's work —technical services, foundations and construction. Technical services is comprised of people who do the planning and initial design work when a project is in the bidding stages. If Amalacorp is awarded the contract to construct the project, technical services follows up with detailed designs and drawings for that particular job. My section is involved with the foundation exploration and preparation of a site for the dam, bridge or whatever is being built there. The third main engineering branch is construction. They're the ones who directly oversee the work in the field."

Belinda nodded and jotted notes quickly. "How many people are under you?"

"There are fifty people working in my section— mainly soils-engineers, geologists, surveyors and inspectors."

"What is your primary responsibility?"

"My main function is as a manager. I review reports, make sure the cross-sections and maps are drawn up with the necessary information for the field offices and contractors, oversee the coordination of design's work with foundation's work. Very often design and foundation are working on different aspects of the same job."

"So you are mainly a manager and you do very little actual engineering?"

Kate nodded.

"Are you tied up in meetings a great deal?"

"Yes. I attend meetings with contractors and other company officials as well as frequently talking with men in my section who stop in my office to give me an informal report of progress or to offer suggestions on how something could be done more efficiently."

The interviewer laid her pen aside and asked candidly, "You're not married, are you?"

"No," Kate acknowledged with a smile.

"Tell me, do you think there is room in a really successful woman's life for a career and a husband and family?" Belinda smiled and added, "Or even a meaningful relationship?"

Kate considered the question for a moment before she said slowly, "I think there is a myth of superwoman who can do all things and be all things to all people. However, I do think with careful planning and an understanding on both sides, a woman could have a fulfilling relationship with a man." Most women could, she amended silently, but she knew she could not. She had not gone to Harvard and worked so hard for nothing. The choice seemed clear to her; either she could devote herself to her work or to building a successful life with a man. Men were nice, of course, but she needed the satisfaction of knowing she was making her own mark on the world and the security of knowing she was not dependent on anyone.

Belinda smiled. "I hope you're right. I've just become engaged," she confided. "One more question. Since you are already in a prestigious position with Amalacorp, what are your goals for yourself from this point on?"

"My goal is to do a satisfying job for my employers. Since I'm new in the company, it's important for me to learn how the company works and to fit my style of doing business to theirs."

"I'm sure you'll do quite well in that," Belinda assured her as she stood to leave. "I've enjoyed talking with you, Kate. As I mentioned on the phone, a photographer will be stopping by later in the week to take a few pictures for the story, and we will send you a tear sheet before the article appears."

Kate rose also and walked to the door with her. "It's been nice talking with you, Belinda."

"Where did you say you were going to next?" Belinda asked.

"Europe," Kate answered.

"Oh, yes. Well, have a nice trip." With a wink, she added, "Maybe you'll meet a handsome man there and have the opportunity to find out if a woman can have it all."

Kate smiled. "Perhaps," she murmured. At any rate she would be seeing Ian Nigel. That was a pleasant prospect, even though she had decided on a strictly-business approach to their meetings. She strongly suspected that he was a man who could make her waver in her decision to pursue her career singlemindedly.

Sunday night Kate left for Italy. She was still a victim of jet lag as the project manager showed her around the generating station that was over half-completed. Around her, the workers chatted to each other in Italian. She left the next day for Spain, where the work on the bridge across a wide river valley was in the first stages of construction. They were still driving pilings for the abutment on one side, although the other was completed and the platform for the deck was being built. She left Spain on Monday morning and flew to England for the last stop of her trip.

Kate knew from reading the background information about the dam site that the Cotswold Hills were a series of whalebacked oolitic limestone crests and valleys that stretched 50 miles from Chipping Campden in the north to the extreme south of the county of Gloucestershire. What the report had failed to convey was an adequate picture of the stone walls that divided the sweeping sheep-pastures of short-cropped fescue grass, the flashing trout-streams and the quaint little villages that dotted the hillsides, their stone buildings covered with lichen and moss.

Kate had a clear view of those sights from the project office, which was set atop a steep hill. She gazed out the window into the distance, appreciatively surveying the scenery before she turned her eyes directly downward. The picture below was in startling contrast to the serene rolling green fields.

She looked down on a wide swath where the grass and trees had been stripped away, leaving the dirt and rock exposed. Eventually a dam nearly a mile long would span the distance between the two hills. Already the first stage of the embankment—up to half of its final height—had been constructed on the other side of the stream. A cofferdam, a temporary dam to prevent flooding during construction, was in place across the creek downstream of where the work was in progress. Another cofferdam, to divert the flow of the water while work was being done in the stream bed, had been built upstream of the work area. In the channel concrete monoliths were tilted upward like rows of dragon's teeth to disperse the energy of the water that would someday come over the dam. Kate's eyes moved to the side of the creek the building was on. Below her, massive, earthmoving machines skirted past each other as they performed their various functions—sprinkling water, rolling and compressing the earth and preparing the foundation for the dam.

"Ready to go back down?" a friendly voice behind her asked.

She turned with a smile to face Stan Watson. He was a simian-looking man with shoulders pushed forward on his short, stocky frame and skin weathered a tough nut-brown. But he was capable. He had worked on complex dams in all parts of the world. To him, Kate realized, Denham dam must seem like a piece of cake after the mile-long dams and arch designs he had supervised.

"I'm ready." She picked up her white hard hat from atop the work table where she had been studying tables of liquid limits. "Does this dam lack challenge for you, Stan?" she asked lightly as she followed him outside and stepped into a mud-spattered green pickup which bore the company's name on the side.

He shook his head. "Nope. Every site has its own problems. You can get into trouble if you think because something isn't on as big a scale that it's not going to present unexpected troubles." He changed the subject as he guided the truck down the steep dirt road into the work area. "I thought you might like to see the archaeological area. We also turned up an unexpected bit of bad foundation. If we have time, I'll take you past it." Stan waved to the heavy-equipment drivers as he swung around them and bounced in and out of pot holes. A sideways glance at him convinced Kate that he was completely at home in the morass of mud and heavy sheep-foot rollers.

He raised his voice as they passed a noisy air compressor and returned to their original discussion as if there had been no interruption. "The thing about building a dam is that each one is different. Even after the specs are drawn up in the office, a lot of things come up in the field that require further modification." He steered sharply to avoid a large pot hole and then started up the hill. Halfway up he stopped the truck with a lurch near a small copse of trees. "We can't bulldoze these until the archaeologists have finished their work," he explained. He jumped out and Kate followed him to a small square area. It had clearly marked boundaries, cordoned off with string running from stake to stake.

"I don't think they've found much, a few shards of pottery or some such," Stan explained disinterestedly. "They should be out of here in a few days, so we can get in to work. They're behind schedule already." With a grin, he added, "To hear them talk, you'd think they'd found the skull of the missing link."

Kate smiled and started back to the truck. The company always hired a consultant, usually a university group, to do an analysis of historic and prehistoric sites. Only rarely did they find anything of real significance.

They drove back down the hillside and alongside the embankment. In its half-completed state it was the height of a levee and had the same wide, flat top. Stan stopped the truck and pointed toward the slide. "Not a bad one," he threw over his shoulder as he walked to the embankment, bent and picked up a small piece of dirt. He rubbed it casually between his thumb and forefinger.

They walked back to the truck and started toward the office. Halfway up the hill, Stan pointed out the window toward a section of the cut-off trench.

"There's where we found some bad foundation," he explained as they wove past a huge sprinkler truck which made their pickup look toy-like.

Kate paid no attention to the mammoth vehicle; she was looking back at the part of the cut-off trench Stan had pointed out. "Did you remove the incompetent material?" she asked.

"No, grouted. We pumped enough concrete into it to get it plenty tight. It won't leak," he assured her.

"Good." She turned back around and grabbed for the dashboard to stabilize herself when Stan hit a particularly deep rut.

Chapter 7

Kate walked into the Ritz, past the round entrance leading into a long promenade that ran the length of the hotel. She stopped only for an instant to glance around at the high ceilings, mirrored and marbled walls and gilded statuary. She had never stayed here before, although she had eaten in the Winter Garden, a room in the center of the hotel that was a journey back into a time when its marble pillars, pink plush chairs and chandeliers dripping crystal had been commonplace. She checked in and followed the bellboy up to her room.

When she had called Ian Nigel from the dam site and informed him she was spending the weekend in London, he had suggested she meet him for dinner Friday night to discuss the project. A quick look at her watch told her she still had two hours before she was to meet him at Annabel's. She showered and changed into an oatmeal-colored suit with contrasting trim of black velvet. The straight skirt fell to just below her knees although a generous slit up each side revealed more of her long legs. She decided it was a nice blend between the business uniform of a working woman who was meeting a business associate for dinner and a dress that was suitable for a restaurant with the élan for which Annabel's was famous. Her dark hair was caught back behind each ear with a mother-of-pearl comb.

Kate arrived at the club to find Ian Nigel waiting in a room with walls full of pictures and crowded sofas full of debs and businessmen sipping apéritifs. He looked the well-groomed English gentleman in a tweed jacket that was slightly nipped at the waist in European style. To complete the effect, he wore a white cotton shirt and oxblood silk tie and a pair of well-tailored gray slacks.

"I hope I'm not late," she greeted him with a smile as he rose.

"You're right on time." He took her arm and led her through a swinging door into a dimly-lit, low-ceilinged dining room. Square columns of polished brass made a stately parade down the room. Tables were lined down the center of the room and set beside mirrored walls that were painted with Poucette figures. They were seated in a table near the front, far from the glassed-off section where dancers were moving on a tiny floor.

As Ian studied the leatherbound wine list, Kate darted an unobtrusive look at him. He looked tall, even sitting down, and in the uncertain light his face was shadowed mysteriously. She noticed a small scar over one eye that she had not seen before, and she wondered idly what had caused it.

"I expect the Cotswolds are lovely. This is just the time of year when the hills are blooming with butterfly-orchids and one can find lilies-of-the-valley in the woods," he said.

"It was quite beautiful," she agreed. "Some of the villages I drove through on the way to London are incredibly quaint. I felt as if I were passing through another century." She laughed lightly. "I almost expected to see monks crossing the roads instead of school children in uniforms."

He smiled pleasantly. He had a most disarming smile, she thought as he laid the menu aside. "I like the Pouilly Fuissé, but they have a very good château-bottled claret if you prefer it."

"Either's fine." She steered the talk toward business. "Have you been out to see the job site?"

"Not for over four months. I've been rather busy lately."

"I see." The hair on the back of his hands was touched with gold, just like his hair, she noted as he folded his hands on the table in front of him.

"Are you enjoying your new job? I recollect that you told me you were new when I spoke with you in Dallas."

"Yes, I've been with Amalacorp just a little over a month." Around them, Kate was conscious that other couples were exchanging light gossip and flirtatious banter. The mood of the restaurant was not conducive to discussing business, but that was why she was here. "Did you have any particular questions about the dam, Mr. Nigel? I think I could answer most of them; I've read quite a lot about the project in addition to the time I just spent there."

"Nothing specific. I merely wondered how the work was progressing." He hesitated. "Mr. Arnold, Denham's man at the project, mentioned a few weeks back that there was some unsuitable foundation material discovered that had to be grouted. I take it the bad material was something Amalacorp had not expected?"

Kate was on firm ground now, and glad to have a specific engineering problem to explain. It put her fully in mind of the fact she was here as a representative of her company. "There was a small problem, but it has been corrected. The core holes Amalacorp drilled were placed at carefully-selected locations to give us the maximum information about the subsurface conditions."

He was watching her with eyes that were a disturbing

steel-blue. "Then it was an isolated occurrence and it doesn't pose any major problems for the dam?"

"No. Once we found the problem, we corrected it." She saw his face relax and he gave her an engaging smile. Frank had compared Ian Nigel to Burke Walters, and when Ian had listened to her words with a calculating look, she had been struck by the similarity between them. But there were surely many ways the two men were different; she would never have expected to see such a charming expression on Burke Walter's face. But then, charm was something she had long since learned to distrust.

"I have every confidence in Amalacorp," Ian assured her.

"I'm glad."

As he gave their orders to the waiter, Kate looked around the room. She recognized a shipping heiress who was seated in a corner of the room with a short, dark man—perhaps he was a candidate for her fourth husband. At another table Kate saw a lovely young princess whose marriage had gone awry; she looked lonely and pensive. All around her she saw the same faces that graced the "People" section of *Time* magazine. She knew Anabel's was a club where only a carefully-selected few were admitted. Kate looked back at Ian Nigel. His position as chairman of the board of Denham would not, by itself, have assured a membership to this exclusive club. He was probably from an old, established family. Kate pushed aside those reflections. She had no way of knowing what kind of private life Ian Nigel led, and it was pointless to speculate. Besides, the fact that the man across the table was undeniably attractive and that she felt tempted to flirt with him only made it the more imperative that she remember that she was here for company reasons.

But even as she made the resolution, the memory of her dream about Ian came into her mind. Kate stole a quick look at him and discovered he was regarding her quizzically. Something about the quiet humor in his eyes—as if he were aware of a secret—brought a touch of color stealing into her cheeks. Of course, he couldn't know about her dream where he had played such an exciting part, but *she* knew. And the remembrance of it was enough to cause her embarrassment. It was unnerving to try to carry on a business discussion with a man about whom she had had such erotic fantasies.

Kate was spared the difficulty of doing so when their waiter delivered their dinners. She had just tasted the Hollandaise sauce atop her Frittata Fiorentina when a man stopped at their table and greeted Ian jovially, "Ian, my dear boy, I didn't expect to see you here."

"A man has to eat," Ian returned genially.

"Precisely," the other man agreed. He was a portly, balding man who turned to Kate with a smile. "You must be Lady Davina."

"No, Martin, this is Kate Justin," Ian intervened.

"My apologies," he continued unabashed. "Pleasure to meet you, Miss Justin. I'm Martin Winchester. I rode in the Quorn with Ian's father."

"How nice," she murmured vaguely, while Ian explained across the table, "It's a fox hunt."

"Well, I must get back to my table or the chocolate ice will have melted—it's the best part of the meal." He excused himself with a nod to both of them and a conspiratorial beam at Ian. Martin Winchester obviously thought they were together under romantic circumstances, Kate realized.

It had happened to Kate before. With a smile at Ian, she lamented, "I hope this doesn't complicate things for you." So Ian was seeing a titled woman? Such a revelation should not have been unexpected. After all, he was attractive and wealthy and very eligible. Still, she was momentarily disheartened by the news; even the realization he was out of her reach because of his professional ties to Amalacorp did not entirely assuage that feeling.

He looked at her in confusion. "What?"

"Mr. Winchester might mention to the wrong person that he saw you here with me."

A light of comprehension dawned in his eyes. "Not to worry; there's no problem in that area."

"Good." Possibly his relationship with the mysterious Lady Davina was not a romantic one. He obviously didn't intend to divulge any more details of his personal life; she recognized the wisdom of his choice, even though she felt a certain curiosity.

"What of you? Is there no one in the States who would view the sight of us sitting in such well-heeled intimacy with some jealousy?" His question sounded completely off-hand.

"I don't date one particular man," she replied evenly. That was certainly true. The fact that she had not dated any one at all since she moved to Dallas was something she did not care to relate. "Besides," she added smoothly, "I'd never date a jealous man. My job requires me to travel and meet too many people; I couldn't be tied to someone who was possessive. Even if it weren't for my job, I want too much freedom for myself."

"I can understand that. One does not willingly surrender one's freedom unless it's for someone who means a very great deal to one."

"Point taken," she murmured, studying the wine in her glass. "For the right person I would surrender *some* of my freedom. I simply wouldn't allow anyone to *take* it from me." She laughed lightly and finished her drink. "So much for philosophy. We seem to have strayed from talk of the dam."

He shrugged. "This is Friday night," he reminded her. "Surely Amalacorp doesn't pay you to spend every spare minute thinking about their projects? You have to have some time to talk of other things—things that interest you."

"They sent me over here on business. Tonight I'm

yours to discuss the dam. Tomorrow I'm going to have my day off to go shopping and sightseeing." Her words were, strictly speaking, true. She had come to dinner with Ian to discuss business, and tomorrow was her day of leisure. But she already knew that her most pleasant moments in London were taking place right now. In fact, she admitted to herself, her evening would be pleasant even if Ian spent the whole time talking about how to rid a yard of gophers or what he thought of the current political-economic climate in light of recent developments in Third World countries. The simple truth was that he fascinated her. Looking at him in the dim light that left his face partially shadowed afforded her an enjoyment she had not felt for a long time.

"What are Americans paying for each other's thoughts now? Is it still a penny, or has inflation edged it up to a nickel?" he asked with a faint smile.

"They're still a penny," she answered lightly. "I want to see cash on the barrelhead before I reveal any information."

He dug into his pocket and extracted a handful of coins. "Take your pick," he invited as he laid them on the table.

Kate picked up a small copper coin and rubbed it between her fingers thoughtfully before she replied, "I was wondering if I should rotate the tires on my car when I return to America."

He stretched his hand forward across the table imperiously. "I want my money back."

"You don't believe me?" she asked with innocent sincerity. "I assure you, a representative of Amalacorp would never lie to anyone in Denham company. In fact," she added, "I may rotate some of the tires on the company cars when I return." The fact that this was a business dinner and even the knowledge there was a certain Lady Davina in his life did not dim her playful spirit. She knew she was flirting, but she couldn't stop herself.

"Let's leave Denham and Amalacorp out of this for

just a few minutes," he said softly. "We'll just be plain Kate Justin and Ian Nigel."

The laughter in her eyes was swept away and she regarded him pensively, trying to read his inscrutable expression. "I can't do that."

"All right." His voice was quiet, but when he spoke again it was in a heartier tone. "Does Amalacorp dance with Denham?" He motioned toward the glass doors that led to the dance floor.

She rose. "I think so."

The dance floor was so crowded that it wasn't realistic to say that they danced together. Still, they touched each other as they were nudged on either side by people around them who elbowed for more space. Kate looked up at Ian from beneath her eyelashes. He must be 6'3" at least, she estimated. He was the first man in a long time who made her feel petite at 5'8".

Ian looked down at her with a grin of resignation. "I don't know which side is winning the battle on this floor, but it's safe to say we are not. Let's sit down where we can talk again."

She nodded her agreement and he took her arm as they walked back to their table. As he pulled her chair out for her, Kate considered how often she had dined with men in a professional capacity. Business luncheons and dinners were a part of her job. The problem of having to separate her personal feelings from company loyalty had never come up before; she simply had never developed an interest in any of the other men. And she ought to have her head examined for doing so now.

"I daresay it's as well the floor was crowded," Ian remarked. "It kept you from seeing that I am not much of a dancer."

"Mr. Winchester mentioned he hunted with your father. Are you a sportsman?"

"I'm afriad I don't have time for such things, and I was never much interested in them. I ride occasionally, but that's about the extent of it. And you, what do you do for relaxation?"

"I play a little tennis, swim when the weather is nice, and I like to sail." Joe had owned a catamaran and had taught her how to sail.

One of the mother-of-pearl combs slipped through her hair and dropped onto the table as her loose curls tumbled forward. She picked up the comb and replaced it before looking up to see Ian smiling at her.

"You didn't get it on quite straight," he noted.

"Oh." Kate pulled the comb out and patted her hair.

"Allow me to assist you," he offered gallantly as he leaned forward across the small table. He smoothed her hair with the ends of the mother-of-pearl comb before pinning it into her hair. "There, you look as good as new."

He had been so close that she could smell the faint musk scent of his aftershave, and the back of his hand had brushed against her cheek for a moment. Those were insignificant things, of course, and she shouldn't have noticed them at all. But she had.

The plain fact of the matter was that there was something about Ian Nigel that made Kate feel an inner radiance. It was, of course, infatuation. The symptoms were plain, even though she had not had such a severe attack since she had fallen violently in love with the high school football captain. It was certainly a good thing that she would not be seeing Ian Nigel after this weekend. . . .

Chapter 8

Three days later, as Kate sat in the conference room at the oversize table, the thought of Ian Nigel was completely erased from her mind. She listened intently to the grim-faced man pacing the length of the table. He whirled at the other end of the room and started back. Kate was conscious of the wariness of the company officials around her.

"Lost it! Is there anyone here who needs a clarification of what that means to Amalacorp?" Burke Walters demanded, catching a few reluctant eyes before dismissing each of them with a contemptuous glare.

No one needed to be told what the loss of a project to build a tunnel beneath a major river meant to an engineering company. With a price tag that floated a million dollars after it like a banner, it was a plum for which several companies had bid ferociously. Kate suspected Burke's bitterness over not winning the contract had been accented because word had been leaked not two weeks ago that Amalacorp was a very strong contender.

Because she had never seen Burke Walters greatly pleased with anything, she had come to the conclusion that he accepted defeat with the same calm he accorded triumph. But it was evident from his present agitation that he did not.

He stopped behind his own chair at the head of the table, gripping its leather back with tense hands. "I think there is a lesson to be learned from this, and I hope you will all take note of it. Our estimate on that project was too goddam high because we overdesigned. We had rock bolts stuffed on top of rock bolts, and we estimated so damn much shotcrete that the weight of it alone would have collapsed the tunnel."

Around her, Kate sensed men tensing at the president's words. The bid for the project had been finalized long before she came to work for Amalacorp, so she knew his criticism did not concern her, but she felt uncomfortable all the same. Burke Walters had reviewed the bid on the tunnel and had approved it at the time. But that made scant difference in his condemnation of those he viewed as having lost the job for Amalacorp. She had a pretty good idea where he fixed the blame by the hard look he bestowed on a few people.

"The cost of construction items is rising so swiftly that we can no longer afford to overcompensate for all minor problems—if, indeed, we ever could. There is no reason to have outlandish safety factors built in." His tone was scathing, as if he were talking to ignorant and unruly children. His look fell on the man beside Kate, as it had a time or two before.

She saw Harold Brown clench his hands together tighter in his lap. She knew he was nearly bursting to answer Burke Walters, but recognized this was not the time to do so. Kate glanced over to see his jaw set in a firm line.

Burke noted Harold's expression as well. "You look as if you have something to say, Brown," he barked.

Harold Brown straightened with dignity. "I do,

Burke." His quiet voice carried through the room, the nervous fluttering of papers ceased. "We lost a bid. I think we need to keep that in perspective. Amalacorp will lose a lot more bids if word gets out that we're going to start slapping our projects together."

"Are you through?" Burke demanded.

"Yes."

"Then let me address myself to your *point*." Burke said the last word with such a heavy load of sarcasm it was evident he didn't believe Harold had made a point. "I didn't say we were going to start 'slapping' anything together. I said we are going to have to stop overloading our estimates with expensive safety factors. You can look at some of our recent bids and see what I mean. We had items on this project that none of the other bidders included."

"That doesn't mean the items weren't necessary for a good project," Harold argued stubbornly.

For a moment Burke eyed the man beside Kate with cold thoughtfulness; then he said in a voice of steel and gravel, "We did not get the contract and they did. In the future Amalacorp will do whatever is necessary to make certain that doesn't happen again." He paused and surveyed the room before announcing, "That's all that needs to be discussed today. If anyone has anything further to say, please see me in my office or bring the matter up at next Monday's meeting."

There were no objections. Kate put her notebook back into her attaché case and pushed her chair back. Around her, men were breaking up into small groups and speaking in low tones, but no one approached Burke. He stood rubbing his hand across his forehead, as if he had a headache and wished to ease the pain.

Kate walked out into the hall and back to her office. Her secretary greeted her with a warm smile. "How was your trip last week?"

The question jolted Kate out of her thoughts about the meeting and back to the memory of England. "It was very productive. How were things here, Nedra?"

"Hectic," the gray-haired secretary replied as she walked to a filing cabinet and began to sort through a sheaf of papers. "I'm sure you'll be able to tell just how busy when you see the stack of work on your desk."

Kate returned the older woman's smile and stepped into her office. There was indeed a pile of work laid out in neat stacks on one corner of her desk, but she did not immediately look through it. Instead, she walked to the window and gazed down at the pedestrians passing below. What a way to start a work week, she thought, especially when she was still suffering from jet lag from her flight back yesterday.

Still, she reminded herself philosophically, Burke Walters might have a right to be angry. She hadn't seen the estimates that went in with the tunnel bid, but perhaps the Amalacorp people had been too cautious when they submitted their proposal and had added costs that could have been shaved enough to win the contract. It wasn't the fact that the president had been so abrasive that bothered her now. What worried her was that he had been so clearly upset about the loss of the job. Did that mean Amalacorp was hurting for work?

"Thinking of jumping?"

Kate turned to see Frank standing in the doorway regarding her with a smile. "No, I wouldn't dare," she replied. "I can imagine what Burke would say if I broke the glass."

He crossed to stand beside her at the window. In an amused voice, he said, "I wouldn't worry about this morning if I were you. Burke gets keyed up now and then, but he never stays that way long. He'll be back to just being plain old blustering, insulting, distrustful Burke in a few more hours. He's annoyed that we didn't get the job," Frank continued mildly, "but he doesn't expect to land every major project. Besides, there are a couple of big jobs still out that we very well may get."

"Of course." But Kate had heard that Amalacorp's chances of landing either of those jobs was very slight.

Frank changed the subject briskly. "What did you think of Denham dam?"

"Everything seems to be going well. They've had a few problems, but nothing major. Stan Watson is quite capable. There's only one place I think we need to do some more work."

"Where's that?" Frank asked casually.

"I think we should do a little more drilling in the area where some incompetent material was uncovered. I realize it was grouted once, but just in case there's a large cavity below ground, it wouldn't hurt to punch down a few more core holes."

He shrugged. "If you think it's necessary. Talk to the explorations people and have them plot a few more holes."

After Frank left, Kate applied herself to the work on her desk. Nedra had been right; a lot had transpired the week she had been gone. There was so much to do that she stayed late that evening. When she arrived at her apartment Jessica was out in front picking up her mail.

"You look beat," her petite friend greeted Kate. Jessica's layered blonde hair was pushed back from her face and she was wearing a lavender jogging outfit.

"I am," Kate replied as she stopped at her own mailbox. "Have you already been running or are you going now?"

"Just going."

"Mind if I join you? I can be ready in fifteen or twenty minutes."

"I'll wait."

Kate walked into her apartment. It had been a rough day, but she was too restless to settle down to an evening of reading or watching television. She exchanged her pale linen skirt and jacket for a pair of gray gym pants and a sweatshirt of the same color. Then she opened a can of cat food for Cuddles and stepped out the front door. Jessica was waiting on the doorstep.

"Ready?"

"Yeah." They started off at an easy pace, talking as they ran.

"So how come you look so tired today? Did you have a wild weekend in London?"

"Hardly," Kate said. "And there was a lot of work waiting for me when I got back."

They separated as they passed a group of people with tennis rackets in hand. "You spend too much time with your work," Jessica said with conviction. "You need to meet a man."

"I'm not sure a man isn't half of my problem now," Kate returned with a rueful laugh. When she had walked onto the plane in London, she thought she had effectively left Ian Nigel behind. Apparently she had not, for thoughts of him or one of his anecdotes had crept in and out of her mind all day.

Jessica glanced at her. "Old flame in Kansas City?"

"No, this is a man who lives in London."

"Forget him," Jessica advised. "Long-distance affairs never work out."

"You're right. Besides, there are other complications." Her voice trailed off in the unsteady laboring of her breathing. For several minutes the only sounds were the thuds of their shoes hitting the hard-packed clay path.

When they stopped to do stretching exercises, Jessica pushed back the headband that had slipped down to just above her eyes and continued, "I know just the man to introduce you to. He's perfect."

Kate straightened and leaned back against a tree, drawing in deep breaths of air as she watched a couple ride past on bicycles. "Perfect men are pretty scarce," she observed. "I'm surprised he hasn't been snatched up."

Jessica laughed. "Okay, a little skepticism is in order. He was married until just over a year ago. His name is Elliot Downey, he owns part of a construction business but he used to work for Amalacorp, so you already have something in common. He's good-looking," Jessica continued, swinging her arms down to touch her toes. "He's in his middle thirties, he drives a Porsche, and he has a lot of style." She drew herself up straight. "Interested?"

"I don't know." Perhaps she was too hesitant to meet men. The one Jessica had described might be the very person to put an end to all thoughts of Ian, she considered.

Jessica started down the path again and Kate followed. "I can introduce you so that it won't be obvious. His parents are giving a cocktail party this weekend. They're very socially visible people; he comes from good stock," she added in an aside, and then paused to regain her breath. A moment later she resumed, "I'll be going to the party to cover it for the paper, and you can go as my guest."

"Is that proper?" Kate asked, pushing back the limp strands of her hair that were floating down into her eyes.

"Of course. I'm always welcome to take a guest. This way you can look Elliot over and have a chance to meet him without it being obvious someone is trying to get you together."

"I might as well, I don't have any plans for this weekend." With a smile, she added, "I suppose that doesn't sound very gracious. What I meant to say was 'I'd be delighted to attend the party with you and thank you for including me.'"

Jessica laughed. "Save the prim and proper comments. And we might as well both save our breath and concentrate on running."

Kate nodded her agreement.

Jessica pointed out Elliot Downey shortly after they entered the room. He was standing near the walnut mantel of the large fireplace in his parents' spacious living room. An hour later Kate had still not been introduced to him, but she was aware that his eyes had rested on her from time to time as she and Jessica mingled with the other guests in the crowded living room.

The decor of the large house, set in an extremely fashionable area of North Dallas, was modern. The walls of the room were adorned with a Dali and two Picassos. Even the furniture seemed like works of art. Bright green and blue chairs were designed to loop back on themselves to form both the seat and support at the floor. They looked as capable of becoming airborne as providing a place to sit, Kate thought. Only the baby grand piano in one corner of the room looked conventional.

Around her, Kate noted the women present were dressed in chic clothes. They obviously had money as well as taste, she reflected as she glanced at a pretty woman wearing a silver lamé tunic with slacks. The other women present wore cream colors with petite ruffles around the neck and wrists or bright silks that molded to slender bodies. The little designer touches on their clothes were as telltale as signatures. Jewels adorned feminine throats left bare by plunging necklines. Dainty movements of their hands sent Cartier emeralds and diamonds sparkling.

Kate was wearing a black Spanish-style blouse and long skirt. Red and white flowers were embroidered around the drawstring of the scooped neckline of the peasant blouse, which was tucked into a flowing skirt with embroidered flowers sprinkled around the hem.

Out of the corner of her eye Kate saw Elliot Downey approach where she stood with Jessica and another couple. She looked up as he stopped near her. He was as good-looking as Jessica had said. Green eyes looked out from beneath a fringe of dark lashes. His hair was a deep, burnished red, almost copper-colored, and he had the body of a man who kept himself in shape.

He smiled at her and then at Jessica. "Well, Jessica, I don't believe you've introduced me to your friend."

"Haven't I?" She was completely off-hand. "This is Kate Justin. She's an engineer with Amalacorp." To Kate, Jessica added, "Elliot has always preferred women with brains, so you're a cinch."

He laughed good-naturedly, "That's for my benefit," he informed Kate. "I've known Jessica for years, and she won't let me forget that I was more interested in cheerleaders in college than I was in a good discussion of the economy. She doesn't realize I've changed a good deal since then."

Jessica leaned forward and gave him an affectionate kiss on the cheek. "No one knows it better than I. Now I'm going to get myself another drink and flirt with Isaac Latimer. Be nice to Kate."

"Jessica mentioned you work for Amalacorp; what do you do now?" Kate asked.

"I'm in construction and land developing. We build apartments and condominiums."

"That's a good field to be in right now," Kate remarked. "It's the only part of the construction industry surviving the economic crunch." She took a sip of her drink. Elliot was studying her with obvious interest.

"Right. I hear there are some pretty big firms teetering on the brink of failure. The cost of loans and interest is making the business pretty chancy."

"I suppose so," Kate murmured politely. Actually, she was not interested in discussing business right now.

"Hanging on to my every word, are you?" he asked genially. "Okay, let's change the subject and talk about you. What's your favorite color?"

She smiled. "Deep somber gray."

"Favorite song?"

"Gregorian chants."

"Mine too! We obviously have much in common.

Why don't we have dinner together next weekend and find out just how much?"

She considered the invitation a moment before nodding. "Sounds lovely." She brought the glass to her lips and took a small sip. "What did you do at Amala-corp?"

"If you asked Burke Walters, he'd tell you I made a damned nuisance of myself, but my official capacity was as his administrative assistant." With a boyish grin, he added, "I was so irreplaceable that when I left he didn't hire another assistant. We're still friends," he added. "He taught me a lot about the industry and even encouraged me to start my own company."

Burke Walters as mentor and paternal figure escaped Kate's imagination, but she said demurely, "I'm sure he's very knowledgeable."

Elliot laughed at her tone. "From what you've seen of him, I doubt he has been very endearing. I think he likes for the people under him to hate him; he figures any emotion toward him is good, and hate is as welcome as love. Just as well he feels that way," Elliot said, "because I don't think he strikes adulation in very many employees' hearts. But he has his good points as well." With a shake of his head, he continued, "Let's forget Burke and get back to you. Do you live alone?"

"With my cat," she replied.

"A feline lover," he murmured. "I have a dog myself. He and I go for a tramp every day in the woods." He took a sip of his drink and concluded with a wide smile, "We enjoy it, but the tramp is getting awfully tired."

Kate laughed lightly. "What an interesting dog you have."

"Yes," he agreed. "I took Fido to a movie the other day and the man behind us was simply astounded when Fido applauded. I was too; Fido hated the book."

Kate rolled her eyes heavenward. "Could we talk of

something else?" she suggested. Elliot was not the most scintillating conversationalist she had ever met, but she found his easy good humor relaxing, and he was not unattractive. If it were not for a man with a pair of blue-gray eyes, Kate thought, she could have found Elliot even more appealing.

Chapter 9

Kate didn't talk to Jessica again until they were in the car on the way home. "Did you like Elliot?" Jessica asked as Kate settled back in the seat and leaned her head against the headrest. A combination of the liquor and the late hour made her sleepy.

"He's nice." She opened her eyes and looked at Jessica. In the darkness of the interior of the car, all she could see was a silhouette. "You two seem to be good friends. Did you ever have any romantic interest in him?"

"Once. Not anymore." Jessica hesitated before continuing, "Do you want to know the truth?"

"Of course."

"We were married."

Kate felt as if someone had thrown ice-water on her. For a moment she couldn't gather the words together to form a question. Finally she said slowly, "You mean when you said Elliot was divorced, you meant he was divorced from *you*? Why didn't you tell me?"

The other woman replied amiably, "It didn't occur to me to say so at the time."

"Oh, didn't it?" Kate retorted.

"You don't understand," Jessica said easily. "I'm not married to Elliot *now*. I used to be. At present he's fair game for any woman who wants him. I happen to think you two have a lot in common and I hope you hit it off. You're new in town and you need to meet some eligible men. Elliot's lonely and he needs to get out more."

"For godsake!" Kate expostulated. "You sound like the social director on a cruise ship instead of his ex-wife."

"How am I supposed to sound?" Jessica asked equably. "He introduced me to a man I dated for several months. Why shouldn't I want you to go out with him? He and I are good friends. The fact we are no longer married hasn't ruined that. As a matter of fact, we stood a far better chance of losing our friendship if we stayed married."

Kate was not convinced. "I hate to sound as if I'm stuck in the last century, but I still find it strange that a man's ex-wife works as a matchmaker for him."

"I told you," Jessica continued patiently, "we didn't have a successful marriage. The same things that led to a break-up between us would still keep us apart. That doesn't mean I don't think you and he would make a great couple. You don't have the same problem I had."

"At the risk of prying, what was it?" Kate asked bluntly.

"Success."

"Could you be a little more specific?"

Jessica sighed audibly. "Not in a way you'd understand. Let's just say that Elliot was going places and I wasn't."

"You're an editor on a big newspaper," Kate pointed out. "You've told me you have nine people working for you and two assistant editors. You *are* successful."

"But I was a lowly copy editor when Elliot and I

split." Jessica waved to the guard in front of their apartment complex and he opened the gate for them. "Anyway, I shouldn't have sprung this on you. We'll talk about it over lunch tomorrow after you've had time to assimilate it." She stopped in front of Kate's door.

Kate slid out of the car. Lunch tomorrow probably would be a good time to talk the matter over. Right now she was battling drowsiness and a slight thumping in her head that belatedly warned her she had consumed too much alcohol. "I'll talk to you then," she said before closing the car door and walking to her apartment.

Upstairs in her bedroom, Kate pulled the drawstring on her blouse and let it fall past her slender hips onto the floor. She didn't even bend to pick it up. So Elliot and Jessica had been married, she thought hazily. She would not have figured them for each other's type. Jessica was so ladylike and Elliot was so brash and self-confident. Of course, it was hard to say what it was that attracted people to one another.

She slid into bed and snuggled beneath the soft poplin sheets. She gave only a brief thought to the man across the sea who so appealed to her before she drifted off to sleep.

The waitress in the fashionable tea room seated Kate and Jessica at a white-clothed table by a window. Outside, Kate could see roses growing in a neat little garden where other diners sat at white wrought-iron tables. They wore hats with chiffon flowers and some of the older women wore white gloves.

Jessica began the conversation directly. "I know I made you uncomfortable last night. There are a few things I'd like to explain today." Jessica looked completely cool and unflappable in a pearl-gray jacket and a flared black skirt. Only the nervous movement of her hands as she lit a cigarette gave away the fact she was not entirely at ease.

"You don't have to tell me anything, Jessica, and certainly not if it makes you nervous," Kate objected.

"I *do* want to," Jessica insisted. "I feel like talking today."

The waitress arrived bearing two cups filled with steaming Earl Grey tea. Jessica waited until she had left before continuing, "Where was I? Oh, yes, Elliot and I have known each other forever." She looked downward with a reflective smile. "He was at my fifth birthday party. All the little girls were there in short pink and blue dresses with frills and ribbons and the boys wore Buster Brown suits with bow ties. That was before designers of any stature got into the children's clothing business," she noted, looking up at Kate with a smile. "Like good little rich kids, we ate ice cream in the garden and played pin-the-tail-on-the-donkey. Elliot won."

"Sounds like the beginning of a torrid affair," Kate noted mildly.

"It didn't get too passionate right away," Jessica admitted. "When I was fourteen, I went to a private school in the East and he stayed here to go to prep school. Anyway, we wrote to each other, and when I was home at Christmases we went to the country club cotillions together. After my father, Elliot was the first man I danced with at my coming out party and—" She broke off with a grin. "I'm sure you're not interested in hearing all about my past. The point is, I grew up in a society world. There was a right and wrong way to do everything. There were tons of rules about how a well-bred couple should conduct themselves. Our marriage broke up over the changing roles of women in our society. Cliché enough? Elliot decided I didn't enhance his image, and I decided he was impeding my career. We were suffocating each other."

Kate nodded sympathetically. It sounded simple enough, and she could certainly understand how a marriage rooted in the 1950's could go awry in today's world. Besides, it sounded as if Jessica and Elliot had known each other almost as brother and sister. That would account for why Jessica still took a deep interest in him, Kate considered. The ties that had bound them together had not been those of marriage but of friendship; they had not been dissolved when the marriage had.

"My parents accept the divorce well enough," Jessica continued, "but I think his parents believe it's just a phase we're going through and we'll get back together."

"Hmmm. His parents must be real art buffs," Kate commented, to steer the conversation away from personal waters. "They had some impressive pieces on their walls."

"You're changing the subject," Jessica accused as the waitress set spinach salads in front of each of them.

"Yes, I am. The point has been made that you want me to feel free to date Elliot. Okay, I do. There's no need for further revelations about your marriage—not to me."

"You're going to date him?"

"I think so," Kate replied.

Jessica smiled in satisfaction. "Good, I feel better. In a curious way I still feel very responsible for his happiness, and he hasn't been particularly happy lately."

"I can't promise to make him happy," Kate warned in amusement. "I'll see how it goes."

"I have some news," Jessica continued enthusiastically. "I'm going to England to visit a friend. Her name is Clariss and she's the success story of my old set of friends. She married an English baronet three years ago. She lives like royalty in an old mansion in the heart of Kent. I'll be able to get several articles out of this trip. Clariss is a hometown girl, so there will be a reader interest in her life. She's not Hope Cooke or Grace Kelly, but she's nobility all the same."

Kate nodded and took a sip of her water. Even

though her thoughts were in England, they did not center around Jessica's friend. Rather, Kate was thinking of Ian again. She could picture him in a stately manor house with hunting dogs at his feet while he sipped bourbon, still dressed in riding pinks. Suddenly she wondered when she would see him again.

Elliot called Kate midway through the week to confirm their date for Saturday. "We'll go out somewhere to eat and get to know each other," he told her. "Somewhere that we won't be hounded by people who use too much breath freshener. I'm convinced they're clones trying to take over the world."

"It's so nice to talk to someone who isn't paranoid," she responded sweetly.

"Right you are. I have to hang up now; the phone is probably bugged."

Saturday night Kate dressed in a sleeveless plum-colored cotton dress with white piping around the neckline and arms. Below a slim white belt the skirt blossomed to a stylish fullness. She had lost a little weight since moving to Dallas, she noted as she moved the belt in another notch. She would try to regain it in the next month or so; her whole wardrobe depended on it.

Elliot arrived right on time. He looked casual but well-groomed in a brown sportscoat and beige trousers. "Since it's such a special evening, I even polished my gold tooth," he greeted her. With a glance at his wristwatch, he continued, "I made reservations at Durham House in Waxahachie. We'd better get going; they won't hold the reservations if we're late."

After a knuckle-whitening ride in Elliot's low-slung red Porsche, they arrived at the restaurant fifteen minutes later. Elliot ushered her into a quaint Victorian house that had been completely restored. It was furnished with antiques and complete with a pewter fish tank in the women's room, where Kate retired to repair her wind-blown hair.

When she returned to the dining room, Elliot had just discovered he had forgotten to bring a bottle of wine. Kate shrugged and dipped into the peanut bisque. "Order something here," she suggested.

He gave her a look of pity. "My dear midwesterner, this is Texas, state of vast empty spaces—many of them in people's heads. Liquor in this state is by local option. Waxahachie is dry."

She looked at him in surprise. "What strange laws."

"I have several words for them, but 'strange' isn't one of them," Elliot replied. He pushed the thought of a wineless meal from his mind and changed the subject. "I ran into Frank Moyer this week; he sings your praises."

Kate smiled. "I like working for Frank." He was one of several of the company officials who had told her he was impressed with the job she was doing. Only Burke Walters had made no comment so far. With him, it might be that no news was good news. Kate suspected it would take a major feat to win Burke's commendation. He probably felt he had paid her the highest compliment when he had hired her.

"I always liked Frank," Elliot told her as the waiter set the stuffed trout in front of him. "He's not one to stab a person in the back."

"Every company has back-stabbers," she observed as she picked up her fork and tasted the beef filet with green peppercorns.

"Sure," he agreed. "That's why I like being my own boss."

"I thought you had a partner?" she asked curiously.

"He's a silent partner; I make all the decisions," Elliot explained.

"That could have good as well as bad points," Kate said. "If everything goes well you look good, but one bad decision and it could all come tumbling down."

"That's why I don't make any wrong decisions," he told her with a brash grin.

"Modest," she murmured.

"No one likes a modest leader. Secretaries and draftsmen have a flair for that, but most presidents don't. Who would vote for a candidate who said, 'I'm afraid I'll go to Washington and botch things up even worse than they already are, but if you think of it in November, why don't you vote for me?'"

Kate smiled. Whatever else Elliot was or was not, he did not lack self-confidence. Not that she objected to that, she liked men who were strong and capable. In fact, there was much about Elliot that she liked. Given time and the right circumstances, she thought she might come to like him even better.

Chapter 10

Monday morning Elliot was far from Kate's mind as she leaned back in the leather chair and gazed thoughtfully at the speaker standing at the end of the long conference table. She heard little of the man's explanation of Amalacorp's technique for thermal mining of oil in Russia; her mind was not on the meeting going on around her. She was recalling Frank's words to her when he had stopped at her office door before they had come to the meeting.

"Stan Watson called me," he had begun. "They've finished drilling those extra holes at the dam site you asked them to do."

Kate said nothing as she picked up her fawn-colored jacket and slipped it on, buttoning it carefully as she composed her face back to a serene expression. In truth, she was far from calm. Stan Watson should have been calling her instead of Frank to report foundation findings. That was an oversight she would discuss with Stan when she talked to him again; and that would be immediately after the meeting. She intended to make her position in the company very clear. Once people under her got the idea they could by-pass her, there was no saying where it would stop, and she was not going to let anyone undermine her authority.

"I'll tell you what Stan said after the meeting," Frank had said as they walked into the conference room together.

"Of course." Her smile was placid, like a smooth lake that gives no indication that the waters beneath are churning. Inwardly, she fumed; it was a hell of a position to be put in to be given a report by the man to whom she should have been delivering the report. Stan was making her look like a fool. What would Burke Walters think if he knew of this?

At the end of the table the company president was listening to the speaker with the cold look of disbelief he accorded everyone. Her eyes moved from Burke to Frank. Frank, tall and distinguished-looking, seemed to be everything Burke was not—he was sympathetic and sincere and he took a genuine interest in everyone in the company.

The speaker continued, "The present recovery rate is sixty percent, but I think we could do better if. . . ."

Kate had already read the report; she was familiar with what the man was saying. What she didn't understand was why Burke seemed to be taking such a great interest in the project. In terms of dollars, Amalacorp wasn't making much on the mining work, but she had heard rumors that Burke wanted to tap heavily into foreign projects. He probably assumed if the Russians were well-satisfied with this job, they would contract more to Amalacorp. With contracts of any size becoming increasingly harder to land, Kate knew Amalacorp could use all they could get. Of course, all large engineering companies were in the same bind.

"The oil has the consistency of molasses," the man continued, "and only about two percent can be recovered with surface drilling but. . . ."

Kate looked at Burke again. He was listening to the

speaker with his chin propped in his hand while he
rubbed his index finger constantly back and forth across
his chin. At one time he might have been a handsome
man, she thought. But now, in his mid-fifties, his hair
had receded back to the middle of his skull and he had a
toughness that made him seem completely unapproach-
able.

She looked up in surprise when the meeting ended
with a rustle of papers. Pushing back her chair, she
rose.

"It's nearly twelve, do you have any plans for
lunch?" Frank asked.

"No."

"Good. Let's take a long break and go down to the
Chinese restaurant."

"Sounds good." Actually, she wasn't very hungry.
What she would have rather done was to have called
England and talked with Stan Watson while all the
things she wanted to say to him were fresh in her mind.
But it was six P.M. in England, so he might not be there.

When Kate and Frank reached the restaurant, customers were already lined up waiting for tables and
they had a short wait before they were seated at a small
table in the center of the room. Kate scanned the menu
while Frank laid it aside and leaned forward. "I didn't
get a chance to tell you about the holes they drilled at
the dam site."

"Is there a problem?" She hated having to ask. She
felt ridiculous and ineffective.

"No, no, not a problem *per se*," he assured her. "At
least nothing of any significance. They did find another
cavity."

Kate waited for him to continue. This was not good
news, but Frank did not seem alarmed. It must have
been a very small cavity, she decided.

"It's nothing of any size, of course," he assured her
quickly.

She relaxed back in her seat. "That's good. Grouting those holes could become expensive if there's a lot of void space." She knew the company had bid low on the job. Any unexpected major work at this point would cost them a considerable sum. "I'm surprised Stan called you instead of me," Kate related honestly.

Frank shrugged. "He might have tried to get you and your number was busy. It doesn't matter who he contacts in the company as long as he gives us word of what's happening. Anyway," Frank continued, "we'll do a little repair work and I think we'll be in fine shape."

"We'll want to schedule more drilling," she said. When he looked at her in surprise, she added, "Since they have turned up another bad area, it's possible there are still more." She was a little puzzled by his look of confusion. Frank knew as well as she that undiscovered cavities beneath the dam could be a source of potential trouble; water traveling beneath the structure would weaken it.

Frank took a drink of his water and carefully made a series of rings on the formica table with the bottom of his glass. "It's nothing serious, Kate. What they found was only a small cavity—really more like a few vugs. At the present time there's no need to continue drilling. After all, we did a thorough drilling program before construction ever began, and I'm confident we didn't miss anything major. Oh, here's our meal now," Frank said cheerfully as the waiter delivered plates of steaming food.

Kate picked up her chopsticks and took a bite of the double sautéed pork. She wasn't sure Frank was correct in not wanting to drill more core holes, but she would wait until she had more details from Stan before she made a decision about further explorations.

"By the way," Frank continued, "Ian Nigel is going to be in town two weeks from now."

"Oh," she murmured blandly. But her thoughts were

far from the disinterest she was portraying. Ian Nigel was coming to Dallas; she was certain to see him then. She felt oddly expectant about that meeting.

The waiter arrived with their check and they rose to leave. "I have to get back to the office for a conference with a man from Pitt Mining," Frank said as he put a generous tip on the table. "Hope you don't mind the rush."

"No, I need to get back too." She wanted to go through the report of explorations for Denham this afternoon; she would see for herself where the holes had been drilled and locate on the map the spot where grouting had been required to seal off cavities. She wanted to be well-informed on that aspect of the project before she talked to Stan tomorrow.

The following morning Kate had her secretary put through a call to England. "Mr. Watson is on the line," she informed Kate at the same time Kate heard Stan say, "Hi, how's the weather in Dallas?"

"Getting hot," she replied briefly.

"It always does in July."

"Yes." She moved right into the subject that was of far greater interest to her than meteorological accounts. "Frank said you called him the other day to tell him the findings from the drilling."

"Yeah. I guess he told you we didn't find much."

Kate paused, leaving Stan an opening to explain why he had called Frank instead of her, but apparently he did not feel any explanations were necessary. She felt exasperation rising inside herself. Stan had seemed like a man used to working in the company—one who knew the chain of command. She hoped she wasn't going to have problems with him. Tackling the situation directly, she said, "Stan, I'm confused as to why you called Frank instead of me."

"He asked me to," Stan returned simply.

For an instant Kate was off balance. She had misunderstood Stan, she decided as she worded her next question carefully. "Frank asked you to call him in matters concerning the foundation at the dam?"

"Not all of them," Stan replied. "He just asked me to let him know what our additional drilling turned up."

"I see." That certainly took the wind out of her sails, she thought. She could hardly upbraid Stan for following directions given to him by someone higher than she in the company. The findings of the drilling had obviously been a matter of interest to Frank, and it appeared he had not thought it would annoy her to be by-passed. "Well," she continued briskly, "what were you saying about your results?"

"Just a few small vugs. We pumped some grout into one hole, but it didn't take much to seal it up. Frank said he would get back with me and let me know if he thought any more drilling would be necessary."

"Oh, he did." Her voice was flat, but her cheeks were flushed with irritation.

"Other than that, everything is fine," he concluded.

"Good," she replied brightly. "I won't keep you, Stan. It was nice talking to you." She hung up. It appeared Frank intended to keep a tight rein on personnel who should have been responsible to her. Was this the first time such a situation had developed, or had she failed to recognize it before? She intended to find out. Kate experienced a fluttering of apprehension that constricted her throat. She hated the idea of a confrontation with Frank, but he must understand she was capable of running her own shop. For a moment she considered the sickening idea that Frank had wanted her in this position in order to use her as a puppet. She pushed that thought from her mind firmly. He would know better. Besides, Frank wasn't the kind of man who was thirsty for all the power he could grab. Yon Cassius has no lean and hungry look, she paraphrased to herself with a wry smile. There had to be a logical explanation, and she would find out from Frank what it was.

Pushing back her chair, she walked to the window. Outside, an azure sky was capped with snowy white clouds. What was the most tactful way to approach Frank? She furrowed her brow as something that had been tickling at the back of her mind came to the front. Frank had told her at lunch yesterday that Stan might have tried to get in touch with her before calling him; but Frank had known that wasn't true. He had *told* Stan to call him.

Kate turned and started purposefully from her office. She might as well talk to Frank directly and let him explain the situation, instead of trying to piece together a puzzle for which she might not have all the pieces. After she took the elevator to his floor, she stopped at the secretary's desk. "Is Frank available?" she asked.

"Yes, go right in."

"Thank you." Kate crossed to Frank's door and opened it. The vice president was seated behind his desk reading a thick volume; he looked up with a smile when she entered.

"Sit down, Kate," he greeted her. "I was just going through this report on the Brazil tunnel. It seems to be coming along well. You'll have to get down there to see it sometime."

"Yes." She settled into the chair in front of his desk. "I just talked with Stan Watson," she began.

"Anything new?" He laid the book aside and waited for her to continue. His expression was one of interest but no guilt.

"No." She smoothed down her slim cinnamon-colored skirt before she added, "Frank, I have a bit of a problem. Stan said you asked him to call you about the core drilling findings. I'm sure you understand that puts me in a rather delicate position. I should be informing *you* how the work is progressing, instead of learning information *from* you."

Frank's silver-gray eyebrows lifted in understanding. "I'm sorry, Kate. I see how you feel and, of course, it won't happen again. I just happened to be talking to Stan on the phone a week or two ago, and I told him to let me know what he found out. He must have interpreted that to mean report to me instead of you. It was all a simple misunderstanding, and I'm definitely not trying to undermine your authority." He smiled in a way that softened his features and made him look paternal. "Not mad, are you?"

She smiled faintly. "I was a little perturbed," she admitted. "But now I understand how it happened. I suppose I made too big a thing out of it." The tenseness she had felt since talking to Stan flowed out of her body like water dripping off her.

"Nonsense. Always feel free to tell me what's bothering you. I'm sure I step on toes now and then—being around Burke must have rubbed off on me." He shook his head in amusement.

Kate rose with a grin and said lightly, "I'll get back to my office so I'll be there if anyone wants to relay some earthshaking information." Had she seemed too jealous of her territorial prerogatives, she wondered as she left. Frank seemed to have taken it in good part and there were no hard feelings. It was nice to work for someone like Frank. She was more appreciative of that fact than she had been before.

In fact, it was good to work for Amalacorp—period. The projects they had under construction were larger and more varied than anything she would ever have done at Higgins, Powers and Barnes. Admittedly, there didn't seem to be many new projects coming up when the present ones were completed, but it was a temporary lull for the whole industry. Something exciting was sure to show up soon. Besides, she wouldn't object if a few months were slow. Once new projects began rolling in, she would be too busy for anything else in her life. A little breathing space from her work would give her more time with Elliot.

As she waited for the elevator, Kate thought about

Elliot for a moment. He was fun to be with and she liked him, but she wasn't sure how far past liking her feelings for him would ever go. Admittedly, he could enliven an evening, but was he ever serious? Perhaps not, but she was content to spend time with him, and no one said it had to end in love.

Chapter 11

Kate stood looking pensively out the window of her kitchen. It was Friday night; Elliot had cancelled their date when a business trip had come up at the last minute. She had been looking forward to the evening; she wished he had not been called out of town.

She shifted her position against the clean white counter and picked up her coffee cup. She had been dating Elliot for five weeks and he was beginning to want more tangible signs of her interest in him than just a few kisses. She sighed. Elliot simply didn't arouse the emotions in her that she would have to feel before she could ever consider going to bed with him.

Absently, she stirred her coffee. There was something else that kept her from giving herself to Elliot. She knew what it was—had known for weeks—but she tried to push the thought from her mind. There was another man whose appeal was stronger than Elliot's, a man whose face she saw now and again when Elliot was kissing her. He appeared unbidden in her fantasies, and until Ian Nigel was banished from her thoughts, nothing could progress between herself and Elliot.

Kate looked up in surprise at the sound of the telephone ringing. It was nearly ten o'clock. The only person who called her at that hour was her mother, and she had talked to Agatha last night. Padding barefoot across the floor, she picked up the wall phone. "Hello," she said tentatively.

"Ian Nigel here," he identified himself briskly.

Kate looked at the receiver in disbelief. For an instant she thought she was hallucinating. Then she put that ridiculous notion firmly from her mind. Ian Nigel was scheduled to be in the office on Monday. His call must have something to do with that. "Hello, Mr. Nigel, what can I do for you?"

"I'm having a bit of a problem," he replied in a voice that sounded apologetic and a little embarrassed.

She must be reading things into his tone, she told herself severely. "How can I help you?" she asked as she reached for the pen and notepad she kept by the phone. She wished she had a copy of the Denham dam report at the house in case he asked a difficult question.

He gave a short, mirthless laugh. "I find I'm in a rather difficult situation. I'm sorry to bother you; I tried to ring up Frank Moyer, but no one answered." He paused and then continued, "I'm in jail and I need someone to come and get me out."

For a split-second Kate wondered if she had understood him correctly. "Jail?" she repeated in confusion.

"Unfortunately, yes. It's a long story and I can't tell you now. The officer who was good enough to let me make this call is hinting there are others who wish to use the phone."

Kate recovered her presence of mind. "Where are you? I'll come right down." Then, as a sudden worry hit her, she asked quickly, "You are all right, aren't you?"

"I have known happier moments," he returned

dryly. "But no, I've not been injured, if that's what you mean."

"Good," she said with relief, and then another fear prompted her to ask, "You haven't been involved in a car accident or a fight, have you?"

"A fight," he repeated with a wry laugh. "I can see my reputation is going to suffer mercilessly from this night. No, I haven't been in a brawl. There was a slight misunderstanding on my part about where it is acceptable—legal, I should say—to consume a glass of port, and where it is strictly illegal. As you may have guessed, I ended up drinking in the wrong place."

Kate was glad Ian couldn't see her smile. "I'll be right over," she assured him before she hung up. Ian Nigel in jail, what was the world coming to? She laughed aloud as she walked to the hall closet and took out a lightweight jacket. Slinging it over her shoulder, she picked up her purse and stepped into her backless sandals. He was in jail and she was going to rescue him! She shook her head with a smile.

The police station Ian had directed her to was outside Dallas, and Kate didn't arrive there until an hour later. She found Ian sitting in a straight chair across from a uniformed officer. When the heavy glass door swung closed behind her, he looked up.

For a moment Kate forgot the policeman entirely as her eyes rested on Ian and she experienced a curious joy. He was dressed casually in a pair of beige duck trousers and a navy and beige striped shirt. The lights in the room picked up the golden tints of his brown hair and gave it a soft sheen; his hair was slightly touseled in a way that made him look less dignified and somehow vulnerable. He gave her a boyish grin that made her feel limp inside.

Ian stood politely. "Officer Kramer, this is Miss Justin." He turned to Kate. "It seems they are reluctant to take a check on my bank in England. If you could write a check for my release, I will repay you."

She corraled her straying thoughts. "Of course."

The policeman stood and looked her over with a neutral gaze, glancing from her faded jeans to her green and white checked shirt. "Follow me," he commanded. Kate threw a backward look at Ian before falling into step behind the policeman. He walked out of the room and into a long hallway.

"I don't understand quite why Mr. Nigel is here, officer," she began courteously. She thought it would be better to find out the details of this episode from the police; she suspected Ian wouldn't want to talk of it any more than was necessary.

"He was in an establishment that served liquor. This is a dry town, ma'am." He led her into a small room and left her with another man at a desk while he returned to the front office. She watched him go with a faint smile. He was a young man, stiff with authority, who was returning to the dangerous man waiting at his desk.

As she wrote a check, she asked, "Were there others brought in here for being in the bar besides Mr. Nigel? I'm relatively new to Texas, but I was under the impression the patrons of a club weren't usually arrested under these circumstances."

The man surveyed her with a lazy grin. He was middle-aged and wore his uniform with a casual air of one who was used to its authority and no longer unduly impressed by it. "Depends on who does the arresting," he explained calmly. "Some men are more strict than others. Officer Kramer," he added as his eyes met hers, "is new to the force."

"I see." Ian had obviously been caught in the net of a rookie who was out to rid the city of crime wherever he found it. It was an affront to Ian's dignity, of course, but Kate thought it was also amusing. As she recalled the unguarded look of warmth Ian had given her when she had first appeared at the station, a softer emotion swept through her and her smile became more pensive.

The policeman broke into her thoughts, "Here's the release ticket, ma'am."

"Thank you," she murmured.

Ian rose as she walked back into the outer office. "I think you can go now," she told him cheerfully. "I have a ticket for your release."

The young policeman stood gravely and looked the receipt over carefully before he nodded. "Everything seems to be in order." To Ian, he added, "I'm sorry if this has been an inconvenience to you, but you do understand we have laws to uphold. Have a good evening," he concluded.

Ian nodded. When they were outside he asked her, "Are you frightened to be alone with such a dangerous criminal?"

"No. In fact, I feel so brave I'll take you back to my apartment for something legal to drink." As she started her car and sped across the vast prairie toward Dallas, Kate considered that she *was* actually a little frightened. What alarmed her was the fact she was so breathlessly thrilled to be with Ian. Surely it had not been wise to invite him to her apartment. But she felt completely unfettered and she did not intend to put the shackles back on herself now. She didn't think she could have if she wanted to. Ian's power over her seemed somehow greater than her power over herself.

"Aren't you curious how I ended up in that bar?" he asked.

She glanced at him in the dark car. He was so very close to her, one hand rested only inches from her hip on the seat beside her. More than that, there was a charged feeling in the air between them. The subtle masculine scent of his cologne hung in the air. What had he asked? She could no longer remember the question clearly. "I'm sorry, what did you say?"

He laughed. "Never mind. It's not important how I got there. My exit was much more interesting than my arrival. You should have seen me being hauled into jail

with the other patrons of the club. We made a whole-
some little group, let me assure you. I could only hear
snatches of the song they were singing, but it sounded
quite bawdy."

She drove off the expressway and down the side
streets leading to her apartment complex. She slowed
at the guard's booth to allow him to identify her and
then continued on. Inside her apartment she walked
briskly down the hall to the kitchen. Ian followed.

As she poured them both a gin and tonic, she was
acutely aware of Ian's presence in her small kitchen.
Odd that she had been thinking about him tonight. Was
there such a thing as mental telepathy? Did he know
the fact he was here filled her with a warm glow and at
the same time made her feel apprehensive? No, she
decided, he couldn't know that; she concealed her
feelings too well.

She turned and handed him a glass. "We'll take them
into the living room," she directed and led the way.
Seating herself on the blue and white patterned chair,
she motioned him toward the sofa.

"Have I thanked you yet?" he asked. "I wouldn't
have bothered you if there had been any other choice. I
tried convincing the policeman to let me go, but I didn't
have much luck. Why are you smiling?" he asked. He
was looking at her over the rim of his glass.

"I was just thinking of how embarrassed you
sounded on the phone."

"I *am* embarrassed. What would the men on my
board think if they knew their chairman had been
hauled into jail like a common criminal?" With a
twinkle in his eye, he added, "It wasn't even a very
respectable bar."

"Wasn't it?" She looked down at her glass. She felt
good just being in the room with him. "You don't have
to worry that I'll tell anyone." Her voice sounded
husky and heavy with shared confidences; she had not
meant for it to sound that way.

"I know."

Kate didn't look up. She was all too certain from the gentleness of his voice that he was looking at her with those changeable blue-gray eyes. She wasn't ready to look into them yet, not until she had schooled herself into being pleasantly impersonal again. At the moment her feelings were much too much in an upheaval.

She took a quick swallow of her drink and looked around the room. She should not have asked him to come here, she realized belatedly. Her meetings with Ian should be confined to boardrooms and business luncheons; certainly the coziness of her living room was too intimate and suggested something she would not allow to happen. Of course, he was attractive, but that was beside the point. These crazy thoughts and feelings floating through her head had no place in the mind of a company executive. And that was what she was first and foremost with Ian Nigel. She looked up at the sound of a scratching at the back door.

"Either your cat wants in, or you have a polite burglar," Ian remarked.

Kate rose. "I think it's my cat. There's a system to the way he scratches, light and unassuming if he merely wants in the house, shrill and demanding if he's hungry."

Ian followed her into the kitchen. "Just in case your cat taught the system to an animal-loving house-breaker," he explained as he unlocked the sliding glass door and slid it open.

Cuddles bounded into the room. Kate watched Ian as he closed the door and relocked it. She liked everything about this man far too much, she realized. The fact he was protective toward her was another plus in his favor. She watched him stoop to pet the cat.

"I used to have a cat," he said, "when I was quite young."

"Really?" Kate tried to picture this tall man who carried so much responsibility as an innocent young boy. He had probably been mischievous, she decided. Had either of his parents had those wonderful chameleon eyes, she wondered.

Ian rose and they started back into the living room. "Jasper was the cat's name," he confided. "My parents owned a yacht and we spent every summer touring on it. We always took Jasper with us. He loved the water even though my dog hated it."

Ian sat down on the sofa and she sank down beside him, watching him with interest. "Where did you travel?"

"Monte Carlo and a few places off the coast of Greece," he said disinterestedly.

"It sounds marvelous!" she said enthusiastically.

"It was all right," he said with a shrug.

"You don't seem very impressed," she chided. "When I was a child, I would have thought I was in heaven if I had gone to any one of those places."

"They become a lot alike after a while, and frankly rather boring."

"But you must have met such glamorous people," she protested.

He studied her for a moment in silence before he said slowly, "Some of them were quite nice, but I met a good many people who were pretenders. At least that was what my mother called them. Phonies is what she meant. I learned to be very wary of them."

He stopped speaking, but his eyes held hers and seemed to be conveying a message as clearly as if he had spoken it aloud. He was looking at her as if he thought she was the most special person in the world. She looked back into his eyes with an expression that returned the compliment.

Kate reined in her wandering thoughts. What was she doing gazing at him like a starry-eyed young girl? "Do your parents still travel aboard their yacht?" she asked.

"They're dead now," he explained simply, and continued before she had a chance to murmur any words of sympathy, "They had stopped traveling long before they died. My mother preferred to stay at our home and entertain, and my father had other interests." He looked reflective for a moment and then continued slowly. "My wife and I used the yacht for a time."

Kate felt herself go cold. No one had ever mentioned that Ian had a wife. A wife! Someone who had the privilege of holding him late at night. Kate felt a sharp ache inside her. She looked up to see he was regarding her with a worried frown.

"Did I say something wrong?" he asked.

She swallowed. "I didn't know you were married." She hoped the words sounded as casual to him as she had meant them to be.

"My wife has been dead for a number of years." He stated the words as a simple fact.

Kate knew her first emotion should have been sympathy, but instead she felt relief. Of course, she was sorry that he had known the tragedy of his wife's death, but she was also glad no woman had rights to him. What was she thinking, she asked herself. It was not her concern whether he had a wife or not. She could not allow her feelings for Ian to run away from her; she had a responsibility to her company.

"What about your parents?" Ian asked.

"My father has been dead since I was six," she answered.

"It must have been difficult for your mother to raise a daughter by herself. And especially one who is such an achiever. There are few enough women engineers who have had all the advantages, but I imagine you had to overcome more obstacles than most."

Kate felt a delicate color rising in her cheeks as he looked at her. She felt almost as if he could see into her soul. She attempted to put the conversation back onto a more casual basis as she replied objectively, "My mother taught me the value of depending on myself. I suppose it all fell into place from there. Engineering is a stable field, and one where a person can always earn a good living," she concluded briskly.

He smiled. "I don't think you're in it for just 'a good living.' I suspect you want more than that." When she did not reply, he continued, "You want a sense of worth and job satisfaction that few people ever require of themselves. It's obvious your professional life is extremely important to you."

"It is," she agreed staunchly.

"What about your personal life?" he asked candidly.

She did not meet his eyes. "You and I are business associates, Mr. Nigel. I don't think I should be discussing my personal life with you." The words sounded absurd even as she spoke them. If there was ever a man with whom she wanted to be intimate, she knew he was sitting beside her now. And he must know it as well.

"Amalacorp had the job to construct Denham dam before you ever came to work for the company," he said practically. "Everything is set down in black and white now, and there is nothing you could do to influence me and no way I could exert any power over you concerning the dam. Doesn't that leave us free to pursue a personal relationship?" His eyes held hers steadily; they were two unfathomable gray orbs that demanded an answer to his question.

She moistened her bottom lip with her tongue and sought rational words to answer him. If only her thoughts weren't so jumbled by his presence.

He reached up and tucked a lock of her hair behind her ear. His hand brushed across her cheek. "I'm interested in knowing you better, Kate."

Kate felt his hands engulf hers and she knew a sleepy kind of satisfaction. Ian Nigel had walked into her apartment tonight and had somehow filled it with himself. Her thoughts were woven all around him now. Even if he walked out into the night without another word, Kate knew he would still own a part of this evening and of her.

She knew he was going to kiss her before he even lowered his lips to hers; she waited expectantly, filled with anticipation. His skin was a healthy golden-tan and the small scar above his eye was nearly covered with a lock of hair falling across it. She focused on the scar as he brought his head down to hers. When his lips touched the coolness of her own, she forgot the scar, the tan and her protests. She was conscious only of the gently insistent pressure of his lips on hers.

Putting his hands around her back, he drew her closer as his kisses deepened. Kate knew he was pulling her into the whirlpool of emotions she had tried so hard to avoid; she felt heady with the excitement of the moment and immensely secure at being so close to him. The increasing fervor of his kisses fueled her own desire, but lacing through that growing longing was a trembling feeling of panic. She was standing on the edge of something very vast, and she knew she had never been there before.

Ian drew back slightly and looked at her solemnly. "You're afraid. Is it me or something else?"

His arms around her were firm and real, something to hold onto in a world that offered few anchors. Suddenly it seemed that the reality of the moment existed only with him, and everything else was fading to black. "It's not you." She drew in a deep breath to steady her wavering voice. "I just feel so uncertain, as if I'm not acting with a level head." There were other things she wanted to say, but she couldn't formulate any thoughts right now. They were creeping about in her mind like men in trench coats; she knew they were there, but she could not call one of them forward.

She felt him touch her bottom lip and trace the curve of it. Then he kissed the corner of her mouth, slowly, working his way inside with seductive patience. Her objections were swept away like sandcastles in a relentless surf.

She closed her eyes and gave herself over to the feeling of his mouth exploring hers with a gentle intensity. If she had ever wanted to believe in fate, this was her chance. And tonight she found she was willing to put more faith in such things than she normally might have. Tonight she wanted to believe in miracles.

He shifted his position, stretching out the length of the sofa and pulling her down beside him. His lips never left hers and his tongue moved invitingly into the recesses of her mouth with delicate probes. His hands moved across her back as he drew her even nearer to him. They were side by side on the narrow sofa facing each other, yet somehow Kate didn't feel they were close enough.

Ian slipped a hand beneath her shirt and ran it across the smoothness of her back. It was joined by his other hand, stroking up and down her spine in a motion that brought prickles of sensation with each journey it made. Unimpeded by a bra, he moved his hands around to her breasts. She felt a surge of pleasure as he cupped a breast in each hand and slowly massaged them. Her fantasies of Ian wove into reality and she could no longer tell where one left off and the other began.

The highway she was on had roads branching off it at frequent intervals. She could get off whenever she chose or she could accelerate and speed toward the inevitable end of the main road. She knew that Ian was proceeding slowly to give her time to make up her mind. She could feel a tenseness in his hands where they touched her. He was holding himself in check, waiting for her.

It was hard to focus on making a decision when her mind was a blur of longings, but she knew tomorrow she would be alone again. Then she would have to look back and know she had made the right choice. His hands left her breasts and returned to the tender skin of her back. She wanted to cry out a protest and beg him to return to her straining breasts.

His lips left hers and trailed a path of kisses across to

her ear. He searched the hollows and untouched places behind her ear, sending messages downward that spiraled through her body and made her tense with desire. Her decision was made swiftly and on intuition. This man beside her was offering to take her somewhere she wanted to go badly. She longed to feel more messages vibrating from his body through hers. If that was wrong, then tonight she wanted to be dreadfully wrong.

Slowly, with deliberate resolve, she unbuttoned the buttons of his shirt and slipped her hands beneath it, stroking across the curly little hairs on his chest and down to the tautness of his stomach. He slid his hands from her back around her to breasts, moving purposefully upward to cup their fullness. Finally a hand rested on each nipple, teasing them with the lightness of his touch. For long moments Kate drank in the taste of his lips on hers and the sensation of being caressed by gentle hands. Then she drew back and stood, reaching down a hand to him.

Wordlessly, she led the way up to her bedroom. She didn't turn on the light. The faint glow of the moon and the street lights filtering in through the window provided a clear path to the bed. They lay down on the bed together, still clothed but so anxious for the touch of each other again that it was more important to be together than it was to take the precious seconds apart to disrobe.

He would undress her, she knew, and she would remove his clothes. She wanted it to happen slowly, so that she would have time to anoint his body with kisses.

He unfastened her blouse and drew it off of her, his head moving down to draw her breast into the soft darkness of his mouth. The warmth from his body spread through hers, and she felt herself relaxing back against the bedspread. There was an unhurried hazy quality to the night. Events happened in slow and sometimes jumbled motion. She saw him take the rest of her clothes off, saw his gaze linger at the triangle of dark hairs, and felt the hardness of his muscles as she ran her fingers up and down his arms and across his chest.

Then they were naked on the bed together, his body practically covering hers like a heavy blanket. His lips searched hers in a more demanding way before he rested his face in the hollow of her neck and breathed deeply in time to the movement of her hands on his body.

She could feel herself being pulled into a vortex of swirling water. She was going to a place where she would have no control and she waited breathlessly for the time when she could enter that world. Pulsating sensations ran up and down her limbs and her mouth felt dry as she savored the feeling of his hands stroking her body. The pleasant yearnings traveling through her were both heightened and appeased by his touch.

And then he moved deliberately and she felt their bodies merging. She opened her eyes to see him looking steadily down at her, his face unreadable in the half-light. She closed her eyes again and gave herself over to the rhythm of their bodies swaying in time. A flame uncoiled and burst into a leaping fire somewhere inside her. She was aware of it and of the nearness of Ian. Everything else was only a shadow in her mind.

They moved together in a dance that had been choreographed expressly for them. She felt ageless sensations well up in her and threaten to spill over. Her desire was fueled by the undulating motion of their coming together and the slight release before their bodies merged even closer.

The eroticism of their movements and the sound of Ian's voice as he whispered incoherent words into her ear sent Kate over the edge of a vast cliff. With a moan, she plummeted into the abyss. Blue-white lights flashed in her mind, she was suffocating in a mindless bliss. Wave after wave of pleasure washed over her, leaving her weak and satiated. Slowly, she touched reality and landed safely at the bottom of the canyon. Below her, the rapid sound of Ian's breathing told her he had made the trip as well.

There were tears in her eyes, but she didn't move to brush them away. She was still holding onto the moment. It could never have been so perfect with anyone else, she reflected. No one else had ever taken over her desires as completely as Ian had. What she felt for him she knew she had never felt for any other man.

He reached out a hand and pulled her closer to him, wrapping her against his body protectively and pulling the rumpled covers up to envelop their cool bodies. She nestled her head against his chest. The crisp hairs prickled against her face and she loved the feel of them. She loved everything about Ian, she thought with a sigh of contentment as she felt herself drifting off to sleep.

Even in her dreams she was conscious of him, and when she awoke in the still hours between night and morning she reached out and touched his face. He had been right. Denham and Amalacorp had nothing to do with tonight. They had been a man and a woman in this bed, and now she was savoring the rewards of abandoning her professional judgment.

Chapter 12

There was an early morning feel in the air when Kate blinked her eyes open and then closed them again. She felt deliciously happy. The memory of last night came back to her in small pieces. She recalled the warmth of a thigh against hers and fingers stroking softly through her hair. With a smile, she opened her eyes again. Her smile faded when she saw that the other side of her bed was empty. A movement by the window drew her attention.

Ian was standing beside it, fully dressed. The corner of the curtain was drawn back and he was looking down onto the street below. He turned back to her. "Did I wake you?"

"What are you doing up so early?"

"I have an appointment to meet someone in Houston today. Don't get up," he protested when she started to throw the covers back. "I've already called a taxi; it'll be here in a minute."

She subsided back onto the bed. "What time is it?"

"Quarter till five."

"In the morning?"

He laughed. "Yes."

"Isn't it Sunday?" she asked as she snuggled back into the warm depths of the covers.

"Yes."

"You get up and go to work on Sunday morning?" She regarded him through half-lowered lashes. He looked tall and impressive standing by the window; it was hard to believe he was the same man who had held her so close last night. He seemed so far removed from her now that she was a little embarrassed to be in her bedroom with him.

He let the curtain fall closed and crossed the room to the bed. Sinking down onto it, he took her hand, and her thoughts of a moment ago fell away like a winter coat when the weather suddenly turned hot. "You are a restless sleeper," he told her.

The sound of a horn blaring outside prevented Kate from replying. He stood and bent to kiss her cheek lightly. "That's my car." Another loud blast sounded as he walked toward the door. "I'm going to be in the country all this week. I'll call you tonight. Will you be free next weekend?"

"Yes."

"Goodbye," he threw back before he closed the bedroom door behind him.

Kate pulled the covers tighter up against her throat. For a moment she felt a constriction there that warned her she was close to tears. Admittedly, it was not the romantic ending she could have wished after such a night. She brushed her fingers across the eyelet lace at the edge of the mint-green sheet. She wished he could have stayed for a few more hours and kept these feelings of loneliness at bay.

But then, she reflected as she brushed away a stray tear, the important thing was that she had been able to spend some time with him and she knew he was coming back. She didn't regret her actions, but she had to acknowledge that she might have started down a road that wasn't leading anywhere. Was this one of those pleasantly shaded lanes one sees in the country on a summer day? The kind that look wonderfully inviting but only lead to a river with a bridge that was long gone? Would she have to turn and retrace her route eventually, or could the path she had chosen last night actually lead her somewhere?

Kate turned on the bed. A faint smile lifted the corners of her mouth. It wasn't a road that occupied her mind right now; it was a man—a man who made her feel incredibly happy at the mere thought of him.

What was it about Ian that she found so compelling? He was handsome, certainly, with his aristocratic features and warm smile, but there were other attractive men whom she came into contact with every day and none had ever affected her as Ian did. He had the bearing of one who is in control, but she was surrounded by men who made important decisions every day without batting an eye. Ian had an underlying softness that surfaced only rarely. Did the combination of those facts add to this roller coaster feeling in her stomach?

Kate knew the answer to that question was no. She didn't have a logical reason for the things that had happened last night, but for this once she didn't care. She closed her eyes and drifted off into a light sleep.

She was still sleeping when the phone rang hours later. She spoke into the receiver in a husky voice. "Hello."

"Hi, did I wake you?"

Kate pulled herself up in bed. "Jessica?" A glance at the clock revealed that it was 9:30. "We're supposed to play tennis this morning, aren't we?" she asked groggily.

"We were, but if you'd rather not, we can put it off."

"No, I'll be ready in a few minutes. Just let me

shower and dress and I'll meet you at the courts." She
hung up and threw back the covers. After pulling a pair
of white shorts and a white sleeveless top from the shelf
of her walk-in closet, she proceeded to the bathroom
and stepped into the tub. She hummed to herself as she
generously lathered a thick cloth with scented soap.

Kate arrived at the courts twenty minutes later.
Jessica was already there, sitting on a bench taking her
racquet from its press. She wore a pale pink tennis
dress. Two tiny pink pompoms protruded at the back of
her tennis shoes. She greeted Kate with a smile.

"I have a feeling I'm going to beat you today," Kate
warned her cheerfully.

"No way."

They walked out onto the court. It was in the middle
of a row of nine. Most of the courts were already
occupied. There was little conversation up and down
the blacktopped squares except for occasional shouts of
"Out!" and "Love."

Kate and Jessica played for half an hour, with Kate
winning easily. Jessica was a good player, but Kate
wasn't surprised that she was winning. Today she felt as
if she could do anything. The balls seemed to seek her
racquet and her returns were predestined to elude
Jessica's. Another ball went out on Jessica's side of the
court and the game ended.

They walked off the court as another couple bounded
on. Jessica sank down onto the bench and reached
down to retie the strings of her shoe. "Did you hear the
cab honking this morning?" she asked casually.

Kate settled onto the bench and looked at her
companion. "I heard it." She was unable to prevent a
smile from spreading across her face. "Do you want to
know about him?"

"Not unless you want to tell me," Jessica returned
practically.

Kate's face became serious as she continued,
"There's nothing much to tell. He was here for the

night and now he's gone." She felt a wistfulness replace the exuberance that had carried her through the first part of the morning.

"Did it end with a fight?" Jessica asked sympathetically.

"No, nothing like that. The truth is that I have a strong attraction for this man, but I'm not sure it's a practical emotion." He would always have to leave early in the morning, she thought in dejection. Theirs could only be a romance wedged in between meetings and other commitments.

Jessica laughed. "No emotion is practical, Kate. Just go with the feeling and don't try to analyze it as if it were the stock market or a business venture."

Kate adjusted the band on her wrist. "You don't understand. He isn't just anybody; he's the chairman of the board of a company Amalacorp is doing work for."

"Do you feel attracted to him because he's the chairman of the board?" Jessica asked.

"Of course not."

"Did he come to see you because he hoped to gain something through you from your company?" she pursued.

"No," Kate denied staunchly.

"Then what's the problem?" Jessica asked prosaically.

Kate watched the tennis balls bouncing back and forth across the courts, landing with dull thuds. "I work for Amalacorp; I should consider their interests when something in my personal life touches on my professional life. There are appearances to be considered."

Jessica ran the tips of her fingers through her hair, and miraculously the blonde strands fell into their carefully-cut layers again. "All I can say is there's no sense in doing something if you're going to feel guilty about it. If you enjoy being with this man, just leave it at that for now. If your position with Amalacorp makes seeing him impractical, then don't see him."

"That's what I like about you, Jessica, you're so damned logical. I've already made a date to see him next weekend," Kate added with a grin.

"Good for you!"

Kate ran her fingers through her thick black hair. "I suppose I should feel funny talking to you about Ian. After all, I am dating Elliot." She glanced at Jessica sideways to study her reaction.

Jessica shook her head firmly. "You've only been seeing Elliot for a little over a month, and that doesn't mean you can't be attracted to another man. There's nothing serious between you and Elliot, so there's no reason to feel guilty about him."

Kate squeezed her companion's hand. "I should have known you'd be understanding." With a radiant smile, she said, "Ian really makes me feel terrific!"

"You hide it so well," Jessica observed. "If you aren't mistaken for a neon sign, I'm sure no one will ever notice how excited you are. By the way," she changed the subject, "your picture and the story are going to be in tomorrow's paper. The picture's great, and the write-up makes you sound terribly important."

"Hmmm." Kate's mind was not completely on Jessica's words. The events of last evening interfered with her concentration. She bit her bottom lip at the memory of a particularly salient detail.

Jessica continued, unaware that she did not have Kate's undivided attention. "Does it ever bother you that you have so much responsibility? I think I'd be worried if I had a hand in designing or approving anything that could collapse or could somehow endanger people's lives."

Kate brought herself out of her reverie and looked at Jessica curiously. "Before Amalacorp or any other engineering company builds anything, we do extensive testing. Every structure is reviewed by dozens of people. There is little room left for any mistakes, let alone a major catastrophe."

"But they do happen," Jessica insisted. "There was a large building that collapsed in Florida not long ago."

"Amalacorp doesn't construct buildings," Kate replied. "We do bigger things, like subway systems, sewer intercepting lines and outfalls, large airports, tunnels for hydropower and large span-bridges and dams."

"But those things fail too."

"Did the stockbroker you're seeing take you to a disaster movie?" Kate teased, and then continued seriously, "There are review boards and federal agencies at every turn. Even in our own company, no major decision is made by any one person. If anything, there are so many safety factors thrown into every project that the idea of a failure is almost inconceivable."

"A dam failed in Georgia three or four years ago," Jessica commented.

"Okay, I concede there are mistakes, but they're few and far between." Kate pushed her hair back again and continued, "In 1963 a section of a mountain in Italy avalanched into a lake, spilling a tidal wave over the top of the dam. The tidal wave killed four thousand people and several small villages were destroyed, but the dam held. That says a lot for the engineering on that dam."

Jessica looked unconvinced. "I'm glad my biggest worry is whether I'm printing an accurate story rather than whether something I'm in charge of could be potentially deadly."

Kate smiled. "You let your imagination run away with you." They both stood and started back toward the apartments, swinging their racquets as they walked. "By the way," Kate said, "you do remember that I'm going to Chile late this evening?"

"Yeah. Bring Cuddles by the apartment whenever you like; I'll be there all afternoon. Will you be back next weekend?"

"I most definitely will," Kate said emphatically. Wild horses could not keep her from being back. Already she was impatient for the week to be over so that she could see Ian again.

Chapter 13

Kate arrived back from Chile and breezed into her office late Friday afternoon. A stack of yellow phone messages awaited her. She leafed through them quickly. Most were from business associates who left curt messages like, "Need to discuss the fill with you," or "Let's talk over the tunnel supports." Her only personal call was from Elliot.

She was picking up the phone to call him when Frank walked into her office.

"Hi," he greeted her easily. "How was the trip?"

"Interesting," she replied vaguely. There were questions she wanted to ask Frank about the company's interest in Chile, but it was already 4:30 in the afternoon and he was carrying his briefcase, an indication he was on his way out of the building. Her questions could wait until Monday, she decided. "I'll give you a complete briefing about the trip next week."

Her mind flitted back to thoughts of Ian. He had been in the office this past week. "Was Ian Nigel satisfied with the work at the dam?" she asked, more to bring his name into the conversation than to find out the answer to that question.

Frank sat down and put his case on the floor beside him before answering casually, "He's concerned about the few little cavities we found in our last set of core borings. He would like to have more drilling done, but I don't think it will be necessary. Further borings will delay work on the embankment and we're a little behind schedule as it is." He dropped his hands to his lap and continued, "Ian doesn't understand that we know our business and there's absolutely nothing to worry about. Since he's not an engineer, he thinks every little problem is a major disaster."

"Still," she observed, "it wouldn't hurt to do a few more core holes. I know there's little likelihood of any more cavities or clay-filled vugs, but it might pay to check just to make absolutely certain, as well as to reassure Denham."

His eyebrows furrowed into a frown. "Kate, I'll level with you. Denham is turning into a costly project. Any work we can avoid doing we should definitely skip. However, if you feel strongly about punching down a couple more holes then talk to Stan about it. But don't get carried away. We're operating on a hell of a slim profit margin and drilling is expensive."

"I don't think we'll need more than one or two holes," she assured him.

"Good." He rose briskly. "My wife is picking me up, so I'd better get downstairs. See you Monday."

After Frank left, Kate picked up the phone and dialed Elliot's number. He answered the phone himself. "Elliot Downey, may I help you?" he rasped out.

"You certainly sound cheery. I'll call you back after hibernating season."

"Hi, Kate." His voice softened. "Sorry I snapped at you. Both of my secretaries are off and I've been manning—that's not a sexist term is it?—the phones all day. Most of the calls have been for the secretaries anyway. It's been an education to see how much personal business is going on over my phone lines."

"This isn't business either," she informed him with a smile.

"Good. I don't like gorgeous women to make business calls to me. Busy this weekend?"

"Sort of. Someone is coming into town and things are a little up in the air about what I may be doing." That sounded too casual, she decided, and she didn't want to look as if she were putting anything over on Elliot. "After you were called out of town last weekend, I ended up seeing another man. You see—"

"Hey!" he interrupted with a laugh. "You don't have to explain to me. After I saw that stunning picture of you in the paper, I'm not surprised you're busy. Even though they didn't pick up those violet eyes, they did get the luscious lips and hair any man would kill for a chance to run his fingers through. There must be a line of guys a block long in front of your office waiting to see you."

She smiled at his words. "Not quite a full block long," she assured him.

"Put on a fake nose and mustache and duck out the back door and meet me for a quick drink to make up for the fact you can't go out with me this weekend," he prompted.

She hesitated. Why not? She wouldn't get much work done tonight anyway; she was too excited about seeing Ian this weekend. "Sure."

"I'm heading for my car right now; tell me where to meet you before I run out of phone cord."

Kate gave him the name of a bar a block from her office and hung up. It was already five o'clock, she noted as she took her maroon cotton jacket from the coat rack and slipped it on. Her work would be here Monday, she decided philosophically. She closed her office door and left the work behind.

Elliot was waiting for her at the bar in a corner booth

when she arrived. She smiled at him and started across
the crowded, dimly-lit room. Around her, men in
business suits talked to each other and celebrated the
end of the work week. She saw several heads turn to
follow her path as she moved past them. The few
women present were dressed like Kate in conservative
suits. She brushed through the crowd and slid into the
booth across from Elliot.

"I've already ordered you a drink," he said.

"Thanks." She took her jacket off and adjusted the
collar of her crisp white blouse before glancing around
her. Golden oak had been used throughout the bar to
give a turn-of-the-century flavor. Stained glass had
been incorporated into part of the mirror behind the
long bar and a brass footrail provided a resting place for
Gucci shoes and tooled-leather boots.

A waitress arrived a moment later with a Bloody
Mary for her and a scotch for Elliot. Kate sipped her
drink and glanced at Elliot. He was dressed in a
well-cut, nut-brown suit with a red striped silk tie. He
looked the successful executive that he was, she reflected. Jessica had said that he was *too* successful, and
that was what had ended their marriage. She had never
talked to Elliot about Jessica, but suddenly Kate was
curious to try to gauge how Elliot really felt about his
ex-wife. Jessica insisted they were good friends, but
could that really be true?

"Jessica may be going to England to visit an old
friend," Kate began casually.

Elliot studied his drink with interest. "Yes, I heard."

When he did not add to that, Kate continued, "I
think she and I may be there at the same time. While
Jessica's dancing with dukes, I'll be running dirt samples through my hands and taking a hard-hat tour of the
dam." Visions of chauffeurs and ladies in feminine,
wispy clothes billowing enticingly in a faint breeze
chased through Kate's mind. She wouldn't want this as
a way of life, of course, but it would be a wonderful
diversion from her Betty Businesswoman's image.

"Jealous?" he probed, watching her with amusement.

"Of course," she replied lightly. "I can see myself now, taking tea with a countess and talking about Ascot." She tried to turn the conversation back to Jessica, but he prevented her by interrupting with a laugh.

"I'll bet you don't know the first thing about horses."

"They have four legs and a tail, don't they?"

"An expert," he murmured.

She studied him again over the rim of her glass. Why did he seem reluctant to talk about Jessica, she wondered. Did he dislike his ex-wife and was it all a front that they were still friends? Or did he feel something deeper?

"You're staring at me," he told her politely.

"That's because you're so debonair and charming," she said lightly.

"I know, some guy in the men's room told me that very thing the other day," he said easily. "And a woman on the street who tried to kiss me said it too."

"Did you kiss her back?" she bantered.

"No, but I kissed her front," he replied promptly.

She shook her head. Elliot could be absolutely infuriating when she wanted to get information out of him. He was clearly not going to discuss Jessica with her, so she might as well forget it.

Ian called her later that night. His voice brought back to life all the breathless urgency she had felt the last time they had been together.

"I got tied up in Chicago," he told her. "I won't arrive in Dallas until late tonight—actually, two in the morning. If you're busy tomorrow," he added with a hint of uncertainty, "I can change my plans and fly back to England."

Kate began to breathe again. He was coming. "I'm free tomorrow," she assured him quickly.

"Good. I'll rent a car and pick you up at ten in the

morning. Bring your bathing suit; we'll drive north to Lake Texoma and see the scenery."

"I'd like that." Or hunting sharks barehanded or anything else she could do with him. She wondered if he could sense her excitement.

After she hung up, she looked down at the receiver. She wasn't sure what the chemical bond was that tied her to Ian, but it was definitely there. Tomorrow, when she was with him, it would be even stronger. Kate hummed to herself as she started up the steps to look through her clothes and select something special to wear tomorrow. She wanted to look stunning.

At ten the next morning Kate was dressed in a pair of burgundy slacks with a matching tank top that had a white cord drawstring at the waist. Over that she wore a hip-length hooded caftan. The fabric was a soft wool blend with vertical stripes of dull pink and burgundy. Her hair was caught atop her head in a loose knot that allowed a few tendrils to float downward near her face. She picked up her sunglasses and beach bag when she heard a car stop outside.

Kate opened the door before Ian had a chance to ring the bell. To hell with being coy, she thought as she greeted him with a sunny smile. "I'm ready," she announced.

"I wish all the people I have appointments with were as punctual as you," he told her as he led her out to a blue Mercedes and opened the passenger door for her. "There's a map in the back seat. You'll have to be the official guide." He walked around to the driver's side and slid in.

She felt boundless enthusiasm as she turned to face him. "How was Chicago?" she asked. Even that ordinary question seemed like a special one because it was an exchange with Ian.

"Windy." He smiled at her before reaching out to touch her hand. "You look very pretty today." He brought a hand up to touch a wisp of her hair.

He had said she was pretty.

His words were not new, but Kate didn't think they had ever sounded as flattering as they did when Ian spoke them. "Thank you," she murmured.

She settled back in the seat as he started the car and drove out onto the streets. Ian made her feel sixteen again, and today that seemed a nice age to be—young and carefree. While they exchanged details of their week, the green prairie slid by outside the window and they sped toward the border between Texas and Oklahoma. They stopped for a leisurely lunch in the town of Sheridan before they finished their drive into the blackjack and post oak forest that surrounded Lake Texoma. It was two o'clock before they arrived at a sandy and secluded little beach. The only other people present were a family with two children and a young couple. Kate looked at the water lapping against the beach as she stepped from the car. It looked tempting, especially in view of the fact the temperature was over 90 degrees.

"Do you mind if we walk around a bit before we swim?" Ian asked.

She looked from the edge of the water to the woods that spread out around them. They looked leafy and green and cool; not as cool as the lake, but that could come later. "That sounds good," she agreed, and fell into step beside him as he started up a steep path leading away from the water and into the woods. They walked for over half an hour before stopping at the top of a cliff that looked over the expanse of blue-green water. Kate sank onto the grass and Ian sat down beside her.

The wind blew softly through his hair, Kate noted as she watched him squint off into the distance. He had a good tan; he must have spent a good deal of time out of doors lately. There was something else about him, she realized suddenly. He seemed as if he were preoccupied, even worried, and she was instantly concerned. "Is something wrong?" she asked.

"No, why do you ask?"

"You seem a little tense, as if something is on your mind."

"I always have things on my mind," he replied diffidently.

Kate watched him for a few moments longer. She knew he was stalling and fending off her questions because he didn't want to answer them. She attacked directly. "It's the dam, isn't it? Frank told me you weren't satisfied with the drilling that had been done so far." When he said nothing, she added, "We're going to do some more drilling."

Ian picked up a small pebble and tossed it into the water below. "That's good," he said without emotion.

"Don't you think it's enough?" she questioned.

He turned to regard her and his eyes were a flat gray as they held hers. "Do you want to know the truth?" he asked sharply. When she nodded, he continued, "Amalacorp keeps telling me everything is fine, but at the same time drilling always reveals areas that need work."

"They don't require more work," she objected. "We're just grouting them as a precautionary measure. So far when we've grouted, the rock has been so tight and impervious that it takes very little cement. Didn't Frank explain that to you?"

"Yes."

"But you don't believe him," she whispered, studying him in dejection. "And you don't believe me either. You think we're both protecting the company and maybe even hiding something from you."

"Kate," he said quietly, "I didn't come here today to talk about the dam."

Kate felt like an animal protecting its territory. Rising quickly to her company's defense, she said, "No, but since the subject has been brought up, let's pursue it. Stan Watson knows everything there is to know about dams and their construction, and so do a lot of other people who are contributing to the design and construction of Denham dam. And Mr. Arnold, your own man at the site, is making sure everything is done according to plans and specs. I don't see what you think anyone could be trying to pull on you." His lack of trust in her company affected her as strongly as his absence of faith in her word. Kate was determined to show him he was wrong if he thought there was anything at all amiss with the way Denham dam was being built.

Ian reached down and took her hand. "I don't want to go into an explanation about my reservations. But Denham dam is very important to me, and I intend to see that it is built properly." He picked up a blade of grass and smoothed his fingers back and forth across it as his face took on a thoughtful expression. "I take an interest in my corporation." He spoke slowly, as if he were choosing each word with care. "Perhaps too much interest. Few board chairmen visit construction sites. I go to all Denham's plants regularly," he continued. "It may not be what most chairmen do, but it is what I choose to do."

Kate waited silently for him to continue. She understood he was confiding in her something he would not have told others. That knowledge made her strangely content, even though she was still under the shadow he had cast by doubting Amalacorp.

"My father had interests outside Denham." Again he paused.

There was sadness in his eyes as he spoke; Kate could tell his thoughts were painful. "You don't have to explain anything to me," she said as she looked out onto the lake.

"Yes, I do," he contradicted. "The truth is that my father paid so little attention to the business that he very nearly lost it entirely. He, and the whole board along with him, met mainly to discuss the best thoroughbreds. Deciding what business ventures were profitable and the running of the company was left to others. Unfortunately, the men to whom the decision-making fell were in no position to make sound judgments."

She glanced at him sideways. His face was set in a hard line. "Denham was having a lot of financial difficulty when you took over?"

He tossed the blade of grass aside brusquely. "That understates the case. It was in danger of being lost to creditors. I was only twenty-four at the time, so I didn't know a great deal more about running a company than my father did, but I could see how things were going. Even he could by then. I convinced him to hire a management expert to set Denham on its feet again."

"Did he?"

"Yes. We started making slow improvements. When my father died five years ago and I became chairman of the board, things began to turn around. I had enough money from my mother's side of the family to buy some of the other members out. After that I was able to change the focus of the meetings to pure business."

"I see," she murmured. Kate plucked a small grasshopper from the hem of her slacks. She was silent, considering what he had related. Ian had gotten where he was today by working hard to shore up a company that was floundering. It was apparent his father's mishandling of the business had galvanized Ian's determination to build a successful one. That explained why he was paying such close attention to the dam. She could even understand his uncertainties about it in view of what he stood to lose if anything went wrong. But nothing would go wrong. When the dam was completed, it would be proof of Amalacorp's engineering skill. What was of more significance to Kate right now was that Ian was opening a fragile line of communication between them. "Thank you for telling me," she said quietly.

They held hands loosely as they began the trek back to the beach. She glanced at him admiringly as they walked. There was much more to Ian than merely a handsome exterior. He was a man committed to his work; she respected that. In addition, he was sensitive to others, and she suspected he was scrupulously fair in his business dealings. She stole another look at him as they walked along. There was little—if anything—about Ian that she did not like.

They emerged from the cool silence of the trees to the sun-bleached sand. During their absence, more swimmers had arrived. Fifteen or so people were now scattered along the sandy stretch sunning themselves or shouting and splashing in the water.

Kate and Ian changed into their bathing suits in the bath house. Kate dressed in a one-piece black suit with modest cut-outs on both sides of the waist. When she walked outside, Ian was already waiting for her looking tanned and trim in a pair of navy trunks. She saw his eyes travel quickly up her long legs and across the bathing suit before ending at her face.

She recognized his look of appreciation and she thought she had detected a hint of surprise too. Good—that meant thoughts of business were behind him. She threw him a backward smile and ran toward the water. Today was her day to be carefree and absolved from any responsibilities. It was a time to be a woman, totally.

She smiled as she plunged into the water and squealed at its coolness. What would her staff think if they could see her now, she wondered as she watched the people around her frolicking in total abandon.

She rolled over onto her back and began to float, letting her hands dip gently into the water as it rose and fell. Even though her eyes were closed to shut out the sun, she knew when Ian came up beside her. He surfaced with deliberate stillness, but she was aware of his presence as surely as if he had caused a tidal wave with his approach. "When you have a lake like this, will you allow recreation?" she asked.

"No, I'll stock it with sharks," he returned promptly. "What a perfectly dreadful man you are." She opened one eye and observed him solemnly as he joined her by floating on his back beside her. "Is that what an Englishman would have said? It's what they say in all the old English movies—that and things like 'devilish hard,' and 'frightfully dull.'"

"I wasn't aware you had such an interest in the English," he said. With one hand he lapped cool water against her.

She retaliated by splashing cold water onto his stomach. "I don't have an interest in *all* Englishmen."

Her eyes met his in a look of teasing that turned quickly into something else. There was an unguarded look on his face for a moment that included warmth as well as something she could not read. And then the instant passed, as a beach ball fell between them.

Ian picked it up to throw it back to the owner and Kate rolled onto her stomach and made a surface dive into the quiet world below. The water stretched out around her, above and below and on both sides. It seemed as endless and perfect as the day that lay before her.

Half an hour later she lay in the warm sand next to Ian. Had she ever felt this way before? She couldn't recall a time when she had been so at peace with life. Still, the feeling did not seem entirely new.

"What are you thinking?" he asked lazily.

Kate watched Ian let the sugary sand sift through his fingers. "I'm wondering if you'll feed me soon and what I should have to eat."

He smiled and scooped up another handful of sand. "Is that a hint that you're hungry? It's only four-thirty."

"I know, but by the time we change our clothes, drive into town and scour it for a good place to eat, it will be six or after. I get ravenous if I'm not fed promptly at five," she warned. "You'll probably have to stop two or three times at grocery stores so I can buy some cookies and candy to tide me over."

He rose. "Come on. I don't want to be responsible for your teeth rotting away." He stretched down a hand and pulled her to her feet with one fluid motion.

Ian's body still glistened from the water and the golden sheen of his tan. There was something so carelessly sensual about him . . . Could he read in her face the effect he had on her, she wondered briefly. No, she decided, she had become an expert at masking her feelings a long time ago.

They found a restaurant in the town by the dam. It was an old railroad depot that had been converted into a hotel and restaurant, and was named, aptly, Down by the Station. Kate and Ian were seated in an upstairs room amid Boston ferns and asparagus plants hanging from the ceiling, and antique oak furniture. Kate looked at Ian over the low-burning candle as their waiter disappeared down the steps that led to the kitchen.

"I wonder how many people left this station in the 1890's and where they were going?" she asked, looking around at the old rooms with a reflective smile.

"I don't know, maybe ten or so people left a day, probably heading further west," he said dispassionately.

Kate leaned forward, caught up with her thoughts of the past and intent on kindling a like interest in him. "Can't you just picture this town the way it was then? There was probably a saloon across the street bustling with women in black stockings and garters dancing for men with shooting irons strapped to their hips. Doesn't it seem almost real to you?"

"No," he answered honestly.

"You lack imagination," she accused.

"That's all right, I think you make up for it." He studied her for a moment in the uncertain light of the room. "I'm a little surprised, because I wouldn't have taken you for a daydreamer. You give the impression of a woman grounded in reality."

Kate took a drink from the cut glass tumbler and

studied a chip in the lip of it. "I do have my feet firmly on the ground," she said thoughtfully. "I only weave stories and daydream about others. My aspirations for myself are for things I can achieve with hard work."

"'A man's reach should exceed his grasp. . . .'"

Kate looked up as the waiter arrived with their Chateaubriand and put a generous slice on each plate. "You're right," she agreed lightly. He wasn't, of course. She didn't aspire to anything that wasn't attainable. It was self-destructive to pursue something one couldn't have. She picked up her fork and tasted the tender meat while the argument continued inside her. Was she pursuing something unattainable by letting her interest in Ian continue? Shouldn't she deliberately try to quell it? After all, it wasn't likely that she and Ian could ever form a serious relationship, separated as they were by company demands and an ocean. She pushed that thought from her mind; there would be time to consider it later. Today was for enjoyment.

It was after midnight when they arrived back at her apartment. Kate opened the door and led the way into the kitchen. "Gin and tonic?" she called back to him.

"No, thanks." He followed her into the kitchen.

Kate didn't realize how close he was standing to her until she turned around and found herself face to face with him. He put a hand on either side of her, blocking her escape—had she wanted to escape. She didn't. There had been a fire burning inside her since this morning. It had been ignited at her first sight of him today, and now it was leaping into full blaze. She dropped her eyes from his and drew tiny circles around the button of his shirt with her finger. "I had a lovely day; I'm glad you were able to come to Dallas."

"I'm glad too," he said in a thick voice. "Dallas has gained a vast appeal for me lately."

She nodded without looking up. "That's probably because the weather has gotten nicer," she suggested.

"No doubt." He tilted her chin upward with the back of his hand. "You have beautiful eyes."

Whoever had coined that ridiculous adage about flattery not advancing a person's cause had never met Ian, Kate reflected as he drew her into his arms. Her eyes fell closed as she raised her lips to his. There was an unspoken agreement that they were going to kiss, and she fell into those plans agreeably. For long moments she was immersed in the quiet thrill of being in his arms, of feeling his lips touching and teasing hers, and of the gentle search of his tongue inside her mouth. She put her arms around his neck and drew him closer to her, fitting her body against his while his hands moved up and down her back in an easy caress. It had been a good day, and it showed every indication of getting even better.

Finally he drew back. Kate met his intent look with an unblinking one of her own. Then he carefully took the pins from her hair and led her up the steps.

Inside the bedroom Ian turned the covers back and they slid, still fully clothed, between the crisp percale sheets. In the darkness Kate could not see the leafy print on the bedsheets, but she knew it was there. The mental picture of the leafy green designs on the sheets brought to her mind the silent forest around Lake Texoma and her mind made the willing leap from reality to fantasy. She was alone with Ian beneath leaf-laden branches. There was something primeval and exciting to her about that thought. It was as if they were the only two people alive, or the only two of any significance at the moment.

For long moments they lay entwined in each other's arms and she tasted the sweetness of his breath as his tongue wove its way around hers. He created longings that palpitated through her like little jolts of electricity. She was only vaguely aware of the warm breeze coming in through a half-open window. In her mind she was feeling the faint breeze sweeping off the lake.

His hands touched her breasts and brought them to little peaks through the cloth that separated them from his touch. Her growing desire was apparent, and she could feel the unmistakable sign of his longing for her. They were alone in the forest of passion that was verdant around them. It was as if it had lain ready and waiting for her and Ian for thousand of years.

Kate raised a hand to touch the tanned triangle at the opening of his shirt before pulling her lips away from his and moving to touch his ear and breathe gently against it. Then her tongue brushed around it in a slow, circular motion. She could feel his body stiffen as he drew in a shallow breath. He was taut with longing, and it gave her a curious sense of power to know that she could make this self-possessed man respond so to her touch. But she knew she was under his influence just as much as he was under hers. That knowledge was reinforced when he slipped his hands beneath the folds of material and moved them slowly over her body.

She knew they were experimenting with each other, both testing to see what caused a stir of excitement in the other. Ian's hand roving freely over her incited wild urges that brought a new, faster tempo to her breathing and a flush of expectation to her face. Then, with a few deft movements, he pulled her clothes from her and his hands moved downward from her breasts. She closed her eyes tightly, hungrily experiencing the sensations he sent through her as he memorized every dip and curve of her body. The breeze stirred again. "Nature, red in tooth and claw," she remembered her Tennyson, and she gave herself over to it gladly as she experienced sensations as old and elusive as the sea breezes.

When he pulled slowly away and stood, she watched him through eyes half-closed with passion. She could hear the soft rustle of his clothes as he took them off and she could see his shadowy form, tall and broad-shouldered. When he lay down beside her again, Kate was eager for him. As if he sensed her urgency, he moved quickly, bringing them together with a gentleness that she knew required restraint.

When she smoothed her hands across his strong back, she could feel the light sheen of perspiration filmed there, and she could hear his unsteady breathing. As they moved together in perfect harmony, Kate thought rapturously that there was something both effortless and demanding about their lovemaking. The sensations swirling around her and through her increased in fervor, and she felt as if she were on a swing that was going higher and higher up into the air. The wind rushed past her with every sweep she made through the sky, and she knew a heady exhilaration at defying gravity and tasting freedom. From where she was, she could touch the sky.

Her lips parted in a soft moan of pleasure and she exploded with passion into a darkness that was as soft as velvet. Whirling sensations of ecstasy drew her into a fast-moving circle, and her whole body lost all orientation and sense of direction except for one place inside her that radiated bliss. The sweet blackness was replaced by a gradual return to the light. Even then, she was so lost in wondrous contentment that she could not speak.

When she was able to talk again, she did not. Words were inadequate to express the way she felt. But she thought Ian understood when she kissed him gently on the lips.

Chapter 14

Sunday was a blur of smiles—across the breakfast table, by the lions' area at the zoo, over the tennis net, and before they turned out the light that night.

Monday morning Kate awoke early and lay quietly for a moment enjoying the presence of Ian beside her. She could tell by the sound of his breathing that he was already awake.

"I have to leave," he said.

She touched his chest with a regretful sigh. "I know."

"I don't know when I'll be back in the States; I'm going to be rather busy the next few weeks." He moved a wisp of hair from her face before continuing, "I can't say when I'll be able to see you again."

That was the thought she had been trying to push from her mind. She would also be busy, and it might be weeks, even months, before she could be with him again.

"I'll call you," he promised softly, "and I'll fly back as soon as I can."

"Okay." The words sounded braver and more cheerful than she felt, Kate thought as she watched him rise from the bed and pull his clothes on. A glance at the clock revealed that it was 5:30 in the morning. If he could just stay a little longer, she would be more able to let him go, she told herself. But she knew that was a lie. She would feel no differently later than she did now.

Buttoning his shirt, he walked back to the bed and sat on the edge of it. He took her hand in his. "I don't like to leave. You know that, don't you? But we're both in positions that demand a great deal of us. When there's a chance for both of us to spend a few days together, we will. Then we can talk."

"Of course." Her hand tightened in his. It might be a long time before she and Ian had a chance to talk and to decide what their relationship was going to be. In the meantime she was left hanging, afraid to put too much emphasis on the brief time they had spent with each other and unwilling to abandon thoughts of how special it had been.

He bent and kissed her cheek. "Go back to sleep." He crossed the room and closed the door behind him.

She couldn't obey his command. Her mind was too alert, too full of thoughts of Ian, of this weekend and of her feelings to push them all aside and give herself over to sleep. She felt a rising sense of panic when she heard the downstairs door close and she knew he had left.

Maybe it had all been an illusion, she reflected. It had been an idyllic two days, but what was left that she could hold onto? There was not even any tangible evidence that he had ever been here. And even if she and Ian came to the understanding they wanted to see a great deal of each other, what then? Pragmatism would set in, and with it the knowledge that thousands of miles stood between them. And time would always be against them—they were both busy in their own worlds. Ian had made it plain that building a successful company was important to him. And she had already firmly established that having a career was more important to her than any relationship could ever be. Even with Ian.

She shut her eyes tightly. She had built her life carefully, struggling hard to rise from the ranks of a working engineer to a manager. Along with the responsibilities of her new job had come the advantage of having enough money that finances would never be a problem again. She could buy the most expensive clothes, live in the best neighborhood and drive a fancy car. Along with those things came a sense of self-worth and an appreciation of the power of her position. She had come a long way from the little girl who had worried over the price of food in an Ohio grocery store.

She was good at her job and she enjoyed the challenge and fulfillment it brought her. She would never give it up, and she knew Ian was just as emphatically entrenched in his work in England. What, then, could the future hold for them except some happy times before the inevitable parting?

She threw back the covers and rose. She was worrying about things that might never come to pass. She would let her relationship with Ian run its course. In the meantime she might as well go to work. There was much to be done at the office.

Kate was at her desk an hour later. She had intended to attack the stack of work waiting for her, but instead she found herself looking reflectively across the room at the pearl-gray walls and then down at the wine-red carpeting. Ian's presence in her life had affected her in dozens of subtle ways. Today, as she sat at her polished oak desk wearing a white silk blouse with a scalloped neck and a powder-blue dirndl skirt, she felt entirely feminine. And what was more, it didn't bother her that she felt that way.

She forced her eyes back to the report on her desk. There would be time later to think of Ian and to sort out her feelings. Right now there was work to be done, and very shortly the Monday morning staff meeting to be attended. After that four of the men in her branch were coming to her office to discuss the status of their various projects. She opened the report resolutely and began to read.

After the staff meeting Kate met with four of the office engineers at the conference table in her office. Rolled up cross-sections and maps and bar graphs lay ready for presentation and comment at one end of the table. At the other end the five of them discussed some of the projects the company was currently bidding on. Then they settled into the business at hand.

Ivan Brooks talked first. He gave a summary of the work being performed at the Italian project. He concluded with a tentative date for completion. Afterwards, one of the other men outlined work being done at the pipeline in Colorado. Then Allan Smith gave a brief outline of the status of work on Denham dam.

"The core drillings which were completed last week revealed the rock to be competent," he reported. "Work will begin this week on the first-stage embankment on the east side of the creek. The second-stage embankment will be placed on the west side. Both these jobs will be completed simultaneously in about three months. December and January are the rainy months in the Cotswolds, so very little work can be done then. Starting around the beginning of February, the second-stage embankment will be transferred to the east side and it will be completed in late April or early May. After that closure will be effected in the stream channel and the dam will be completed."

Kate waited for him to finish before she said, "I'm afraid our schedule may be thrown off by a week or so. I think we need to drill at least three more holes."

"But the last set of borings showed practically nothing wrong," Allan objected. "There were just a few scattered vugs, and they were so small it really wasn't necessary to grout them. We only did to make absolutely certain nothing down there was left unsealed."

"I know the holes didn't take much cement," Kate

replied. "Still, we haven't started work on the embankment on that side of the creek yet, and if we're ever going to do any more drilling there, it will have to be now. We can have a drilling rig in there that can put down all three holes in a day. What may take a little longer is the borehole camera."

All four men looked at her in surprise. "Is that necessary?" Allan asked. "What do we expect to pick up with a camera that isn't evident from the core samples?"

"It is the responsibility of this company to assure Denham company that there is absolutely no cause for worry. Their chairman of the board has taken a personal interest in this dam, and he has expressed reservations to Frank and to myself. In view of that, I think we should take the extra time and spend a few extra dollars to convince Denham that everything is going smoothly," she concluded as she looked around the table.

There was a grumble from Allan as he shuffled some papers. "I agree that we should make every effort to do a good job, but Denham has their own man on the site. It's his responsibility to oversee the work and convince his employers that everything is going according to the specs."

"Denham does have an engineer overseeing construction," Kate agreed. "However, Mr. Nigel has made his own trips to the site and has drawn his own conclusions. It would be nice if we didn't have to do more drilling, but the fact is we did uncover some unsuitable foundation. In view of the fact we are being paid fifty million dollars to construct this dam, we can absorb the cost of an additional week of work at a thousand dollars a day. What we are buying is confidence in our company. While we may not see any return from that investment in the immediate future, I can assure you other companies will be more willing to do business with someone who makes it clear they will go out of their way to insure satisfaction. Believe me,

Denham has associations with plenty of other corporations who may use us in the future."

"I suppose so," Allan replied.

Kate could see that he was not convinced, but she ignored that and changed the subject. "Right now it looks like the dam will be completed in May?"

"That's the tentative schedule," Allan agreed.

Kate settled back in her chair with a smile. "Good." It was ridiculous, of course, but she felt there was still a slight wedge between herself and Ian in the shape of this dam. Once the work on it was completed, they would both be free of the shadow of their professional lives interfering with their personal lives. If, that is, they were still seeing each other next May.

She stayed late at work that evening. There was a lot to be done and she threw herself into it with fervor. After all, the more work she finished, the freer she would be to take a few days off should she decide to go somewhere—England, for example. It was after 7:30 before she finally pushed her chair back from her desk and rose. She raised her arms over her head in a languorous stretch and then, picking up her jacket and attaché case, started for the door.

She walked down the long hall, noting the Renaissance paintings for the first time in ages. She was taking time to enjoy things more, she noted with a smile. Another of Ian's subtle influences. She stopped at the end of the hall, pushed the elevator button, and waited for a door to open. When one did, the janitor walked out, pushing a bucket on wheels and carrying a mop.

"Everybody must be working late tonight," he said.

"We're an industrious crowd," she told him cheerfully.

"Must be. Mr. Moyer is still here, and Mr. Walters and Mr. Rodgers."

"Are they?" she asked disinterestedly as she stepped onto the elevator and started to push the button for the ground floor. On an impulse, she pushed the one for

Frank's floor instead. He had not been at the staff meeting this morning, and she had not seen him today although she had sent him a memo telling him of the additional holes that would be drilled at the dam site. She had also told him of the plans to use a borehole camera to do further tests on the core holes.

Kate stepped off the elevator at Frank's floor and walked down the long hall into his secretary's office. The light was out, and for a moment she thought the janitor had been wrong and Frank was not here. Then she heard the sound of his voice coming over the secretary's intercom.

"I don't know what to say, Burke. I've explained to her that further testing is expensive and that we're running close to the bid amount now."

Kate stopped, frozen, as Frank continued.

"I can't tie her hands. After all, foundation work at Denham is her responsibility, and she's being conscientious about it."

"The hell we can't tie her hands!" Kate recognized the voice as Duane Rodgers'. "Just tell her we're not doing any more drilling and we're cutting back on extravagant spending like running cameras down bore holes. If she's a photography nut, she'll have to find some other place to indulge her hobby."

Kate listened transfixed. A dull pain was starting in the hollow of her stomach and overcoming her initial shock. What were these men doing talking about her like this? She was a company manager, not some temporary help they had dragged in off the street.

"The poor kid probably thinks the camera thing is a good idea," Frank said in a placating voice.

Kate felt her cheeks turn crimson and an angry surge welled up inside her. The urge to storm into Frank's office was counterbalanced by a childish desire to flee. But leaving could not erase the fact that she had overheard their words. Her anger returned as she thought of Frank, Burke and Duane, and possibly more men, talking about her in this manner. She could picture them now, the "good ole boys," grouped around Frank's desk.

Kate didn't go into the office and she didn't leave. Instead, she stood, almost rooted to the spot, listening to the men talk.

"I've always liked people under me to understand what their function in the company is, and I don't want anyone who will overstep that boundary," Burke said in a ponderous voice laden with displeasure. "I'm not sure we didn't make one hell of a mistake in hiring that girl."

"That's easily fixed," Duane interjected.

"You mean fire her?" Frank asked calmly.

Kate felt as if someone had thrust a sharp knife into her stomach. Her very job was on the line, she realized in alarm. It was her future that was being discussed, and it was being done with the word "fire." The very word singed her with shame. She had excelled in college and she had a glowing record from her other employers; she had always done well. Now she had failed. It was evident the company officials were dissatisfied with her performance. Even the fact that they met in secret to talk about her filled her with despair. Did they think her actions in the company had been so fraught with errors that they could not have met with her to discuss any problems they thought she was having?

"I don't think firing is an option we should resort to just yet," Burke said. His tone was judicious, as if he had not dismissed the idea totally. "There are better ways. Frank, you drop a few hints to her about how we want this organization run. Another thing, slam the checkbook closed. Tell her all drilling will have to be cleared through accounting to make sure we have the funds. Then instruct accounting to tell her the funds aren't available."

"I don't think we need a beauty queen in that job anyway," Duane muttered. "She's certainly the only company official whose picture was in the paper with an article depicting her lifestyle. *Lifestyle,*" he sneered. "What the hell kind of publicity was that for us?"

Burke gave a cold laugh. "Don't worry about that story. No one reads the Dallas papers anyway. You know what they say—Texas is a state where men are men and newspapers are awful. I think that write-up proves it."

Frank was speaking again, but Kate didn't wait to hear what he said. Instead, she slipped quietly out the door and walked quickly down the hall to the elevator. There was an overriding sense of humiliation and hurt struggling to surface, but she stifled it successfully until she was downstairs. Walking into the parking garage, she even managed to smile at the night attendant as she crossed the empty parking spaces to her car. It was only when she was inside it that she rested her head in her hands and let silent tears course down her cheeks.

Chapter 15

Kate sat for long moments before she forced herself to place the key in the ignition and turn it. With the jerky, uncoordinated movements of a marionette, she pulled out of her parking space and drove back to her apartment. Inside the living room, she sank numbly onto the sofa.

Fired! She had worked too hard and too long for her career to be smeared with a brand like that. What had she done wrong, anyway? Frank had never given the least indication he was unhappy with her performance, nor had Duane. Although Burke had not raved about her work, he had treated her the same as everyone else. As she recalled what the men had said about her and the tone of their voices, she felt a new surge of anger and betrayal.

Frank had been there. She had trusted him and thought of him as her friend, even as a mentor. It was true he had not said anything particularly damning, but he had been present. What sort of friend would discuss her with the company president behind her back and worse, let his colleagues abuse her without rising to her defense?

Kate looked up listlessly when the telephone rang. For a moment she was tempted to ignore it; she didn't feel like talking to anyone right now. Still, it might be important. She walked to the kitchen and picked up the receiver. "Hello," she said faintly.

"Kate, it's Elliot. Busy?"

"A little," she replied as she traced figure eights on the clean white counter with her finger.

"I know it's after eight, but I was hoping we could get together for a little while. I just landed the job to build Northway Apartments and I want to celebrate!"

"Congratulations." It was a big job, and one she knew he had wanted badly. She tried to sound cheerful, but the ache that was beginning in the back of her throat made it difficult. The effort to talk somehow compounded her hurt feelings and tangled emotions. She was going to cry and she hated herself for the weakness.

"Is something wrong?" Elliot asked.

"No," she said quickly. Nothing she could talk about yet. It would take her the rest of the evening to collect herself enough just to go to work tomorrow and act as if nothing had happened.

"You sound a little funny," he persevered.

"I may be getting a cold," she mumbled. Tears were spilling over and rolling down her cheeks and it was an effort to keep her chin from trembling. She had tried so hard at her job! She had put all her effort into being successful at Amalacorp, and she had thought she was doing well. It was a sharp blow to learn how disappointed everyone was with her.

"Listen, how about if I just come by your apartment and we'll have a drink to celebrate the contract," Elliot suggested.

"I don't think so, I'm rather tired and you could catch my cold."

He laughed good-naturedly. "I never catch colds and

I don't mind if you fall asleep in my lap. I won't take 'no' for an answer, so you may as well get out the ice cubes."

"Okay," she capitulated. It seemed easier than arguing with him. She knew he was excited; he had landed a big fish. She could go through the motions of having a pleasant drink with him, she resolved as she walked into the bathroom and splashed cold water on her face. There would be plenty of time for crying and feeling hurt later.

Upstairs in her bedroom she took off her office clothes and let them fall into an ignominious heap on the floor. She didn't bother to hang them up neatly as she always did. They seemed somehow contaminated; she wanted to be out of them as quickly as possible. After pulling on a print blouse and a pair of jeans, she walked back down the steps.

The sound of a scratching on the back door startled her at first, and then she remembered Cuddles. She opened the sliding glass door and he leaped into the kitchen and darted directly to the cabinet where his food was kept. When Kate did not follow, he looked back curiously, then returned to her and walked around her purring and threading back and forth through her legs. Kate sat down on the floor and drew Cuddles onto her lap, putting her head down against his soft fur.

She was still holding the bemused cat and thinking about what she had overheard when the doorbell rang a few minutes later. She put Cuddles gently on the floor and rose, brushing off her jeans as she walked down the hall and opened the door.

Elliot smiled at her. "I thought this was a special occasion so I brought my best cognac—" He broke off, lowering the bottle he was holding aloft. "Hey, you don't look too good, Kate."

"I'm fine." She turned quickly and led the way into the living room. "Sit down. I'll bring the glasses."

Elliot watched her walk to the breakfront china cabinet and take out two cordial glasses. "Is it the cold or what? Your eyes are all puffy, like you're going to cry." In mock horror, he added, "Don't go to pieces on me, I can't handle it when women do that."

She closed the china cabinet door and stood perfectly still, looking intently at a tiny bubble in the crystal of one of the glasses. "I had a hard day at the office," she explained tersely.

"It couldn't have been that hard," he said with a laugh. "You look like they ran over you with a Mack truck and then backed up."

"That's how I feel." She walked back into the living room and set the glasses on the coffee table in front of the sofa. The rest of the story spilled out. "I overheard Burke and Frank and Duane talking about me this evening. What I heard wasn't very flattering."

"What did they say?"

She drew in a deep breath. Part of her didn't want to discuss the matter and another part wanted to confess all that she had heard and have Elliot reassure her. "They said I am investing far too much money in a certain project." She swallowed. "Burke suggested they might have been better off not to have hired me. Someone else said I could be fired, but Burke shelved that idea temporarily."

"Christ!" He let out a low whistle. "No wonder you look so down and out." He stood and pushed her gently onto the sofa. "I'll bring you something to drink. It'll soothe your nerves." A moment later she heard liquor being poured into glasses and then he returned. She didn't look up; she was staring at the blue shag carpeting as if it held the secret to all her troubles.

"Here." Elliot put a drink into her hands. "Take a stiff drink."

Kate obeyed mechanically, letting the expensive liquid flow down her throat without even tasting it. "It's good," she murmured politely.

Elliot sat down beside her and began in rallying tones, "I know this won't make you feel much better, but getting fired is an occupational hazard. The higher a person goes on the corporate ladder, the greater the risk of being canned, because the pressures are greater and more people have to be pleased."

"That's just it," Kate objected. "I didn't know anyone wasn't pleased with my work. No one had given the least indication . . ." She paused and continued more slowly, "Frank had mentioned a time or two that we were going over the estimates on Denham dam, but I had no idea he meant it was a problem to the extent we couldn't afford to spend ten or twelve thousand. My God, that's nothing compared to the cost of the project."

Elliot set his glass on the table and fisted his hands on his knees. He was silent for a moment before he said, "Did you ever wonder whether Amalacorp might be having financial problems?"

She considered the question carefully. "I know they haven't been awarded any really lucrative contracts lately, but there's a lull in the whole industry. Do you know something?"

"No, of course not, but I have heard rumors that Amalacorp is having some difficulties money-wise. Your spending may have scared them if that's true. And maybe you've been authorizing more spending than you realize. A few thousand here and there can add up fast."

She didn't think she had authorized that much spending, but she didn't argue. It suddenly seemed very pointless to be defending herself to Elliot. "Maybe I should just resign," she said wearily. "I don't know if I can work for people who aren't satisfied with me, and I'll always feel as if I'm walking on eggshells. Burke didn't throw out the possibility of firing me, he simply put it on hold. That would be a big weight hanging over my head."

"Hold on there just one minute! You're talking about the quitter's way out."

"Should I wait and be fired?" she flared. Being called

a quitter stung almost as much as realizing she had failed at Amalacorp.

"What you should do," Elliot said firmly, "is take a good, long drink of your cognac and try to calm down. You can't think rationally yet. I realize it was a blow to your ego to overhear what you did, but you can't be beaten that easily." He waited until she picked up her glass dutifully and took a sip. "Good," he said approvingly. "Now then, let's approach this objectively. Has anyone at Amalacorp ever hinted there was anything they didn't like about the way you were running your branch?"

"No. Of course, I've had disagreements with the managers of other sections, especially with design because we work so closely with them, but there's been no dispute that hasn't been resolved happily. I think I work well with the others in the company too."

"Then let's assume that Burke and the others were a little keyed up tonight—they may have even been sipping a little Jack Daniels—and they said some things they might not really mean."

"Judging from the tone of their voices, they were dead serious," Kate said morosely.

Elliot looked at her speculatively for a moment before asking, "Have you been poking into company secrets or prying around for information that anyone seems reluctant to give?"

"No!" she replied, affronted. "As a manager of projects I have access to the information I need without resorting to snooping around for it. I work for an engineering firm, not Cloak and Dagger, Inc. Certainly I don't sniff around looking for skeletons in the corporate closet."

"Maybe you did it unintentionally," he persisted.

"You worked for Amalacorp," she returned. "Are you trying to say the company has anything to hide?"

He shrugged and leaned back on the sofa. "Every large organization has a few little secrets that are better swept under a rug or locked in the company vault," he replied. "Amalacorp has made as many deals under the table as any other big outfit. They're not honest or dishonest; when it comes to money, I think every large firm is amoral."

Kate was only half-listening. She was thinking of other words she had overheard from Frank's secretary's office. "They're going to have funding cut off through accounting so that my ability to authorize spending will be curtailed. I guess Burke figured I'd never guess he was behind the maneuver. It's all so sneaking and low!"

Elliot eyed her impassively. "What are you going to do?"

"I ought to march right in there first thing in the morning and confront Burke with what I know. If he wants to fire me, at least I can have the dignity of having him do it out in the open."

"That's the anger speaking," Elliot said with maddening calm. "But what are you *really* going to do?"

Kate finished her drink and smiled wanly at him. "I'm going to be twice as conscientious, work even harder, and pare expenses to the bone. I'll make Burke and all the others realize they've judged me wrong and that I don't spend indiscriminately or foolishly." She felt some of the fire and indignation go out of her as she added, "I may have learned a good lesson from this. I've been too trusting and I haven't been vigilant enough for enemies in the corporate world. From now on I'll be a lot more careful whom I trust."

"If you mean Frank, don't be too hard on him," Elliot warned. "After all, he has to work for Burke, and that entails doing what it takes to get along with Burke. We both know how hard that can be, and you only heard a part of the conversation," he continued. "Don't be too judgmental." He changed the subject abruptly as he pulled her into his arms and kissed her firmly on the mouth. "I hate to sound male chauvinistic, but you do look awfully appealing when you're mad and those pretty violet eyes sparkle." He shifted his body closer to hers and kissed her again.

Kate pushed him gently away. She hadn't intended to talk to Elliot about their relationship tonight, but she could not allow him to think it could develop into anything more than it was. He was a nice person, light and funny, but deep attraction was simply not there. That had been made even more evident by her glorious weekend with Ian.

"What's wrong?" he asked.

"Elliot, I think we need to discuss our feelings for each other. I like you a lot, but—"

He held up a hand. "Don't tell me. I'm a great guy and you want us to be friends, but you don't see anything more intimate ever developing between us."

She sighed and met his eyes. "I'm afraid that's about the size of it. I didn't mean to tell you quite like this, but I can't let you continue thinking we can be anything more than friends." She searched his face. Did he understand? Her fears were set at rest when he grinned ruefully.

"Don't look at me like you think I'm going to throw myself off a twenty-story building. I'm not *that* disappointed. I like you and I'm sorry things didn't work out better between us. I'm glad you've put everything up front." He rose. "I've got to go now, but I'm going to hold you to that promise of being friends. If you need to talk to someone tomorrow, call me. I'll give you another locker-room pep talk."

She smiled. "Thanks, Elliot."

Chapter 16

Kate strode into her office the next day with deliberate dignity. She smiled at her secretary and stepped inside her office, stopping inside the door to survey the room impartially. The conference table with its beige chairs, the wooden bookcases with neat rows of reports, the plush red rug and the picture window that laid downtown Dallas at her feet were all just as they had been the first time she had seen the office. Then they had impressed her as an outward symbol of her success, but now they no longer affected her. It was nothing but a room to which she had been assigned; when she was gone it would be given to someone else. But while she was here to do the job, she intended to throw herself into her work completely, she resolved as she marched to the desk.

She pulled out yesterday's memo detailing the work to be done at Denham and began to write another one rescinding it. She would not authorize any more money for core drilling at Denham. If Amalacorp's higher executives wanted to convince Denham that they were building a good dam, then someone other than herself would have to decide that.

Frank Moyer stopped by her office at a little after ten. She greeted him with a composed smile. He looked the same, she thought as he crossed the room toward her desk. His tall, proud bearing was the same, and the silver-white hair and a handsome, mature face were all intact. It was only her trust in him that had been shattered.

"Hi, how are things going?" His words were friendly and he settled comfortably into the chair in front of her desk.

"Fine," she answered brightly.

"This August heat is killing me," he complained.

For a moment Kate's irritation rose inside her. Didn't Frank have anything better to talk to her about than the weather? Why didn't he talk about the quality of her work and the reservations he had about how well she was doing her job? But she stifled her feelings and agreed blandly, "It's awfully hot."

He leaned back and crossed his legs casually before continuing, "I noticed you sent a memo up about doing a little more explorations on the foundation at Denham."

He's quite a politician, she noted to herself. He was easing himself into a discussion about Denham gradually. "I've decided that further drilling won't be necessary. We've invested enought money there on core sampling already," she began. She saw Frank look at her sharply, as if he wondered at the fact that she was echoing the same sentiments that had been expressed in his office last night. Let him wonder, she thought defiantly. She hoped she made him uncomfortable. "Don't you agree?" she asked politely, deliberately giving the impression she had misinterpreted his look of surprise.

"I do agree," he said hastily.

"Good." With a touch of bitterness, she reflected that canceling the drilling had saved Burke the trouble

of feeding the message back to her through accounting.
Her tone was carefully unrevealing as she continued,
"By the way, I haven't heard any final word on the
contract being let for the suspension bridges in the
northeast. Wasn't that bid going to be awarded last
Thursday?"

"They've delayed awarding it," he answered. "But as
far as I know, we're one of the leading contenders."

Kate was listening intently for any doubt in Frank's
voice. Was he worried about the company's finances?
Just how badly did Amalacorp need that half a billion
dollar bridge contract? Before last night Kate might
have asked Frank that question; now she didn't. He
was no longer a friend, he was simply a business
acquaintance. While they would continue to work
together, he was not a person she would confide in, and
she didn't invite him to speculate on anything with her.

"I've got to get back to my desk. I never know when
Burke might come storming into my office wanting
something." He delivered that statement with a conspiratorial wink as he rose.

She smiled and watched him leave. She wasn't the
innocent she had been yesterday, Kate thought, and
she wished she could tell Frank as much. She certainly
wasn't taken in by his attempt to make her feel that he
and she were in the same boat together. *Esprit de corps*
was all very well when everyone was in the same vessel,
but she had the distinct feeling that she was a lone
person on a raft looking up at an oncoming super-
tanker. That feeling was especially strong when she
thought of Burke's words about her last evening.

She mentally slammed the door on such thoughts.
She had resolved that she was going to work as hard as
she could to please Burke with her work. It wasn't
going to be easy, she reflected as she turned her eyes
back to the correspondence in front of her. For a
moment she toyed with the idea of looking for a job
elsewhere. But positions like this did not grow on trees.
And it would be too great a blow to her pride to return

to Higgins, Powers and Barnes or to take a lesser position elsewhere.

In spite of her attempt to immerse herself in her work, when Jessica called late that afternoon Kate was glad for the break.

"Let's have dinner together," Jessica suggested gaily.

"I'm rather busy," Kate began, looking at the stacks of work on her desk and the volumes of reports to be read.

"Shelve it. You can do it tomorrow. Better yet, leave everything on the edge of your desk and maybe the cleaning lady will tip it off into the wastebasket."

Kate looked around her. The pearl-gray walls that had once seemed so large now gave the impression they were closing in on her. "Yes, I'll meet you," she said decisively. Getting away from here would do her a world of good.

Kate stepped into the restaurant and looked around. A salad bar in the center of the room was set beneath a pretty white gazebo. The whole interior was designed to look like a summer in Newport, with vine and trellis wallpaper and white latticework that separated glass-topped tables and white wrought-iron chairs from other groups of tables. Kate spied Jessica and started across the room toward her.

"Hi," she greeted Jessica as she seated herself. "I like your hair." It had been cut and curled into small, loose waves that looked dainty and feminine on her petite friend.

"Do you? I'm not sure if it's me. I wanted something *très chic*–looking for England, but I may have it changed before I leave."

"Keep it that way; it's cute."

Jessica made a face. "I'm thirty. I don't want to be 'cute.' I want to be cosmopolitan, supersuave or stunning, but I definitely don't want to be cute."

"Okay, it's *ravissant*," Kate obliged.

Jessica settled back in her chair. "That's better," she

approved. "I'm getting a whole new set of clothes too."
She glanced down at the candy-striped jersey that fit
her slender figure well. "I've decided the ones I have
are too American-looking, so I'm scouring Neiman's
and Sanger Harris for some extremely svelte clothes. I
want a couple of evening gowns that look like I walked
out of the Paris designer's shop where they were made
exclusively for me."

The waiter arrived and Jessica gave their order while
Kate studied her. Even though Jessica had spent her
junior year at the Sorbonne and had traveled exten-
sively in Europe, she was still looking forward to going
to England like a child awaiting Christmas.

After the waiter left, Jessica continued. "There's
another reason I'm looking forward to this trip. A
man," she confided.

Kate raised her eyebrows in surprise.

"I knew him years ago. He's recently divorced from
his wife and he'll be at Clariss's while I'm there. She
called yesterday just to tell me he's coming."

"A mysterious man from the past," Kate murmured.
"Sounds interesting."

"He is. Or he used to be," she amended. "I knew
him in Paris when we were both in college."

"You haven't seen him since?" Kate asked curiously.

"I did for a year or two after I returned to the States,
but we lost touch after I moved back to Dallas and
started working. Now he's a free-lance writer."

"And connoisseur of women's clothing?"

Jessica laughed. "His name is Matthew," she continued enthusiastically. "Elliot met him once; he hated
him." She smiled at the memory. "I think Elliot was
jealous because I was so interested in Matthew."

Kate tasted her fresh spinach omelette and added a
dash of black pepper to it.

"So what's new with you?" Jessica asked.

"The usual. I'm pretty busy at work." Kate took
another bite of her salad before turning the conversation back to Jessica. She didn't want to talk about her

problems. Jessica was in far too good a mood for Kate to depress her with her story. "When are you leaving?"

"Next Friday. I still need a really smashing bathing suit and an evening gown that will make the other women at Clariss's party hide their unfashionable heads in shame."

Kate smiled. "I hope this guy is worth all the trouble. I wouldn't want you to be disappointed by finding a balding man with a paunch forming at his waistline."

"He wasn't the type ever to go to seed," Jessica said confidently. "He's like Elliot. You know, keeps himself in shape and looks better as he gets older. He was a little like Elliot in personality too," she added as she took a bite of her quiche.

Kate glanced at Jessica curiously. How much like Elliot, she wondered. It was odd that a divorced woman would display such an interest in a man who by her own admission was much like her former husband. Was the attraction between Elliot and Jessica still strong? That was what she had tried, without success, to find out from Elliot. Certainly few divorced people remained such good friends as Jessica and Elliot were.

"I know what you're thinking," Jessica said with an amused look. "But you're wrong. I'm not trying to substitute another Elliot for the real one. I told you, I had a thing for Matthew years ago."

Kate raised her glass in a toast. "To old friends, may we never be disappointed in them." An image of Frank flashed through her mind, but she pushed it resolutely aside.

"I wish you could go to England too," Jessica said impulsively. "I know you'd love Clariss, and spending time at her house would be great for you. It's really grand, living in the finest sense of the word."

"It sounds like fun, but I could never get off work. I haven't been with the company that long."

Jessica waved her hand dismissively. "I don't care that you haven't been with Amalacorp very long, you've certainly worked hard enough to deserve a break. You drag home stacks of those monstrous volumes every night, and you're always staying late at the office. You ought to just breeze into the president's office and tell him you want a little time off. He'd be glad to give it to you, I'll bet. He's smart enough to appreciate what he's got."

"I'm sure he is," Kate murmured, and wondered absently if that would give Burke and the others just the opening they were looking for. Were they waiting for her to make one misstep before they lowered the boom on her? For the first time in her career she was experiencing the pressure of walking a very thin line. A false step in either direction and she could topple from the company tightrope and plunge downward.

Kate straightened in her chair. Stop it, she chided herself. She would not be where she was today if she had ever doubted her ability, and she had always performed her job well under stress. This was not the time to even consider losing her position. That had simply been idle talk. She was a success; she had built herself into one. All that remained was to convey that image to Burke Walters and Frank Moyer and Duane Rodgers.

"You're rather quiet tonight," Jessica observed as the waiter arrived to clear their plates and offer them a choice of desserts.

"Thinking over my past sins," Kate explained lightly.

"Well, if you decide to ask for a little time off, let me know. I'm sure Clariss would be glad to have you at her house."

"It's nice of you to offer, but I really don't think so right now. When things at work are a little less hectic, I can take some time off. Maybe we can go somewhere together then."

"Sure," Jessica said. "The Bahamas or the Keys." Jessica watched Kate line her silverware up carefully. "What's wrong?" she asked bluntly. The tone of her voice told Kate that Jessica would not be put off with evasions.

"Things aren't going too well at my job." Kate paused. "The truth is that I've found out the president and two of the vice presidents are unhappy with my work. It might even result in them asking for my resignation."

Jessica looked startled. "Are you sure? Where would you hear something like that?"

Kate flushed. "I know it sounds gothic, but I overheard it. I was in Frank's outer office after work and the secretary's intercom had been left on. I heard some pretty uncomplimentary things about myself."

"But you work so hard!" Jessica exclaimed. "Is it because you're a woman?"

Kate shook her head. "I don't think so, although they did mention the article in the paper. I think I'm just not shaping up as their ideal of the perfect company official; I'm not their style of executive."

"What are you going to do?" Jessica asked sympathetically.

"What can I do? I'll just have to try harder and give more thought to my decisions and make certain they're consistent with the company's method of operation. I'm probably just going through a period of adjustment that I haven't completed," Kate said, more to pacify herself than to convince Jessica. "Once I'm in tune with how Amalacorp operates, then things will smoothe out." Kate hoped so. She had already canceled the drilling that she had promised Ian would be done at Denham. She wondered fleetingly how Ian would view that when he learned of it.

It did not take Kate long to discover how Ian regarded the fact that Amalacorp would not be doing further drilling at the Denham dam site. Frank was in her office shortly after she arrived the next Monday morning.

"I talked with Ian Nigel," he began abruptly. "He wasn't happy when he learned no further drilling is scheduled."

"Oh." Kate pushed her pen aside and rested her chin on her hand, waiting for Frank to speak again. He didn't know the real reason she had canceled the drilling, but was he now implying it was her fault that Ian Nigel was dissatisfied with Amalacorp? That was galling, Kate thought as she felt her temper rising. But Frank quickly put to rest the idea he was making any accusations against her.

"I told Ian there's simply no reason to do more work. I think I've about half-convinced him." Frank picked a speck of lint from his immaculate gray jacket. "Still, I think we ought to keep Ian satisfied."

Kate suppressed a sigh of exasperation. Frank seemed to be going up and down like a seesaw. Was he now trying to suggest further drilling *should* be done? She was not going to walk into the trap; she would wait for him to make that decision. The choice she had made concerning coring had definitely been the wrong one. She was not going to put her job on the line again when she had been burned once. "What do you think we should do?" she asked, putting the ball squarely back into his court.

"It's important to have good communications with Denham," Frank observed placidly. "I know that Ian Nigel was just in Dallas and you were in England not too long ago. Still, since he is taking such a personal interest in this project, it wouldn't hurt for you to go back to England and try to massage his ego."

That statement set Kate's temper up again. In her view, it was not Ian Nigel's ego that was bruised. What had been damaged was Ian's faith in Amalacorp. Kate resented the fact Frank was distorting the focus of Ian's worry. Some of her feelings were reflected in her words. "I don't think Mr. Nigel's demands have been unrealistic. In view of the fact that there were problems with the foundation earlier, I believe he has every right to be concerned." As soon as the words were out, Kate regretted them. She had promised herself she would concentrate on fitting into the company, and already she was making waves.

But Frank did not appear perturbed by her words. "I agree that he has a right to express reservations; that's why I think it would be a good idea for someone to go to England and explain the situation to him. I think you are the ideal person to do that. You understand foundations and you're sympathetic to his concerns—that's obvious from your last statement. It will be easier for him to get an idea of what's going on if he is actually at the project instead of looking at plan views and cross-sections. Since he's not an engineer, those things probably don't mean much to him anyway," Frank continued. "You can cancel whatever you have scheduled for next week and fly over. It would be even better if you could go at the end of this week, but talk to Ian first and find out when he's free."

Kate started to argue and then stopped herself. She would clear her calendar, just as Frank directed, even though she saw no reason for the trip. After all, a phone call to Ian Nigel would surely do. Another voice inside her drowned out that objection. It was precisely the attitude she was showing now that must have caused Burke to wonder if he had been well-advised to hire her. "I have a couple of meetings next week, but Allan or Ivan can take over."

"Good." He stood and walked toward the door. "I'll see you before you leave and we can review the latest information on the dam. But, basically, you only need to reassure Ian that everything is going well."

Chapter 17

Kate was in the air four days later. As she looked out the window of the plane, all she could see was endless blue. There was no way of distinguishing where the sky stopped and the ocean started, she thought as she peered downward. She settled back in her seat and flipped open the book she held on her lap. She had been trying to read it off and on since she had boarded the flight five hours ago, but her mind was not on the words printed on the page. Instead, she found herself mentally reviewing the conversation she had had with Ian when she had called to tell him she was coming to England and would meet him at the dam site.

"Is it something we can discuss over the phone?" he had asked bluntly.

"No, I think it would be better to be at the site. Can you be available, say, next week?" She wondered what thoughts were going through his mind as a silence fell on the other end of the line.

"I suppose I can," he finally said reluctantly.

"Good, then I'll meet you there. I'll be arriving on Friday."

"I can't make it until Monday."

"That's all right. I'm coming early to have a chance to look over the site myself so that I can explain everything to you," she explained.

"I see."

Kate adjusted her seat back further and closed her eyes. Her talk with Ian had left her feeling confused. She knew that he was busy, but she had expected a little more enthusiasm from him at the prospect of seeing her. For herself, she was both looking forward to seeing him and dreading it. She was sure he was going to present the hard-driving business side of his personality during this trip. She already knew he wanted more drilling done, and she also knew she would have to explain why she had changed her mind about that additional drilling.

Of course, she must do so in a way that was convincing. She could not let him know the painful truth—that she no longer felt she had the authority to make that decision. Even if she told Ian further corings would be taken, she knew the job would never be performed. Accounting would be instructed not to approve money for it. In view of that, she could only undermine her position by promising something she couldn't give. None of those thoughts were pretty ones. It was almost intolerable to work at a job where such restraints were placed on her, but she knew it was only temporary. Apparently money was tight for Amalacorp.

Jessica had left for England only a day earlier. Although she had insisted Kate come to Clariss's at least for a day, Kate didn't think it was likely that she would. She would be at the dam site this weekend and the following week. Although she had no concrete plans for next weekend, she didn't want to make a commitment to go to Kent until she had seen Ian. She thought it probable she would be spending the next weekend with him.

The following day Kate made a leisurely drive to the Cotswolds. Driving west through the Home Counties, she passed silent beechwoods and eighteenth century flint and brick houses with thatched roofs. The seventeen hundreds seemed a long time ago, she considered, but such dates paled in significance when she realized the oldest rocks in Britain dated back at least 3400 million years. She had read that in a geological summary of the project area. Millions of years ago the Midlands that she was now driving through had been submerged in an ocean trough. Even later in geologic time Britain had been a desert wasteland. It had been a scant 10,000 years ago when the last glaciers had retreated and Stone Age men had pushed into the virgin forests.

Although no clear boundary separated the Cotswolds from surrounding land, Kate knew she was well into them when she passed through deep green valleys enriched with placid trout streams and embellished with villages built of the golden oolitic limestone peculiar to the Cotswolds. The houses in the villages looked as natural as if they had grown there, like the willows, generations ago.

When she drove into the small village of Chipping Down, she was almost disappointed that her trip was at an end. She was glad she had driven instead of chartering a plane. Even after the drive she felt rested and at peace. The feeling of serenity continued as she checked into the Hound and Heath Inn. It was a honey-brown Cotswold stone building with leaded glass windows fronting a formal gravel entryway. Inside were oak-paneled rooms with stone fireplaces where logs burned and a high-ceilinged hall furnished with antiques.

Kate's room overlooked a terraced garden. Flagstone walks and roses blooming in carefully tended plots offered a place of retreat. The room itself was paneled in mellow oak, with a four-poster bed and a tapestry on one wall. She unpacked her suitcase and hung up her clothes, stopping now and then to admire the delicately-wrought brass handle on her wardrobe door. Amidst all the quiet the room seemed to offer, it was hard for Kate to keep in mind that her purpose for being here was to see a structure far removed from this tranquility. She was staying in the sixteenth century, but she had come to see the work of the twentieth, she thought as she prepared for bed.

The next morning Kate was at the dam site early. She parked her car and walked away from the construction work and down into the valley below. The stream purled lazily beneath great oaks and wound through lush meadows before it reached a confluence with a larger stream—the Churn River, she knew from her reading.

Kate paused near the side of the bank and bent to pick a blue delphinium. It grew tall and straight with its sisters. Kate wondered if a Saxon maiden, thick blonde braids plaited down each shoulder, had once picked flowers like these. She smiled to herself; the beauty of the countryside was bringing out the romantic side of her nature. She turned and started back toward the dam site, to the real world of cutoff trenches, embankments and spillways.

She spent the rest of the day and part of Sunday dressed in jeans, a plaid shirt and a hard hat. Stan took her on a thorough tour of the dam. Along the almost mile-long length of the dam work was proceeding vigorously, with workmen pursuing their own special tasks. Everywhere Kate looked, men bustled about doing their assigned jobs; she marveled at the efficiency with which all the work had been planned so that one crew did not interfere with another.

By the time Ian was due to arrive Monday, Kate felt confident to discuss all aspects of the dam with him. Still, she was nervous—for personal, not business reasons. Ian had sounded curt on the phone with her. But, she told herself, he was a busy man and it was possible she had caught him at a bad time. Memories of their day at the beach and the night they had spent together flooded back. He was warm and understanding, surely he would be glad to see her.

It was the middle of Monday afternoon before Ian stepped out of a white and tan company car outside Amalacorp's office and walked inside.

Kate looked up with a smile from her study of an oversize set of drawings. "Hi." She searched his face quickly.

"Hello." Ian gave no answering smile, she noted as she rose. Instead, his mouth was set in a firm line and his eyes were a cool and impersonal gray. With a slight sinking of spirits, she realized this was going to be a difficult encounter. If he was glad to see her, he gave no indication.

"Did you drive from London?" she asked conversationally as she gestured toward a swivel chair near her.

"No, I flew in the company plane," he replied without leaving his post by the door. "Do you mind if we proceed immediately to look at the project?"

"Of course." Kate picked up her hard hat and handed one to him as she started out the door. He was not going to make her job any easier, she could see. Not that she had expected he would. She only wished she had a better explanation to give him about the question she knew was in his mind—why Amalacorp was not going to drill more holes. "Pretty day," she commented as she stepped outside. The sun was half-covered by thin clouds that filtered through a soft light.

"It's nice," he agreed shortly as he seated himself beside her in the company truck.

"There's a lot of work going on," she said with more enthusiasm than was called for. "I thought you might want to see the earthfill activities that are being done to raise the closure section to the height of the first-stage embankment." She started the truck down the steep road. "Or was there something you want to see in particular?"

"I'd like to see the area where the bad foundation was discovered," he said coolly. He did not look at her.

Kate steeled herself against his tone. It wasn't meant to be cool to her personally, she reminded herself. She moistened her lips and explained, "Actually, you won't be able to see much there. Work has already begun on the first-stage embankment on this side of the stream. That means fill material is being placed over the foundation. I don't know how familiar you are with dams—"

"Not very," he cut through her words crisply. "What I would like to know is what happens if a dam is placed on poor foundation?" This time he looked at her directly.

Kate avoided his eyes and continued to watch the road as she maneuvered past the giant earthmoving machines, driving aimlessly across the site. "There are several things that could happen in that unlikely event. First the dam would probably compact itself enough to hold the water. If that did not happen, it's possible the dam would never fill because the water would constantly seep through the embankment. Of course, how a structure will react is contingent on the type of soil, the plasticity of it, the weight of the overlying material and other factors."

"I see. Since I cannot see the foundation that was in question, could we return to the office?"

She nodded and turned the truck around. He was angry, she could tell by the rigid way he held himself and the clipped way he spoke. She felt helpless and frustrated. What was she going to do now? It was her job to make certain he was satisfied with the work being done, but she didn't see how that was going to be possible without further drilling.

When they arrived back at the office, he did not immediately get out of the truck. Instead, he sat facing the other abutment and asked frankly, "Why did you call and ask to meet me here?"

"I understood you were expressing some concern

that we won't be doing further drilling," she replied in a tone that was beginning to match his own. Damn him, anyway. Did he think she enjoyed this?

"I'll let the drilling pass for a moment," he said. "What I'd like to know is why *you* met me here. It seems that Stan Watson could have explained anything to me I might have wanted to know."

"I am in charge of foundation work," she told him tersely. "It is my responsibility to oversee all work on it; this was an opportune time for me to come to England to see the work in progress, and I thought you might wish to be here to discuss any reservations you had."

"As long as we're discussing my 'reservations,' we might as well begin with the major one. You told me your company would be drilling more holes, and the next thing I know not only are they not going to but everyone is back to square one, including you, explaining to me how unnecessary such drilling is. What changed your mind about further work?"

Kate straightened and gripped the wheel. "I apologize for having told you that. I'm afraid I spoke before I had consulted all parties. I wasn't fully aware of how futile more core holes would be, and frankly, they are expensive. There is absolutely no need to do work that serves no purpose, and that was the category more drilling was falling into. It was wrong of me to speak without making certain I had all the facts."

"How do I know I'm getting the quality I'm paying for? I don't know anything about dams; Amalacorp could be pulling the wool over my eyes."

"You can take my word that you are getting a quality product. Amalacorp builds nothing else. And if you don't know anything about dams, that doesn't matter. The people who work on this project know *everything* about them. In addition, Mr. Arnold is at the site supervising work in progress for Denham, so you don't have to take our word if you don't want to."

For the first time his lips curved upward into an

almost-smile. "Still smarting over the matter of trust and distrust?"

"It's easier to do business with people who have confidence in what we can do and who respect our expertise," she answered stiffly.

"Look," he said reasonably, "I'd love to trust you, but I'm enough of a doubting Thomas that I have to see some proof—just a little. What would it hurt to drill a few more holes?"

He had asked the question she had readied herself for. "It isn't feasible," she answered calmly. Although he could not see it, her hands tightened even further on the steering wheel.

"Dammit!" he exploded. "How the hell much does drilling cost? The way you are resisting, one would think it's a million dollars a hole."

"Money is not the issue here. Time and unnecessary work are. We are working on the embankment, and it would be fruitless to stop work and bring in a rig, drill a hole and throw the whole schedule off. This dam is carefully scheduled with weather conditions and the rainy season taken into account. Any delay in work is expensive. I'm sure you understand that," she concluded firmly.

"I understand that you are saying a definite no. It just happens that I don't accept that." He regarded her speculatively. "Perhaps I should be talking to someone with more authority than you." His words were scathing.

"That's entirely your decision," she told him with more bravado than she felt. Inside, she was deflated. She was as frustrated as he; she knew she could not give an inch, even though he had logic on his side. It was not a pretty feeling to be ineffective, and her pride was suffering. Added to that, she felt a curious pain at Ian's attitude. It was becoming harder and harder to remind herself their disagreement was over a business matter and should not be taken personally.

"Then I will talk to Burke Walters. I'm afraid I'll

have no choice but to tell him that I could make no headway with you. I don't see why not, truthfully. I refuse to believe it's such a large matter that it will throw the construction dates off that much."

"Then talk to Burke." She was thankful she was able to maintain a cool exterior, one that did not reflect the turbulent emotions beneath.

"That's exactly what I am forced to do." He hesitated. "There is something else I'd like to know. Did you originally tell me there would be more drilling done simply to appease me?"

"I told you what my thoughts were at the time," she said crisply.

"Yes, but I find it hard to accept there has been such a turnaround in your thoughts."

"We've already agreed that since you are not satisfied with my answers, you will discuss this whole affair with someone else," she said woodenly.

"I'm going to talk to Mr. Arnold; I'll be back before you leave." He got out of the truck. "I can see there is nothing more to say." He closed the door and walked back to his car.

Kate sat rigidly and watched him drive off down the hill, a small cloud of dust following in the wake of the car. Anger warred with pain for dominance within her. She felt like an animal caught in a trap who must sacrifice a leg in order to escape. There was no way she could emerge from this confrontation unblemished. And it was beginning to look as if she was going to lose on all fronts.

She hardly needed a bad report to Burke from Ian; it might be the final straw that cost her her job. And then there was Ian. Who was she kidding that this was not personal? He saw her as stubborn and ungiving in this instance, and he was bound to assume that she was in other areas as well. How strongly would this color his feelings toward her? Slowly, she pushed open the door of the truck and slid out. She felt completely miserable.

Chapter 18

Ian did return to Amalacorp's office late that afternoon. If there had been any hope in Kate's mind that he might want to see her that weekend, it was completely killed after they discussed a few matters about the dam and he prepared to leave.

"Perhaps I'll see you in Dallas the next time I'm there," he said, but his tone was indifferent. If they did see each other, Kate had the distinct impression it would be under business circumstances.

"That's possible," she agreed diffidently and watched him leave. "Have a good trip," she muttered after the door had already closed behind him. Her hurt feelings were giving way to a bitterness that encompassed Ian as well as Amalacorp officials. Even though Ian did not know the position she had been placed in, he could be more understanding. He had not even cared if he saw her again or not. How much did that say for how fond he was of her? Not much, she decided, with a touch of wrath.

She sat down at the secretary's desk and drank a cup

of half-cooled coffee. She wanted to see him, she recognized regretfully. She could always call him when she was in London. She set the cup down abruptly. To hell with that! Why should she go crawling back to him? She hadn't done anything wrong. No, she would not call him, and she would spend a very enjoyable weekend.

Impulsively, she picked up the phone and called Jessica. There was no reason she should cut her trip short and fly back to the States when she could have a lovely time in Kent. A few days in a country house would take her mind off Ian. That was exactly what she needed.

A woman answered the phone.

"May I speak to Jessica Holmes?" Kate asked.

"Can you hold one minute please?"

Jessica was breathless when she finally came to the line. "Hello."

"It's Kate. What in the world have you been doing?"

"Playing tennis," Jessica panted.

"I hope you're winning. I'd hate to think that you were that exhausted and losing."

Jessica laughed. "I'm doing okay. I hope this call means you'll be able to come to Kent this weekend. Clariss has an absolutely fabulous party planned."

Kate pushed the coffee cup around gently on the desk. "I can come."

"Good. You already have directions, but give us a call if you have any problem finding the house. It shouldn't be too hard. It's set on a huge acreage, and the stone gates leading up to it look like they lead to a royal palace. Listen, I have to go; Clariss is motioning to me from the court. See you then. Bye."

"Goodbye." Kate hung up the phone and took another drink of the coffee. She wished Jessica had had more time to talk. She felt the need to unburden herself of her feelings. Not that she was sure that she could even explain them aloud, but she would have liked to try.

Standing, she walked to the door and looked down at the work going on at the bottom of the hill. Even though it was after six, people were still working, driving the huge crawlers and bouncing across the rough dirt roads in giant sprinkling trucks. Everything on the dam was going just as scheduled. It was only in her own life that things had gone a little awry, she thought with a forlorn smile to herself.

Kate arrived at Roxhall Manor late Friday evening. Jessica was right; there was no missing the gates, tall wrought-iron grilles supported by massive limestone columns on either side. Beside the gates stood a square brick gatehouse with lichen growing around the base.

She drove through the open gates and followed a blacktop road that wound through lush green trees and up and down little rises before it emerged into an open area. The view that met her eyes was so magnificent that she stopped the car for a moment to gaze in awe. The house itself was Georgian, built of a warm red brick, and was approached between great yew hedges. It was a perfectly symmetrical house with Greek columns across the front and graceful, arched windows on the lower floor. To Kate it looked more like an exclusive boarding school than a private residence. She eased her foot off the brake and drove forward past the carefully-sculpted yews and up the circular drive that led to the front door.

A uniformed man appeared from nowhere as she stepped from the car. "I will park your automobile," he explained deferentially as he held out his hand for the keys.

"Of course," she murmured, and started up the marble steps that led to the front door. It opened before her hand even touched the elaborately-carved doorknocker. A man in the same blue livery held the door for her, and she stepped into a house that was as grand inside as out. Porphyry columns rose majestically to the tall ceiling. Niches of marble provided a place for the busts around the room, and elegant Chippendale chairs flanked an ornate Spanish writing desk. Kate stared upward at a ceiling lavish with frescoes and friezes in bold browns, golds and crimsons.

"Are you here for the tour of the Sistine Chapel?"

Kate turned to see Jessica smiling at her. She embraced Kate warmly and then stepped back and gestured around her. "What do you think?"

Kate's eyes took in the room again. "To tell the truth, I had been reading about how bad the economy is here in England and I had been feeling sorry for the British people because they're going to have to lower their standard of living. That was before I knew how well they were living to begin with."

Jessica laughed. "Clariss has it better than most," she admitted. "She isn't here now, but you'll meet her later. In the meantime you and I will have a chance to talk."

Jessica led the way through the vast hall and into a smaller one. A grand staircase at the end of it curled upwards. Kate looked at the pictures on the wall as they ascended. There were regal-looking ladies in elegant ballgowns and elaborate hairstyles and men who looked stern and forbidding in cravats and morning coats.

"Are all these people relatives of Clariss's husband?" Kate asked curiously.

"Yes." Jessica pointed to a picture of a woman in a somber gray gown. "That was painted in 1620. That's when the family had this house built. Clariss says the style was originally Elizabethan, but one of the later owners had the Georgian façade constructed. Some of these portraits are Gainsboroughs, and there's a Reynolds as well."

Kate stepped off the top riser and followed Jessica down the thick Oriental carpet runner. Pastoral pictures and hunting scenes lined the walls of the wide hall.

"This is your room," Jessica announced as she flung

open the door to a spacious bedroom. Kate stepped
inside. The walls were a light blue while a deep blue
and burgundy Aubusson carpet covered the floor. A
carved four-poster bed had a canopy and draperies of a
pretty burgundy print. The ceiling was decorated with
friezes, and the walls were hung with paintings in lavish
gilt frames. There were Chippendale chairs covered in
burgundy and blue flowered patterns and her suitcase
had been placed beside an elegant mahogany writing
desk.

"Please don't pinch me," Kate said as she walked to
the center of the room and turned slowly around,
"because if this is a dream I'm rather enjoying it."

"I told you Clariss had all the trappings of wealth."

"If this is a trap, it's a lovely one," Kate replied. She
crossed the thick rug to an arched window that faced
out onto the back of the house. Below she could see a
garden that seemed to stretch for several acres. It was
neatly divided into geometric shapes radiating out from
a central fountain, with clipped hedges and paths of
white gravel and well-trimmed flower beds.

"It is nice," Jessica agreed. She walked to a white
Sheraton sofa near a marble fireplace. "Sit down and
tell me how your week was," she invited as she patted
the empty place beside her.

Kate crossed to the sofa and sank onto it. For a few
moments she had been swept away into the world of
dukes and duchesses, but Jessica's question had
brought the preceding week tumbling back. With it was
the unhappy memory of how she and Ian had parted.
Her day no longer seemed quite so pleasant nor the
house so grand. "My week was okay," she replied
casually.

"Did you see Ian Nigel?"

Kate ran her long nails over the smooth white
brocade of the sofa. "Yes, I saw him."

Jessica peered closer at her. "You don't have any
plans to see him this weekend?"

Kate met her eyes directly. "I'm afraid he and I

didn't part on very good terms." She bit her bottom lip and looked down again.

"Does he know that you're staying in England this weekend?" Jessica pressed.

Kate shrugged. "He might. He could find me if he wanted to since I left this phone number at the dam." Kate knew as she related that fact that it gave away how much she wanted him to get in touch with her. She was leaving a trail of crumbs behind.

"Do you want to talk about what went wrong between you?" Jessica asked sympathetically.

"We had a disagreement over the dam," Kate said simply. With a half-smile at Jessica, she added, "I keep telling myself I should just say 'to hell with him,' but I can't seem to get him out of my mind."

"He might call," Jessica suggested.

"He might," Kate agreed, but she didn't think so. She stood abruptly and walked to her suitcase. She put it on the bed and began to take clothes from it.

"You don't have to unpack; Clariss will send a maid to do it for you."

"I don't have many things," Kate replied. She continued pulling folded garments from the suitcase. More than a desire to unpack, Kate felt a need to keep busy, as if by doing so she could keep her thoughts at bay.

"There'll be about four hundred guests coming to the party tomorrow night," Jessica changed the subject. "I thought the servants would be going crazy getting ready for it, but I can't even see any signs of increased activity." With a slight laugh, she continued, "I think the servants are all third or fourth generation with the family, and they're so polished that I do believe if an expressway were built through the entry hall, they would handle it with dispatch and discretion and a minimum of inconvenience to the guests."

"I'm looking forward to the party." At the moment, however, her thoughts were once again with Ian. Four hundred people. Did Ian give lavish parties like this? In fact, would he be coming tomorrow? Clariss's party would surely be composed of the cream of society, and she was certain Ian ranked among that elite group. Still, with 400 people present, she certainly wouldn't be thrown into intimate contact with him.

Kate met Clariss for the first time at dinner that evening. Her hostess was a tall redhead with almond-shaped green eyes, a full mouth and a lingering trace of a Texas accent. "I'm always glad to see someone from home," she told Kate as she enfolded her in a cordial embrace.

"It was kind of you to invite me," Kate replied.

"I want you to meet my other guests," Clariss continued enthusiastically, and took Kate's arm and introduced her to the dozen other people assembled in the red drawing room. She did not catch all of their names, but she was aware of a large number of titles.

The guests blended well with their surroundings, Kate considered as she glanced around at the swag red velvet draperies, the red and gold striped Hepplewhite settee, and Adams fireplace and the delicately-carved walnut chairs. Although their clothes were contemporary, the women in jersey and silk dresses and the men in jackets and trousers, there was still something about the way they held themselves and their speech that seemed distinctly upper class.

The dining room they adjourned to had sand-colored walls with stippled panels and a beautiful navy, beige and red Oriental rug. The ruched curtains were a deep beige. In the center of the room a long table covered with damask was set with fine china that Kate recognized as Limoges. The gold flatware and the crystal goblets and glasses beside the plates caught the glitter from the chandelier and twinkled. For a moment, as Kate was seated in a magnificent Queen Anne chair, she knew the panic of one sitting down to a formal dinner for the first time. It was true she had been to superb dinner parties before, but she had certainly never dined in such stateliness as this and never with such aristocratic companions. What if she made a mistake or spilled her wine?

But her fears were put to rest by the relaxed manner of those around her. At one end of the table she could hear a distinguished-looking matron talking about her grandchildren with all the pride of any other grandparent. And at the other end two men were engaged in a spirited discussion of the merits of their favorite jockey. Soon she found herself chatting easily with her right hand neighbor, a tall, light-haired marquess.

Later Jessica sat on Kate's canopied bed and waved her hand to dry her newly-applied polish. "I must say, Brian Duringham is taking quite an interest in you. He's shown you around the house and grounds and he certainly seemed disappointed to see you come upstairs to go to bed."

Kate sat in front of a low dressing table, brushing her hair absently. Brian Duringham *had* shown an interest in her, and once she had gotten over her initial awe at his being a marquess, she had realized he was a warm and witty person. "What does he do for a living?" Kate asked, looking at Jessica in the mirror. "I asked him, but he didn't quite answer."

"He's an art collector," Jessica replied. "I don't think he has an actual job. He's not like the rest of us mortals; he has enough family money that he will never have to work at a daily grind."

Kate put the brush aside and stood. Her lemon silk robe floated back behind her as she crossed the thick, soft rug to the bed and sat down beside Jessica. "What about you? You didn't seem to be spending much time with Matthew. After coming all the way across the ocean to see him, I thought the pair of you would be inseparable."

Jessica put the cap on the nailpolish and set it on a table beside the bed. "I guess people change; he's not quite what I remembered."

Kate looked at her shrewdly. "Is he too much like Elliot or not enough?"

"I don't know," Jessica answered candidly. "But he simply doesn't intrigue me. I'm going to bed," she announced as she rose. "Tomorrow we're planning a ride early in the morning and after that a few games of tennis and swimming if it's warm enough. And then, of course, the ball in the evening." With a smile, she added, "It should be a full day—full enough that you won't have a chance to think of Ian Nigel. But then, I think Brian will keep your thoughts from straying to Ian anyway." She crossed to the door and closed it behind her.

Kate sat for a moment on the bed looking at the closed door and then at the luxury that surrounded her. Nothing she had encountered so far had made her forget Ian, but she almost hoped Brian could. The growing worry that she might never see Ian again was singularly depressing, and she needed something or someone to push that thought from her mind while she was in England. Once she was back in America, she could forget Ian by throwing herself into her job.

Chapter 19

The ballroom that ran the length of the back of the mansion was a fabulous salon, long and narrow with a fan-vaulted ceiling. It had French doors hung with rose silk draperies, dusky-rose Savonnerie rugs over the parquet floor and splendid delft-tiled fireplaces at either end of the room. The furniture was grand baroque, exquisitely carved deep green chairs and rose-patterned sofas mixed with fine cherry tables that held Waterford crystal lamps and pale green Wedgwood vases full of freshly-cut white roses.

Across the crowded hall elegant men and women were assembled. Their jewels flashed as they talked and laughed, holding drinks in one hand or touching each other lightly on the wrist as they exchanged amusing stories. Kate's eyes swept the room. If there were not 400 people present, spilling out onto the balcony through some of the open French doors, walking in the garden, and dancing to the soft strains of the orchestra on the terrace, there must at least be very close to that number.

"Imagine," Jessica murmured beside Kate, "most of these people's grandmothers and great-grandmothers knew each other. They might have been present in this very room a hundred and fifty years ago for a Regency soirée or before that for a Georgian ball."

"Please! You're making me feel like an intruder," Kate protested. But she didn't really. With her hair pulled back away from her face in a thick braid that was coiled atop her head and rimmed with tiny sprigs of baby's breath, she felt quite regal. She wore a white eyelet gown with a high waist accented by a pale purple satin sash, and a tear-drop amethyst necklace and matching earrings were her only jewelry.

Clariss walked up to them, smiling brightly and weaving just a little. "You girls aren't circulating. Half the male eyes in the room are on you," she admonished. Turning to Kate, she continued, "You poor dear, I saw that Sir Robert had you buttonholed for half an hour. He's a crashing bore, but I simply had to invite him." Her eyes searched the room. "Have either of you seen Arthur? He was a bit late arriving; he just made it in time for the party."

"No, I haven't seen him yet," Jessica replied.

Clariss waved a hand dismissively. "Well, you will. He's bound to be here somewhere and he always finds the prettiest women." She raised her hand toward a waiter as he walked past. "I'll just have a half a glass," she said as she took a full one from the silver tray. "Oh, there's Princess Marie-Louise. I haven't spoken with her yet."

Kate watched Clariss thread through the crowd toward a very tall, striking woman dressed in deep crimson.

"She's crocked," Jessica murmured. "I wonder if Arthur even came at all."

"She said he did," Kate answered.

Jessica laughed shortly. "That's known as 'saving face.' If he is here, he has probably already enticed some nymphet into the bedroom and they're in the ancestral bed right now."

Kate looked at her in surprise. "Would Clariss's husband really do that?"

"Don't look so shocked. Everyone knows their marriage is strictly a formality. Why else do you think he hasn't been here until tonight?" Jessica turned toward Clariss and indicated the tall woman beside the hostess. "The princess is stunning, isn't she? Several couturiers, Robert Ricci for one, dress her for free, but she certainly is a marvelous advertisement for them."

"Who is she?" Kate asked curiously.

"She's an Austrian woman who is married to Prince Michael of Kent; he's a relative of the Queen, I believe."

Kate looked from the tall beauty back to Jessica. "You know a great deal about the English nobility, don't you?"

Jessica shook her head with a grin. "Just enough to get by. But I'm trying to pick up some interesting tidbits tonight. I think the Dallas readers would be enthralled by a party of this dimension. After all, the scale is weighted heavily with titles, and that's always a fascinating element for Americans."

"Do you mind if I join you?" a man asked.

Kate looked up with a smile at Brian Duringham. She had danced with him earlier on the terrace. While the orchestra had played a slow, formal waltz, they had moved in perfect time beneath the stars. Afterwards, another man had claimed Kate for a dance and then another. In their black bow ties, crisp white shirts and formal black evening clothes, all of the men had been courtly and pleasant. But none had been Ian Nigel.

"Ah, my lord," Jessica greeted him with a warm smile. "We were just talking about the intrigue and romance of a title. You can surely give us the inside story about how glamorous life is for a marquess. I understand you were an earl before you inherited your father's title."

He smiled. "I *was* an earl before I became a marquess, but then, as now, I live like anyone else."

"In a house like this?" Jessica pressed, gesturing around her.

He glanced about, looking past the ladies in elegant gowns and the couples talking in low voices. His eyes traveled upward along the hand-painted walls to the fan-vaulted ceiling before he said judiciously, "My house is a bit smaller. You needn't smile at me like that," he chided Jessica lightly. "Such houses as this are handed down for generations. I couldn't afford to buy such a mansion today, and I doubt Arthur could either. It's a terrible expense just to maintain such residences."

Kate looked up as another pair joined them. It was a man and woman whose names she could not recall. But the woman smiled at her and Jessica before addressing Lady Augusta, who had joined them a moment before. "Did you see Lady Davina? I haven't seen her since the SAS ball; she looks positively ravishing in that white gown."

Kate's eyes followed Lady Augusta's toward a group of people by a fireplace. She saw two middle-aged women in heavy dark brocades, a portly older man and a younger man and two young women. One of them, a tall blonde-haired woman of classic beauty, was dressed in a white gown that draped Grecian-style across her neckline before it was caught at the waist with a gold chain and fell in soft layers to the floor.

"Who is Lady Davina?" she asked. It was a question she had thought of ever since the man at Anabel's had mistaken her for the other woman, but she had never asked Ian.

"She's a widow. Her husband was killed in the Grand Prix a few years ago. Charming woman," Lady Augusta pronounced.

"Indeed," the other woman agreed. "Who is that man she is with? I thought she and Ian Nigel were seeing each other quite regularly."

"That's the Honorable Mr. Edmund Lindser. She hasn't been dating Ian Nigel for some time."

"Really? What happened between them? I thought he was finally going to marry again."

Lady Augusta laughed lightly. "I don't think we'll ever see the day Ian Nigel remarries. Lady Davina went the way of all his other inamoratas. He kissed her softly on the cheek and exited with a charming look backward, I daresay."

Kate listened to their words and tried to incorporate them into her picture of Ian. Was that what he was like? Would he use a woman and then toss her aside when his interest waned or she showed signs of becoming too serious? Kate thought of how cold and unyielding Ian had been when they parted. For the first time she considered that Ian might have used the dispute over more corings as an excuse to rid himself of her. After all, their conflict had not been a personal one but a business one. Yet she knew when they parted it had interfered with their private lives as well.

Had Ian dumped her as well as Lady Davina and possibly countless other women before? Certainly, from the talk going on around her, she gained the impression he was not a man who stayed with one woman for any length of time.

"It's a pity Ian will never remarry," Lady Augusta noted as she took a glass of sherry from a waiter in an impeccable white coat.

"I don't know," the marquess observed. "I rather think he enjoys being a bachelor. After all, he is most eligible, so he has his choice of women; he's certainly not lonely. He can enjoy feminine company when he chooses without having anyone making demands that will take him away from his business. He's worked long and hard to build his company. I think he would take a hard look at any woman before he thought of marrying again; he wouldn't want her to interfere with that aspect of his life."

"Would you excuse me?" Kate murmured. "I think

I'll step out onto the terrace for a breath of air." As she moved past little groups of people, she smiled and nodded, but she was intent only on making her escape. Stepping outside the French doors, she walked past the long arched windows that flooded the balcony with light. She avoided the dancers and followed the balustrade to a far end of the balcony. Then she stopped and gazed downward into the moonlit garden. Leaning against the balustrade, she ran her fingers across the gritty edge of the limestone ledge.

She had been hurt by the way things had stood when Ian left last Monday, but she had held out the hope that it was only a temporary misunderstanding that would be cleared up by a phone call. But that had been before tonight. Now, in light of what she had just heard, she realized there was a deeper rift between her and Ian. Lady Davina could probably tell her about it more fully. The man Kate was so strongly attracted to apparently would not allow himself to return those feelings. Had something devastating happened between Ian and his wife? Kate wondered. Did that account for why he avoided marriage? Perhaps, she reflected, his marriage had had nothing to do with it. Possibly Ian saw women only as objects of passion, not of lasting affection.

"There you are."

Kate looked up to see Jessica coming toward her. "Pretty night, isn't it?" She turned to look up at the dark, cloudless sky lit with a soft moon.

Jessica joined her at the balustrade. "Don't try to con me; I heard what they said and I saw the look on your face."

"What look?" Kate returned.

"As if you had been shot and were momentarily stunned by the noise and pain."

"You read too much into my expression," Kate demurred with a laugh. "The look you saw was actually caused by too much *croquant aux prunes* at dinner this evening."

Jessica leaned against the balcony beside Kate. "You don't know that there is a word of truth to what you heard tonight about Ian. The fact he hasn't remarried may simply mean he hasn't found the right woman," Jessica said firmly.

"Possibly, or maybe there was something so overwhelmingly awful about his marriage that he will never allow himself to feel anything for another woman."

Jessica laid a hand on Kate's. "You're putting too much emphasis on what you heard. I know you're upset about the way things stood when you left Ian, and I know you're thinking he used you. But you don't know that. Let me talk to Clariss and ask a few discreet questions of some of the others about him. I'll find out what happened in his marriage, and what happened with Lady Davina."

"It isn't necessary," Kate protested. She wasn't sure she wanted to know more than she now did about Ian's affairs.

"It is," Jessica contradicted. "You've found him guilty of philandering with every available woman without giving him the benefit of a judge or jury."

Kate nodded. "You're right. I guess I was a little quick to believe the worst of him. I'd appreciate it if you can discover what his marriage was like. It's possible he still holds the memory of his wife very dear and will never love anyone as much as he loved her. I'd like to know; I think it would help me understand him better."

"Let's go in now. The orchestra is picking up the pace a little. They might even go full-fledged disco here in a minute." They walked back into the ballroom—back into the world of women in high fashion and important men, to a fairytale land where everyone was beautiful and gay and happy and there was no place for heartaches.

Chapter 20

The smaller dining room where breakfast was served was as impressive as the rest of the house. A bay window gave a view of the garden below, while inside the room a Sheraton-style sideboard was filled with covered silver serving dishes containing eggs, pork, steak, ham and an assortment of jams and breads. Kate took a seat at the table while a footman in livery served her coffee in a Limoges cup and poured orange juice into a glass.

She looked around at the empty chairs. It was early yet, not quite nine, and she did not think the other guests would be up for several more hours. The party had lasted until past three in the morning.

Kate was spreading butter on a slice of toast when Jessica stepped into the room. Her blonde curls were falling limply around her face and there were shadows under her eyes, but she looked cheerful.

"What are you doing up so early?" Kate asked her, as Jessica dismissed the footman.

"I wanted to talk to you alone," Jessica confessed as

she took a seat across from Kate. "I found out something about Ian last night. I mean about his first marriage." She cut a piece of ham and continued, "It was definitely a love match. I thought perhaps they married because of some sort of long-standing arrangement between the families—those things still happen occasionally—but that wasn't it at all. They say she was a beautiful woman. Actually, she was little more than a girl. Her name was Elizabeth. She was tiny and doe-eyed and Ian absolutely worshipped her when they married."

Kate traced the lines of her cut-glass orange juice goblet with the tip of one long nail. "Is that why everyone believes he'll never marry again? Because he was so in love with her?"

Jessica shook her head. "I talked to a few different people. Their stories conflicted somewhat, but the nearest I could figure out is that the flame of romance died quickly between them. Something went terribly wrong in their marriage early on. I don't know what—some say he realized what a stubborn and self-centered person she was, and others say he was to blame because he was too possessive and unable to understand her young and capricious ways. Actually, they were both young, perhaps too young to sort out their misunderstandings. By the time they had been married less than a year, there was already talk of a divorce. I'm sure her death would have been wrenching enough under ordinary circumstances, but she was killed after she and Ian had had a terrific row and she had stormed out of the house."

Visions of smashed cars and crumpled bodies flashed through Kate's mind. Her hand tightened involuntarily around the glass. "Think how guilty he must have felt." She wasn't sure she had spoken the thought aloud until Jessica answered.

"Yes. Anyway, it was a long time ago, and much of what I heard could have been colored by people's memories, but I think that's very close to what happened."

Kate said nothing. She was thinking of Lady Davina, the lovely blonde Kate had been introduced to late in the evening. Up close Kate had observed that she was even lovelier than from a distance with porcelain skin and wide-set amber eyes. Lady Davina had seemed a woman of warmth and gentle humor and yet Ian had left her, apparently to move on to someone else. After what Jessica had just told her about Ian's marriage, Kate thought she better understood why he didn't settle with one woman long. That thought aroused a fluttering in her stomach. Did that mean her too?

"Kate, don't make any judgments until you've seen Ian again. Just because he's never been serious about a woman since his wife was killed doesn't mean you won't be the exception."

"I wonder if Lady Davina thought as much," Kate murmured.

Jessica cut another piece of ham. "Lady Davina was a new widow when Ian started seeing her. Her husband had been a good friend of Ian's. He probably began taking her places because she was lonely and he wanted to help her get over the shock of her husband's death. After that it might have been her own idea to start seeing other men."

"That's possible," Kate agreed. There had been other women, surely a good number more, judging from what Kate had heard last night. Even if Lady Davina had made the decision not to see Ian any more, Kate didn't believe that was true of all the others.

"What are you going to do when he calls you again?" Jessica asked.

"I don't know," Kate replied. Would he call? Should she call him? Oddly, among the many emotions she was experiencing at the moment the strongest of all was a keen longing to feel his hands on her waist and experience the touch of his lips on hers.

"My, we do have a couple of early birds," a man said cheerfully.

They both looked up to see Matthew standing in the doorway, looking natty in a tweed jacket and dark pants. "Mind if I join you?"

"Be my guest," Jessica replied.

Kate nodded agreement as she stood. "I think I'll go for a short walk in the garden, if you'll excuse me." She closed the doors quietly and walked back to her room for a sweater. The morning chill was still in the air when she strolled out into the garden and started down the deserted paths where lovers had embraced and walked hand in hand last night. It was a beautiful place to be in love, she considered as she stopped to pick a flower.

She walked slowly down the path toward the fountain. The nights she had spent in Ian's arms had been more special to her than any she had ever known. Surely if that felt so right, then everything else would fall into place. She paused on the gravel path. She would *make* it fall into place. If Ian did not want to see her in the future, then he would have to tell her so himself, because that was the only way she would accept it. With a resolve in her step, she turned and walked back to the house. She would call him and suggest that they spend the afternoon together. It would give them time to talk over whatever stood between them. Perhaps it was simply the work at the dam that was at the root of their troubles and she was complicating the matter in her own mind, influenced by what she had heard last night.

Kate stepped into the house and started down the long hall toward the stairs. A footman stopped her. "You had a call, Miss Justin. I did not know where you were."

"Who was it?" she asked breathlessly.

"A gentleman. He did not give his name, but he left this number." He held out a piece of paper with a number she did not recognize. She thanked him quickly. "Where is the nearest phone?"

"In the library." He indicated a closed door near her.

"Thank you." She hurried into the deserted room. Around her, rows of leatherbound books lined the walls. Two recessed windows looked out over the emerald-green front lawn and busts on columns watched with dignity as she seated herself behind a massive Queen Anne desk and picked up the ivory-colored receiver. She didn't remember the number of the office at the dam, but something told her this was not it. And if not, it must be Ian. She held her breath as she heard the phone ringing. Once, twice, three times. Let Ian answer it, she prayed silently.

"Hello."

She drew a breath of relief. Last night and everything she had heard about him fell away. There was only the sound of his voice and the excitement rising inside herself. "It's Kate. I had a message to call you."

"I'm glad you did; I was afraid you wouldn't." He sounded tentative, as if he were waiting to hear her reaction.

"Why wouldn't I?" she asked gaily.

"You mean my strategy of not leaving my name was wasted?" he asked. There was a warmth in his words she had not expected, and she smiled in delight to hear it. Everything was all right. There was nothing between them that couldn't be resolved by a few apologies and explanations. No, she didn't even demand that. They could start fresh and go from there. "How's the house party?"

"Great!" She would not have responded so enthusiastically to that question five minutes ago, but just the sound of his voice had changed her whole perspective on everything. She felt like singing.

"Listen." His voice was less certain now, as if he were picking his words with care. "I didn't want to leave things between us the way they were when you left. We were both a little irrational and angry."

"We could have been calmer," she agreed cheerfully.

"If you're not enjoying yourself *too* much in Kent, I was hoping you could pull yourself away and we could get together. Can you leave?"

It was the question she had been waiting for. "I think that could be arranged," she said warmly. "Today?"

"Immediately," he returned decisively.

For a morning that had started so badly, it really was turning into a wonderful one, Kate thought. Ian wanted to see her as soon as possible. The initial joy of hearing from him and knowing that everything was all right between them had passed, and now she felt weak with relief. She had not realized until that moment how frightened she had been that he would not call her again or want to see her if she called him.

"Why don't you come to the Cotswolds?" he continued. "I'll fly over and pick you up."

"No, I have my car. I'll drive out; it won't take long."

"Then I'll meet you at the inn in Chipping Down."

"Okay." There was nothing more to say, but she was reluctant to hang up and sever her connection with Ian, even though it would only be for a short time.

As if he understood her thoughts, he laughed softly and said, "It'll only be a little while before you are here and we'll have lots of time to talk then."

"Goodbye." The word was a caress. Kate hung up the phone and raced back to the breakfast room. Jessica was still there with Matthew. They were laughing when she entered. "Sorry to interrupt, but I'm going to have to leave. Since Clariss isn't up yet, will you explain to her that I've gone and tell her I had a lovely time."

"What happened?" Jessica asked quickly. "Is anything wrong?"

"Things couldn't be more right!" Kate assured her with a smile and left for her room. She was already packing when Jessica trailed in behind her.

"What's up?" she demanded.

"Ian called."

"Is this the same Ian you were so down on this morning?" Jessica asked as she took a position beside Kate and picked up a navy top to fold.

"Mmmm. I think I'll change into my gray slacks and the blue silk blouse with the lace collar," Kate mused, and then looked at Jessica. "Sorry I interrupted you and Matthew. You don't have to see me off if you want to be alone with him."

"Who wants to be alone with him?" Jessica quipped.

"I know you said you weren't interested in him, but you did spend time with him last night and you seemed to be getting along well just now in the breakfast room."

Jessica pushed aside a pair of slacks and sat down on the bed. "It sounds crazy because I do keep flirting with him, but I realized after five minutes that I really have no interest in Matthew. I think I'm using him to ward off loneliness."

"Really?" Kate looked at her in surprise.

Jessica shrugged. "Okay, it might have been a little longer than five minutes, but it was definitely under ten."

"Be serious," Kate chided. "Are you really lonely?"

"If I tell you, then you must promise you'll never bring it up again."

"I promise."

Jessica studied the pattern of the rug. "The truth is, sometimes I miss Elliot. I think I try to find other men to ease the ache."

Kate looked at her in amazement. "But if you miss him, then why don't you discuss it with him? Maybe the whole divorce was a mistake and he feels the same way you do."

Jessica shook her head firmly. "There's no chance of us getting back together," she said with conviction. Changing the subject with a bright smile, she added, "I'd tell you to have a good time with Ian, but I know that would be a waste of breath; it's obvious you're going to."

"But Elliot—"

"Ah-ah, you promised you wouldn't bring his name up again, and the matter is closed. I'll help you finish packing."

Kate thought about Jessica's confession briefly as the miles fell behind her and she headed for the Cotswolds. Then she forgot Jessica and Elliot completely to devote her thoughts to the man she would soon be seeing.

The drive took her through Ashdown Forest, thousands of acres of lofty, undulating heath and woodland interspersed with lovely streams and ponds. Despite its name there were few ashes, although there was an abundance of oaks, Scots pines, hazel and sweet chestnuts.

She followed the road into Marlborough Down. South of Swindon the scenery changed abruptly as the rolling Marlborough Down, with its dramatic, wooded heights, swept southward toward the Vale of Pewsey. Then she wound up into the Cotswolds Hills through short turf and beech woods. Finally she arrived at Chipping Down, where Ian was waiting for her. He was seated on a stone bench in front of the quaint old inn.

As she emerged from the car, suitcase in hand, he came toward her. His hair was tossed by a gentle breeze and he gave her a wide smile of welcome. For a moment Kate felt like throwing the suitcase aside and running into his arms. But she didn't. She proceeded at a dignified pace until they stood face to face, gazing at each other as if afraid the other person would vanish into thin air if they blinked.

Finally Ian broke the silence as he reached down to take the suitcase. "You must be the new schoolmarm," he drawled.

She laughed. "That's absolutely the worst imitation of a Texas accent I've ever heard!"

Then they were both suddenly serious again. "I'm glad to see you. Even after talking to you on the phone, I wasn't sure you would come." He took her hand and squeezed it tightly before he bent and kissed her briefly on the lips.

She felt as elated as an emperor who had just conquered a city. Ian had missed her as much as she had missed him! All of their problems were behind them. The pleasure of just being with him seemed immeasurable.

"We'll leave your car here and take mine," he said as he led her to a low-slung car across the street. He opened the door for her and she slid inside, glancing around at the walnut trim, the plush leather seats and the fleece mats on the floor before she looked out the front window, down the long hood to the distinctive ornament. She knew the initials RR were just above the grille, proclaiming to the world that this was a Rolls. Glancing toward the back seat, her eyes took in the ample leg room, small television and portable bar. She looked up when Ian got in on the driver's side and started the engine.

"Where are we going?" she asked.

"To my cottage up in the hills," he said as he navigated a narrow, twisting spiral of road that led out of the village past mellow Cotswold stone houses with limestone slate roofs.

"I didn't know you had a cottage."

"I bought it when we purchased the land for the reservoir," he explained. "I haven't been able to spend much time at it, but it's a nice retreat. You'll like it." He pressed her hand again.

"I'm sure I will." But then, she thought, she would have liked a cave if Ian were going to be there with her. She relaxed back in the seat and enjoyed the warm feel of his hand on hers. It was almost as if through that contact the happiness inside her was flowing through her fingertips into his.

Chapter 21

Ian's cottage was tucked into a vest pocket of the Cotswolds; its stone walls were nearly covered with rambling vines and moss. The house was of golden-gray limestone with two dormer windows in the second story that looked out onto the dirt road winding past the front of the house. Through the back windows Kate could see the valley below. In the distance the dam was visible. When it was completed and water impounded behind it, the back of the house would look out over the lake.

The inside of the house was cozy and charming. The living room had a cheerful blue and white handmade rug on the wide plank floor as well as a settee, two Windsor chairs and two small tables. The kitchen had a huge hearth and gleaming copper pans hanging from the ceiling. It had been partially modernized, with a small stove and refrigerator, but the sink still had a hand pump and the table and four chairs were antiques.

Ian showed her through the downstairs of the house and then led her to the settee in the living room and drew her down beside him. "There's something I haven't told you yet." His voice became serious and Kate felt tension well up inside her. "When I left you last Monday, I told you I was going to call Burke to insist that more drilling be done." He paused. "I didn't call him."

She felt the tenseness evaporate. "Why not?"

He ran his hand across the back of hers. "I gave it a great deal of thought and I decided it was possible I was being too demanding about the extra drilling. It's true I would like to be convinced beyond the shadow of a doubt, but when I put that into perspective I realized that if the engineers are satisfied, I should be too. To tell the truth," he continued, "the fact that you were so adamant against the drilling swayed me. I know you wouldn't take such a firm stand unless you felt strongly that everything was okay." His hand closed over hers.

Kate looked up at his face. It was odd how abruptly he could change from a hard-nosed executive into a gentle, almost vulnerable man. She studied his face, taking in the firm line of his mouth and the healthy glow of his skin. Her eyes rested on the scar above his right eyebrow.

She touched the scar. "How did you get it?"

Ian stood, walked to the window and pulled back the blue wool curtains that covered the leaded window. "A riding accident. It happened years ago." He turned back to her. "There's a lovely old church not far from here. It's part Norman, and before that it was Saxon. I'd like to show it to you if you're interested."

"Of course," she agreed, rising. She followed him out to the car and they started for the church. As he drove, Ian talked about the history of the area. "The Romans began their conquest of Britain in A.D. Forty-three. They were here until the fifth century. The Anglo-Saxon people who came in around the fifth century used place names that ended with '-ing,' '-ton' or '-ham.' They were a bloodthirsty lot, but they weren't barbarians. They were converted to Christianity around Six hundred A.D. The Normans were the last successful invaders; they came in the eleventh century."

Kate was only half-listening. She was preoccupied with wondering why Ian had changed the subject at the cottage so abruptly. Was he embarrassed by his scar? She wouldn't have thought he was a vain man, but the scar certainly seemed to be a subject he did not wish to talk about. Perhaps the memory of how he had received it was painful.

Ian continued speaking as they traveled through the hilly country laced with wandering country lanes, deep valleys, lofty hills and occasional big estates complete with manor houses.

She looked at him. Would she ever understand him? Would they ever reach the point of closeness where he did not have to avoid certain subjects but could speak openly? She hoped so, but she wasn't sure. In many ways he was an enigma, and as changeable as his blue-gray eyes.

As they continued their drive, he pointed out the window. "We're near Sapperton now. It overlooks the Golden Valley. There's an overgrown entrance to a long tunnel which was part of the Thames-Severn Canal. We'll see it when we go past it on A419."

"What happened to the canals?" she asked.

"Railroads," he explained briefly. "In the early eighteen hundreds there was a man named Bridgwater who had an absolute passion for canals. People thought he was crazy, but they would have been very profitable if the rails hadn't come."

She nodded and looked back out the window. The canals had been replaced by rails, and they in turn had lost their position to improved roads and the automobile. It seemed things were always changing. Roman to Saxon to Norman. Lady Davina to her.

Ian drove into a village set high on a hill. "This is Bisley," he told her. "It's at the mercy of the winter wind up here, but it has some interesting historical objects. The Bear Inn has two secret passages and a priest's hole."

Kate looked at him in confusion. "A what?"

"It was a hiding place for priests during Cromwell's reign." He directed his conversation back to the village they were passing through. "As you can see, Bisley is a pleasant little group of typical Cotswold houses—all corners, gables, roofs and chimneys." He parked in front of the church and walked inside. "The most impressive thing about the church is the Norman font," he said, indicating a highly-decorated chirstening font. "It's on a modern pedestal," he continued. "The vicar did considerable restoration in the middle eighteen hundreds. During the restoration two Roman altars were discovered."

Kate walked down the aisle, stopping to touch the curved edge of a wooden pew and then to look at a cloverleaf-shaped stained-glass window. "It's all so lovely and quaint," she murmured. She crossed to a stone statue of a man lying with his hands clasped before him in an attitude of prayer.

"This is his tomb?"

"Yes."

"It must be hundreds of years old," she said in awe.

"It's thirteenth century."

Kate and Ian walked outside the church and back to the car. They drove back toward the Cotswolds in contented silence.

Ian pulled up in front of the cottage again and they got out, walking hand in hand up the flagstone walk. "Have I shown you the upstairs?" he asked as they stepped inside the house.

"No, you haven't." She looked up at him coquettishly through lowered lashes. She was most interested in seeing the upstairs.

"Come on." He motioned for her to follow him up the winding flight of stairs to the second floor.

It was exactly what she had expected—two small bedrooms with the roof of the house sloping in on one wall of each room. A colorful handmade quilt covered one bed and a wool spread the other. The furniture was a serviceable pine. A white bowl and pitcher were set on the table next to the bed. Her eyes rested on the bed and she felt longing well up within her.

Ian was standing close to her when she looked back at him. She knew his thoughts were following the same path as hers. Slowly, he touched her cheek with the back of his hand and then stroked down to the column of her throat. Then he moved even closer to her while his fingers trailed down past the base of her throat and reached beneath her blouse to cup a breast in his hand.

"Are you trying to seduce me?" she whispered.

He kissed the edge of her mouth. "The idea had occurred to me." He unfastened the top button of her blouse as he spoke.

The idea did not seem without merit, she mused as he drew her against him and their lips touched. Yes, it was an idea whose time had come. The possessive but tender way he held her and the way he kissed her, like a man in the desert who had thought he would never see water again, sent a thrill of pleasure and excitement through her.

When they lay down on the bed together it was his urgency, his need to be as close to her as he could, that propelled them forward. Kate felt as if she were running along beside someone she could not possibly keep pace with. But she didn't object. It was exhilarating to know that he found her so exciting, and she certainly found him so. Ian stood and yanked his clothes off before she even had time to remove her blouse. Then he lay beside her on the narrow bed again. His impatient hands helped her remove the remainder of her clothes.

She closed her eyes and ran her fingers across his bare back. She didn't think anything else had ever felt so perfect to her as the strong muscles beneath her fingers. Here in this remote cottage he was hers completely, and she felt she belonged to him just as totally. When they merged it felt as perfect as if they had always been together. They were the lovers who had fled out into the storm on the eve of St. Agnes, and theirs were the first two bodies coming together on the morning of Creation.

Kate heard Ian whisper something to her, but she did not assimilate the words. She was wandering through the quiet halls of history, knowing the emotions of all women who had encompassed the body of the man they loved. The sensations coursing through her at every touch of his fingers were as ageless as water flowing down a stream. He was arousing her to a fever of expectation; she was impatient for the dark odyssey of pleasure to take her to the place she could not describe but could only experience again.

His mouth moved lovingly over her and his hands returned to massage one bud-hard nipple. She felt like a runner who was straining past the turn in the road with all her strength, trying to reach the elusive reward at the finish. Her breath was abbreviated and harsh, but she pushed onward with the singlemindedness of one who is oblivious to everything but the goal. Then, suddenly, she felt as if she had stepped onto a higher plateau where the air was pure and life-giving. She was part of the race and yet somehow above it, where everything was easy and perfect.

She pressed her fingers tightly into Ian's skin as incredibly pleasant sensations throbbed through her. Gradually, she slid from the top of the mountain into a sunlit vale. In her mind she was still reliving the glory of the peak.

As her breathing steadied, she was aware of Ian's strong hands moving over her back and then through her hair. Without opening her eyes, she tried to determine what his expression would be. She gave a lazy smile at the thought—he would be regarding her with tenderness and a hint of a smile. She opened her eyes to confirm her guess. With a start, she realized he was looking at her somberly.

"What's wrong?" she asked quickly.

"You want the truth?"

She nodded and ran her lips across her mouth nervously.

"I'm thinking that you'll be leaving shortly."

Kate felt herself relax. For a moment she had thought he had been dissatisfied with their lovemaking. "This is the jet age," she told him lightly. "Travel is easier now than it's ever been. Besides, we can always pick up the telephone and be in touch with each other in the space of seconds." She wondered if her rallying words cheered him any more than they did her. It might be the jet age, but an ocean was still an ocean, and lonely nights were not offset by hearing a voice in the void, no matter how dear the voice.

"Of course," he agreed listlessly. He rose and drew on his clothes. "I'm going downstairs to make something for us to eat. You must be starved."

"I'm a little hungry," she admitted.

His footsteps faded away as he walked down the narrow stairs to the kitchen. Kate rolled onto her back and put her hands behind her head, looking up at the ceiling and then out the mullioned window. Ian had spoken to her while they were wrapped in each other's arms, but she had been so involved in the pure feeling of the moment that she had not understood his words. Or had she? As she thought back, it seemed to her that he had told her he loved her. She shook her head to clear it. Maybe he had not told her that. It was possible she was substituting the words she was beginning to long to hear. But if he loved her and if she loved him, then surely that changed a great many things.

Kate closed her eyes. *If* she loved him. Who was she kidding? She had loved him from the moment she had met him. Certainly he was never far from her thoughts now. The emotions that were conjured up at the mention of his name and the anticipation she felt each time she knew she was going to see him were not in a league with those she had ever felt for any other man. However, the fact remained they were two people who were building successful careers and lives of their own. Besides, she was not certain that he had said, softly, and in a husky voice, "I love you."

Chapter 22

Kate called Jessica later that evening to give her the phone number at the cottage.

"Your boss called," Jessica related.

"Burke?"

"No, some guy named Wayne, or Duane. I have it written down here somewhere." Kate could hear papers rustling before Jessica came on the line again. "Duane Rodgers. He wants you to get in touch with him or Frank."

Kate glanced at the clock ticking loudly on the rough-hewn beam that served as a mantel above the fireplace. It was eight o'clock Sunday night. It would be two in the afternoon in Dallas. She hated to interrupt Duane's weekend, but it must be something important for him to call her from America.

She put the call through to Duane and waited for him to answer. When no one did, she called Frank. He picked up the phone on the second ring.

"It's Kate. I had a message to call Duane, but I was

away when he called. Do you have any idea what he wanted?"

"I think he wanted to know how you were making out with Ian."

Kate glanced across the room to where Ian sat comfortably ensconced in a Windsor chair with his feet propped up reading a book. She was making out quite well indeed with Ian, thank you, but she knew that was not what Frank was referring to.

"I mean, did you convince him everything at the site is fine?"

"Not totally," she said honestly. "I think he still has some niggling reservations. Certainly he would not be averse to further drilling." She saw Ian look up; he had heard her.

"We've already taken a stand on that. Still, if he's not completely happy, why don't you stay there for another week? There's nothing hot going on here, and there's no reason not to make sure he's perfectly happy with the work we're doing. Take him around and give him a first-class tour of the dam site. You could even drive up to the North country and show him the dam we constructed there a few years back. You know, just keep up the PR work," he concluded cheerfully.

"But I have meetings scheduled this week and I'm to confer with the man from Bechtel on—"

He cut through her objections. "That's been put on the back burner for a while. Don't worry about a thing." With a laugh, he added, "Do you think we can't handle your meetings?"

"No, it isn't that, it's just that I feel as if I'm more or less on vacation here and I should be back there doing some work."

"You deserve a vacation," he said firmly. "You've been working too hard as it is. Stay another week, then you can get back here in the thick of things again. I have to go now, I think my youngest is burning the hot dogs on the grill. Talk to you later." He hung up.

"Who was that?" Ian asked after she put the receiver down.

"Frank."

"What did he say?"

She hesitated. Frank had been so insistent that she stay in the Cotswolds that she was beginning to feel nervous. After all, this came hard on the heels of the talk of firing her. Were the two connected? Even if they weren't, it certainly made her feel like an unnecessary appendage to be told she wasn't needed back at her desk for at least another week. She wondered if Ian would think the same thing. She phrased her answer carefully. "Frank had a few things he wanted me to look into while I'm here. I may even end up staying the rest of the week to take care of all of them." She should have felt guilty for lying to him, but she didn't. She was more intent on saving her pride in front of him; she wanted Ian to have no indication that her career might be on the line.

"That's good," he said pleasantly. "See if you can stretch it to last the whole week and we can go somewhere next weekend and be by ourselves." He grinned conspiratorially. "I'm going to be tied up most of the week, but it sounds like you'll be busy anyway."

Kate realized her mistake in making it sound as if she had a number of things to do in England. Casually, she mentioned, "One of the things Frank suggested I do was to make sure you're perfectly happy with the way the work on the dam is progressing. If you're not booked for the whole week, I could spend some time with you reviewing the construction procedures."

Ian looked at her suspiciously. "Frank wanted you to make sure I'm satisfied?" There was an edge to his voice; she could tell he was not pleased.

"He didn't put it that way," she hastened to assure him. "He just thought there might be some questions about the dam that I could answer." Damn! she thought silently. She was being caught up in the story she was fabricating. Oh what a tangled web we weave . . . But she could not tell him the truth—that she had been ordered to pacify him. On the other hand, she would not have any reason to remain in England if Ian were not at the dam site. She had the distinct impression her presence would not be welcome back in Dallas just now.

Kate stood and walked to the door. Pulling her navy cardigan sweater closer to her, she opened the door. "I think I'll just go for a brief walk." She closed the door behind her without asking Ian to join her. She didn't want to discuss the situation with him; she wanted some time alone to think it out.

Kate paid little attention to where she was going as she followed a narrow path off into the trees across from the cottage. Did Burke want her out of the office because he was actually interviewing a successor for her? No, she didn't believe he would do that as long as she was officially employed with Amalacorp. Perhaps she was making too much of nothing. Frank had not told her *not* to return to Dallas; he had simply suggested that she stay at the dam site and make certain Ian was content with the work that had been done thus far. But why?

She stopped to pick a snowy-white flower, inhaling its fragrance as she walked slowly along. It was apparent that Amalacorp had not sent her to England because they were so in awe of her engineering prowess, she thought with wry humor. After all, they had been discussing firing her not three weeks ago. And that was odd, she considered, thinking of the occasion unemotionally for the first time. She might not be the best engineer or executive ever to hit Amalacorp, but she didn't think she was doing too badly either. In fact, looking at it as objectively as she could, she thought they were lucky to have her. She was young and ambitious and had been educated at the best schools with grades that took a back seat to none.

But why had Frank insisted she stay in England? The thought continued to nag her. She remembered sud-

denly that it was Frank who had introduced her to Ian
at the Rodgers' party, and he seemed to be almost
pushing her on Ian ever since. She knew that Frank had
an avuncular fondness for her, and it crossed her mind
that he was trying to make a romantic match between
her and Ian. But she quickly dismissed the idea as
absurd; Frank was not romantic to the point of being
unprofessional, and it would hardly be businesslike to
fix her up with the chairman of the board of a company
Amalacorp was under contract to. Unless—no, she
tried to push the sinister thought from her mind, but
she knew she had to face it. Could Frank be using her
as a lure? Perhaps it was no accident that the only
woman at Amalacorp, and a very attractive woman at
that, had been delegated to deal with the handsome,
unattached head of Denham company, whose reputation as a playboy was undoubtedly known to Amalacorp. Had Frank asked her to remain in England to
snow Ian, distract him perhaps from something serious
that was taking place at Denham dam? She shook her
head; she couldn't believe Frank capable of such
Machiavellian tactics. Besides, if there were anything
wrong at the dam, Frank must realize that she was
likely to find out about it if she stayed.

She stopped when the woods led out into a flat
pasture where sheep grazed contently. Turning, she
started back toward the cottage, still trying to decipher
the riddle of what was in the minds of the highest-
ranking men in her company. There was the possibility,
as Elliot had suggested, that she had stuck her nose in
somewhere it was not wanted. The talk she had overheard between Frank and Burke and Duane had cen-
tered around Denham dam. But if that were the case,
wouldn't they have taken her off the project instead of
having her remain at the dam site?

Kate gave up in confusion. She didn't know what
Frank had had in mind when he had requested she stay
in England. Maybe everything had been on the level
and he had only wanted her to give Ian a thorough tour

of the site. She wondered what Frank would think if he knew Ian wasn't even going to be at the dam? But she would take the opportunity of being here to look further into the incompetent foundation that had been uncovered and repaired. It was certainly a long shot that there was anything the least bit objectionable about it, but she was stuck here for the week and she had little else to do.

Monday Kate walked into the project office carrying her hard hat and wearing thick boots, jeans and a red and blue plaid shirt. "Hi, Doris," she greeted the secretary. "Is Stan here?"

"He's down on the fill," the secretary replied without looking up from her typewriter.

"I'll see him later then. You might tell him that I'm going to be here for the rest of the week." Kate started for the door. "By the way, Doris, where are the rock cores stored?"

"In the small shed behind the soils lab. Watch out for mice; they get into the boxes sometimes," she warned.

Kate nodded and walked across the tiny compound behind the soils lab to a metal structure. She opened the door and stepped into the dim shed. Flipping on the light, she walked down the row of neatly-stacked core boxes.

After an hour of checking, she confirmed that some of the boxes were missing. Perhaps all of the core had not been stored in this shed.

She closed the door and walked back to the office. "Doris, do you know where the remainder of the core is located?" she asked as she stepped inside.

The secretary glanced up from her filing. "Everything I know about is in that shed."

"Oh." Apparently Doris didn't keep completely abreast of what went on at the dam, but Stan would know. "Has Stan come back yet?"

"Yes, come and gone. He had to drive into town to see about something," Doris replied.

Kate walked outside the building and stood for a moment uncertainly. The geologist's report on the missing holes indicated the rock had been good. Still, she would have liked to see for herself. Since she could not find the rock samples to actually look at the rock herself, she might as well ask someone who had been present when the core was drilled. One person who would have been there was Denham's engineer. He could verify that the core had been good. Of course, she would have to ask him in such a way that he never knew there was any doubt in her mind about it.

She slid into one of the company trucks, drove down the steep dirt road past the construction work and up the steep hill on the other abutment to Denham's office.

Mr. Arnold looked up in surprise when she entered. "Hello, Kate. I didn't know you were still here."

She glossed over that. "I convinced Amalacorp that I needed the vacation." Walking casually toward his cluttered desk, she seated herself in front of him. "Do you really get through this whole stack of work?" she teased.

He shrugged. "Some of it. If I get behind, I just sweep the whole pile off into the wastebasket and start over."

"I'll have to remember that technique the next time I get behind. Poor Stan is snowed too. Of course, he has inspectors, but even so, he has to see to a great deal of the work himself."

"Sure he does."

"Do you have that problem? I mean, do you get stuck behind a desk when you need to be out watching the work?" she asked.

"Sometimes."

"The one job I always hated in the field was watching the drilling. It's usually an hour or two of coring before they bring up any core samples, and there's nothing to do while they're drilling," she commented, edging around to the subject of interest to her.

He nodded. "I was gone the week they did most of the drilling and even when they cored the last few holes. My wife's mother died," he explained. "The company sent some new trainee to oversee it." With a laugh, he noted, "To tell the truth, I don't think the kid knew shale from schist, but Amalacorp's inspector and geologist were there."

"Of course," she murmured. "I can remember the first job I was on . . ." Kate led easily into a story about her early experiences, but she was paying little attention to her own words. Instead, she was considering the information that Mr. Arnold had unwittingly given her. The man who would have recognized bad rock had been gone during the drilling and now the core was gone as well. That was certainly a curious coincidence.

Another voice inside herself told her she was making a mountain out of a molehill. Just because Mr. Arnold had not been present did not mean that there had been anything irregular taking place. And as to the core being gone, it might have been destroyed because there was a shortage of core boxes, or possible someone had misnumbered the boxes.

Back at Amalacorp's office, she went directly to the files. She took out the geologist's copy of the geologic logs. It explained the type of rock present, its appearance and physical condition at each depth and other noteworthy facts. She knew the geologist was no longer with the company, but the inspector, Lester Peters, had been present during the drilling and was still here.

"Doris, is Lester around?"

"Sure. I think I just saw him go into the soils lab a few minutes ago."

"Thanks." Kate closed the files and walked back to the soils lab. Inside the large rectangular building, she wrinkled her nose at the melting sulfur smell that permeated the room. The center of the room was given over to two long work benches. Kate saw a short, thin man standing near the second work table weighing a sample on a small scale. This was Lester Peters. She crossed the room toward Lester. Seating herself on a high stool next to him, she began in a friendly manner, "Can I talk to you?"

"I suppose you can, you've got the run of the place."

There was no humor in his remark, but it was without bitterness either, Kate noted. He conveyed an impression of complete apathy toward her. "I was at the core shed earlier," she began. "I couldn't find the boxes that contained some of the rock, particularly from the last borings. I see from the geologic log that you were the inspector."

"I was," he agreed levelly. He took the sample from the scale and set it aside.

"I'd like to get a little firsthand information about the rock. What was your evaluation of it?" Kate asked.

"What do the geologist's logs show?" he countered.

"That it was a firm limestone with a very few small vugs."

"Then I guess that's what the rock was like." Lester turned away from her and crossed the room to the sink.

Kate followed with rising exasperation. She had seen this attitude before in men who had worked all their lives as inspectors or assistants and never moved up the ladder while young engineers were constantly being brought in over them. He resented her because of her position in the company. But she wouldn't let his attitude get to her.

"How long have you been an inspector?" she asked.

"Since before you were born," he said promptly.

"Then you must know quite a bit about the soils and rocks," she noted.

"Yeah," he agreed, with no false modesty.

"And your opinion of the rock samples taken during the last testing is that they represent good rock?" she continued.

"Do you understand how grout works?" he asked impatiently. "We pour cement into a hole to fill up all the vugs and cavities. If a hole doesn't take much grout, then that means the rock is firm and doesn't have any spaces in it to be filled. The holes took little or no grout, so that means they're firm," he concluded brusquely. He turned and walked away.

Kate walked toward the door. Talking to Lester had left her even more dissatisfied than she had been from not finding the core and from discovering that the rock had been sampled while Denham's engineer had been absent from the site. The idea that had been only a fleeting thought last night was taking deeper root in her brain. It was possible that embankment was being placed over an unstable foundation. If the limestone were vug-ridden, the water that would eventually be impounded behind the dam would surely find those vugs and travel through them. For all she knew, they were building a dam that would never hold water. And she had the distinct impression that Ian Nigel didn't want to pay for the world's largest sieve.

Chapter 23

Kate spent the remainder of the week at the dam site. The thought of the faint cloak of mystery surrounding the missing core nagged at the back of her mind. The matter was not something she felt she could call and discuss with anyone in the company. The rapport she had once had with Frank had been shattered; the simple truth was that she no longer trusted him. In the end she decided to wait and discuss her findings with Ian. It was possible she was letting her imagination run away with her, she told herself. Certainly work was progressing steadily on the dam, and Stan Watson seemed calm enough. When she had inquired about the missing core to Stan, he had shrugged off its disappearance.

Friday, after work, she drove to Ian's cottage. He arrived a short time later, looking tired and drawn, but he gave her a welcoming smile that erased the lines of worry from his face momentarily. "Did you have a good week?" he asked as they walked into the living room of the cottage.

"So-so," she replied. She would get into the details of her apprehensions later. Just now he looked as if he needed rest and a cold drink more than he needed further worries. "How about some iced tea?" she suggested.

"Please!" he said in mock horror. "This is England. I'll have hot tea, if you please."

"Of course." She returned to the kitchen and put a copper tea kettle with a blue and white delft handle on the burner. "How was your week?" she called back into the living room.

"I've had better," he answered. "Those damned managers have got some stubborn idea into their heads about increasing productivity by—"

Kate didn't hear the end of his sentence. She was taking the heavy blue cups and saucers from the pine cabinet as the kettle began to whistle. She made the tea and carried a cup into the living room for each of them. "I didn't hear you, what were you saying?"

He waved a hand dismissively. "It doesn't matter. Let's forget work for a while and talk about our weekend. We'll go to my home in Cornwall. You'll love it there." His face became more relaxed as he leaned back in the wooden chair and smiled reflectively. "It's always peaceful in Cornwall. Now that's getting back to the land of legends. King Arthur was Cornish, you know."

She stood beside the mantel leaning slightly against it. "That sounds good." He was in a better mood and already he looked more relaxed. She might as well tell him what was on her mind now instead of waiting until they were at his family mansion. She plunged into her story. "This may not be a good time to get into this, but there's something I think you should know about. It has to do with the cores that were drilled last month."

"What about them?" He set his tea aside and looked at her.

"I wanted to see them, just to double-check the description of them on the geologist's log. I couldn't find them," she concluded, and waited for him to speak. When he did not, she continued, a little defensively, "Later I found out that Denham's engineer wasn't at the site when they were drilled. A less experienced man was there to take Mr. Arnold's place. Then I talked to the inspector who was there during the drilling and he seemed rather—I don't want to use the word 'suspicious,' but he didn't quite convince me he was telling the truth."

"The truth about what?" he asked in confusion. "I don't understand what you're getting at."

Kate began to feel uncertain, as if she were advancing lame arguments. She shouldn't be talking to Ian anyway. She should have discussed her concerns with Burke or Frank. Once they learned the cores were missing, they might even have authorized some further drilling. Of course, if the highest company officials were part of some kind of cover-up, then they would hardly be the people to talk to. It was all so confusing!

"What is it you're saying?" Ian asked again.

"Nothing," she murmured. "I'm probably making a big deal out of nothing."

"Tell me what it is," he pressed.

"I wonder if there's any chance that the rock sampled wasn't good and that the logs and reports about them are wrong. I mean, perhaps someone made the determination to cover up the fact the cores indicated unsuitable foundation material." Her voice trailed off limply.

He stared at her speculatively for a moment before he spoke. "I understood grout was injected into the holes to plug up the cavities. There was little grout take. That indicates there were no cavities to be plugged, doesn't it?"

"That's right, of course," she agreed, "but those reports might not be accurate either." She could tell by the way he was looking at her that he thought it highly improbable someone was going to such trouble to conceal something.

"Do you have any reasons to suspect Amalacorp of being involved in anything like this?" he asked bluntly.

"No," she replied. Woman's intuition hardly seemed a good reason to base her suspicions on, and neither did the fact that her company had talked of firing her. She was letting her feelings about that color her judgment, Kate decided. Certainly she should not have discussed the matter with Ian. "I guess it does sound pretty far-fetched," she concluded as she pushed herself away from the mantel.

"It doesn't seem to me that the evidence points to a cover-up so much as to shoddy management," Ian commented. "It's true that the cores should be there, but the fact they're not proves nothing. Still, it wouldn't hurt for both of us to be alert for anything suspicious that may happen in the future."

"Of course," she agreed, and started for the door.

As if he sensed her thoughts, Ian stopped her. Putting his hand on her waist, he turned her to him. "Kate, I don't want you to be uncomfortable or feel you've made yourself look foolish to me."

"I don't," she assured him with more haste than truth.

"But you do," he contradicted. He drew her closer to him. "I don't want any friction between us this weekend. Understand?"

She smiled slowly. "You're a tyrant," she said in a low voice as she fingered the point of his shirtcollar. "I promise," she told him, looking up just as he brought his mouth down to hers. For long moments she was lost in the heady delight of kissing him, inhaling his manly cologne and feeling his strong arms around her. Finally she pulled back. "I think we'd better go before we get distracted." Not that the idea of curling up in bed with him seemed unappealing, but they would never get to Cornwall this way. "Come on," she called gaily as she broke away and started out the door. "I want to get on the road so I can sit in the back seat and watch television."

He laughed as he took her hand and led her to the car. Kate relaxed in the seat beside him.

As they drove through the Mendip Hills, Ian pointed out sights of interest. "The finest views of Cheddar Gorge are seen from the north," he told her.

As they came in sight of the towering limestone cliffs, Kate reflected that there was a lonely majesty about driving through the canyon. Around them the limestone walls rose straight and silent, their starkness interrupted by the green trees that grew wherever they could gain a foothold on the nearly vertical walls of buff-colored rock.

They continued southward through the pastoral moors and forests of Exmoor, where the grouse, ponies and sheep grazed as contently as they had for centuries. Then they journeyed through Dartmoor, famous for its rugged, desolate beauty. Finally they reached Cornwall. Kate discovered it was a pasture land divided into many little fields by stone walls.

"All of Cornwall isn't like this, of course," Ian explained. "There are granite moors covered with heather, rough grass and boulders in places, and bogs too. What we have few of are natural forests or woods, except along the river valleys. Cornwall's beauty is in the height and ruggedness of its sea cliffs."

"I know that it's very wild and stark near the coast," Kate told him with a suppressed smile. "I saw the movie *Rebecca* three times." She looked at him solemnly.

He laughed. "I can see your education about England has been sadly neglected. Cornwall," he continued in a professorial voice, "is almost an island. It's separated from Devon by a river for all but five miles of their common border. On the other three sides, it's surrounded by water. Its history is ancient; there are barrows, cairns, standing stones and hut circles from the Bronze and Iron Ages. When the Saxons invaded and drove the Britons west, Cornwall became a bastion of the old Celtic ways. There was a separate Celtic language until the Middle Ages."

Kate looked out the window, watching the countryside change as they came within sight of the sea. The white-crested Atlantic breakers roared in and beat against the craggy rock wall. Kate gazed at it with a thrill of exhilaration. Glancing at Ian, she saw there was a half-smile on his lips as he looked off from the narrow ribbon of road and over the precipice that plunged down to the sea below.

"'I must go down to the sea again,'" Kate quoted. "Imagine how many millenia the waves have beat against those black cliffs. Like a stranger begging entrance to a house whose doors are closed." She did not take her eyes from the view below. She felt awed, realizing how insignificant all man's works were in the face of such power. It even seemed somehow presumptuous to try to capture a small part of this terrible energy behind the dam they were building.

When they reached Ian's house, the setting sun was just reflecting off some of the window panes and bringing them to a golden glow. It was a large, square structure with long, narrow windows and capped by a roof of dark blue slate. In front a vast circular pond reflected the stone house in its peaceful waters.

She walked with Ian up the flight of steps and into an entry hall paneled in rich brown, with lavish stuccowork on the ceiling. Directly in front of them a staircase ascended to a landing and then branched into two sets of stairs going off in opposite directions. A balcony on the second floor looked over the large entryway.

"Very nice," she said as she walked slowly across the white marble floor.

"Yes," he agreed with noticeable pride.

Ian led her to the foot of the staircase. "Your room is at the top on the left. I'll send a maid up to help you unpack. Your luggage should be up shortly."

She nodded and proceeded upward. Her bedroom

was enormous, with swag draperies of rose and gold and a thick gold rug. The furniture was a fine Queen Anne. It was a beautiful room, she thought, but like the rest of this elegant house, it had a cold and formal appearance.

A middle-aged woman appeared followed by a man carrying Kate's suitcase. When he left, the woman set about unpacking Kate's clothes, hanging them neatly in a cherry wardrobe and putting the intimate apparel carefully in a drawer of a handsome highboy. Kate walked to the window and looked out.

Below she could see formal gardens, and to one side a large building she guessed was the stables. In the distance she could see the ocean; from outside she was sure she could hear the surf pounding on the land. The door closed quietly, and she turned to see that the maid had left.

The house was not as grand as the one Clariss lived in, but it was far from modest. She had known Ian was rich, of course, but somehow actually seeing this house and the servants brought home the fact she and Ian were from totally different backgrounds. For a moment she wondered if that was a factor she had dismissed too lightly. With a smile, she recalled their last night together. There were other equalizers, she decided.

It was an hour later when she met Ian downstairs again. She was dressed in a white silk shirtwaist with silver threads woven delicately into the fabric. He was standing in front of the fireplace in a blue drawing room, beneath a portrait of one of his ancestors, looking dashing in a double-breasted navy jacket with gold buttons.

He took her arm and led her across the hall. She paused inside the dining room. Beneath two gigantic crystal chandeliers were a long trestle table and dark Tudor chairs. Silver candlebra and an epergne were set atop the white damask tablecloth. A formal place setting of gold-rimmed china and Waterford crystal wine and water goblets were laid at either end of the table.

"A bit much, I agree, but I thought you might want to do it up in style tonight. Tomorrow we can use the smaller, informal dining room." He seated her at one end of the table and took a place beside her. "No sense shouting to each other to pass the butter," he explained as he motioned a footman to move his plate and silverware.

After the cold asparagus vinaigrette, while the butler served them sole Florentine, Kate turned to Ian. "Do you keep this house open all the time? I mean, it seems extravagant to have a complete staff of servants if you are seldom here."

"Actually, there are very few servants. I only keep an agent who looks after the land and house, the butler, three maids, two footmen who also help the two gardeners and a groom."

"Did I hear 'a partridge in a pear tree?' " Becoming serious again, she continued, "It sounds like a lot to me considering you rarely come here."

He took a bite of his food before replying slowly, "I bring business contacts here from time to time to settle a delicate deal. Besides, the town has little industry and jobs are hard to come by."

"I see." She suspected he seldom brought business contacts here. She further guessed the only reason he kept the house open at all was to provide employment for some of the townspeople.

"What are you thinking?" he asked, watching her with an amused expression.

She looked down at her lap and smoothed her linen napkin. "I was thinking that I'm finding out more and more about you. Some of it is rather a surprise," she confided. "I had decided you were a hard-nose businessman who paid little attention to anything but profit. Now it appears there is a softer side to your personality."

"Don't get carried away," he cautioned lightly. "I have a certain responsibility to the servants who have worked for my family for some time. Other than that, your estimation of me is right on target. I'm very much a hard-nosed mogul," he assured her, with a twinkle in his eye.

"Can I think of you as a softie if I want to?" she asked, touching his hand as she spoke to him.

"If you like, but don't spread any rumors to that effect."

She was enjoying flirting with him and having him alone in this fabulous dining room; she was glad that the weekend stretched out before them with time to be together. "I saw your stables from the window. I'd love to ride tomorrow."

"I thought we might drive to Land's End tomorrow."

"Will that take all day?" She was anxious to explore the countryside on a spirited horse and race beside Ian alongside the ocean. Besides, there would be people at Land's End, and she wanted him to herself.

"No, but then I thought we would go to St. Michael's Mount."

She was not willing to give up so easily. "We could both get up early. The morning is a lovely time for a ride anyway." Her eyes sparkled at the thought.

He shook his head firmly. "No, the fogs are sometimes thick and it's quite dangerous to ride in them. We can do it another time," he concluded.

Kate watched him in confusion. Ian definitely considered the subject closed, and she was not certain why. It was no big deal, really, that she wanted to ride out and see the countryside, but she could see he was deliberately putting obstacles in her way. "If you don't wish to go with me, I can go alone or with a groom," she said.

"Kate, I really would rather not discuss it," he said coolly. "If you have such an avid interest in riding, you'll have to indulge it somewhere else. I don't wish for you to ride here with or without me; that is all I wish to say on the subject."

She stared at him in disbelief. Had she heard him right? He sounded as if he were talking to a child who was asking for something outrageous. "I'm sorry," she said in a frosty tone. "I won't make any more suggestions. In the future I will wait for your recommendation on how we should spend our time and, of course, I will abide by it."

He laid his napkin aside and looked at his plate in indecision before he spoke. "I'm sorry. I was rude, but please humor me on this one point."

Wordlessly, she nodded. She was too surprised to marshal her thoughts clearly. What was it about riding that seemed to upset him so, she wondered. But now did not seem like the time to ask him.

When the meal was completed, Ian pushed his chair back and stood. "Why don't we go for a walk in the gallery? There are some interesting paintings I would like to show you."

"I'd love to see them," she replied automatically.

Inside the long gallery were row upon row of pictures framed in gold leaf and carved wooden frames. Some were landscapes of the wild and rocky Cornish coast, but most were portraits. Ian did not take her hand as they walked into the room. Instead, she thought he seemed almost to have forgotten she was present.

"I daresay you have heard something of my marriage," he began, stopping to examine a picture of a huge wave splashing into a secluded cove.

She hesitated. "A little."

"Do you know how my wife died?"

"No."

"It was after she and I had an argument—a rather violent one. That was a difficult time in our marriage," he explained. "Anyway, she became very angry at something I had said. We were riding at the time, you see. She galloped off—very fast. I saw her urging her horse even faster, and I saw her go over the first wall." He paused. His voice was completely calm, but he was running his hand restlessly back and forth over the carved leaf at the corner of the frame. "She did not make the second wall." He touched the scar above his eye. "Her horse had to be destroyed. I got a rather nasty kick from him when I tried to get to her. Really, I suppose it was too late even then. The doctor said she broke her neck and died instantly." He removed his hand from the frame and took hers.

Kate said nothing—there was nothing to say. But she entwined her fingers in his securely, as if she never meant to let go.

Chapter 24

Ian led her up the steps and wordlessly down the hall to his room. It was a large and masculine room of tan and brown. Kate saw little more of it before Ian turned out the lights and led her unerringly to the wide bed.

There was something bittersweet about the moment when their lips first touched. There was passion in Kate's kiss but there was also a new gentleness, as if she now felt responsible for his happiness. He had been hurt—deeply, she now realized—during his marriage. If she could have, she would have turned back the clock so that she could have been there to soothe away the pain when he was lonely and confused after his wife's death. That wasn't possible, of course, but now she tried to express her sympathy for the anguish he had known.

When he removed her clothes and she helped him remove his, her tender thoughts were pushed further to the back of her mind. His restless, insistent hands gave her the feeling of standing in front of a powerful force—like the sea—something that could draw her under in its strong current. She swam willingly out to meet the surf.

"Do you know how soft your skin is?" he whispered against her neck.

His mouth seized hers, preventing her from replying. His lips tasted hers with hungry ferocity and his hands on her body now were more demanding, almost rough. He was forgetting how much bigger and stronger than she he was, she realized. He drew her closer to him, crushing her tightly against him. She could scarcely breath as she lay against his chest held by arms as strong as steel bands. But she did not protest; she could feel his desire for her in every movement he made.

His lips wandered down the column of her throat and he took one of her breasts into his mouth, causing her to jump with a stab of pleasure and then pain when his teeth seemed to bite into the tender skin. She recognized the passion he felt for her had somehow been affected by his talk of his wife's death earlier in the evening. His lovemaking was that of a man who has loved and lost. Tonight, Kate realized, he was holding her tightly to keep her from slipping away from him the way his wife had.

Kate reached out a hand and touched the back of his neck gently. She wanted to reassure him that she was not leaving, but no words would come. How could she say that? She would be gone in just two short days. Weren't they really making love tonight with an intensity to carry them through the days and nights they would spend alone? She wound her arms tighter against him.

His lips returned to hers and his hands searched lower, exploring and caressing intimately while his tongue sought new depths. Unyielding arms and hard thighs pressed her closer to him, and then she was completely encompassed by him.

Ian was holding her so tightly she knew in the morning her delicate skin would be bruised. She didn't care. His passionate hunger was kindling her own desire to greater heights. Her mind began to jumble thoughts together. Visions of the surf pounding relentlessly against the shore came to mind, followed by images of raging tropical storms. Then she was swept away into the storm within, feeling the strong winds and the hard rains before she felt the perfect calm of one who is in the eye of a hurricane.

Gentle waves of pleasure dripped off her as she touched pure ecstasy, embraced it wildly, and gradually felt a tingling warmth flow all through her body, ending at her fingers and toes. Slowly, the feeling ebbed away, leaving her spent and happy.

She heard Ian move beside her and then lift a cover and put it over her. "I'm sorry," he said in a shaky voice. "You'll probably be black and blue tomorrow." He drew in a ragged breath. "My God, Kate, say something! I was so carried away I might have seriously hurt you without even knowing it."

She laughed softly. "You must have been carried away if you thought that could happen." She pulled him down beside her. As their lips met, she felt passion begin to blossom again.

By the time Kate left England three days later, she had much to ponder. Ian had made it plain he considered her much more special than a casual date. Still, he had said nothing of anything permanent between them. In fact, he seemed to subtly reaffirm what she had heard at Clariss's party, that he would be reluctant to become involved in any committed relationship with a woman. So where did that leave her?

Kate asked herself that question as she sat at her desk in Dallas on Tuesday morning. On one side of her there was a stack of memos, reports and notes awaiting attention; on the other was correspondence waiting to be read.

The ringing of the phone brought her back to the realities of day-to-day life in corporate America. She was plunged into a dispute with a subcontractor over his interpretation of a contract specification. It was not until late that day that Ian entered her mind at all, and that was in conjunction with talk of Denham dam. Frank had stopped by her office to ask her how work was progressing.

"Fine," she answered evasively. She studied him. His brown slacks were perfectly creased and his tie exactly in place, while his gray hair was carefully combed. Everything about him seemed perfect; only his face showed lines of strain. For the first time since Kate had overheard the talk about being fired, she began to feel some sympathy for Frank. He was not in an enviable position. No one could be who worked so closely with Burke. Besides, Frank had been the only man in the room who had not actually said anything damning about her. Duane had suggested she be fired and Burke had said it might have been a mistake to have hired her. But Frank had said nothing derogatory.

He walked to the large plate glass window and looked out before turning and walking back to the chair. "Stan mentioned something about you wanting to see some core that had been mislaid."

"Did he find it then?" she asked, her eyes never leaving Frank's face.

"No, I don't think so." He crossed to the window again and thrust his hands into his pockets.

"I talked to the inspector who was there during the drilling." Kate did not add that Lester had given her no information contrary to what was on the logs. Instead, she waited to see Frank's reaction to her words. She was not disappointed; he turned and walked back to the desk, seating himself abruptly in the chair.

"What did he tell you?"

She shrugged. "Not much." Her look was calculated to convey the impression she was not telling all she knew.

"All right." Frank slumped a little in the chair. "I might as well tell you everything."

"I'd appreciate that," she said calmly. Inwardly, she was steeling herself. What was *everything?* Was he even going to go so far as to tell her that the decision had been made to replace her with someone else? Assuming a look of indifference, she settled back in her chair.

"The core samples were not misplaced, they were never saved."

"Why not?"

"Kate, how long have we been acquainted? Six years? Seven? I think you know me personally and by reputation well enough to realize that deception is not my game. However, circumstances can force people into situations they would normally avoid. Well, I'm leveling with you. The core was destroyed because it revealed a few vugs. There were so few that it took next to no grout to plug the holes. You can check that yourself on the grout report. However, Ian Nigel has shown such an intense interest in the project that it began to seem like a matter of diplomacy not to show him anything that was not one hundred percent perfect. Do you understand what I'm saying?"

"Yes," she said tonelessly. She felt a swell of anxiety rising inside her. Was Frank telling her the truth? Was the core acceptable, or was he lying?

"I'm disclosing this because I think you have a right to know. There has never been a deliberate attempt to conceal the facts from you. It was simply more logical to have as few people as possible know. That's why we didn't inform you."

"Whose idea was it, Frank?"

"I can't say," he replied quickly.

Burke's, she decided. Frank would have told her if he had made the choice. She pushed her hand through her hair in confusion; she almost wished he hadn't told her. "I don't understand. Was this necessary? Even if the cores showed nothing irregular, it *looks* so fishy to have rock samples missing. What would Denham company think if they ever found out about this?"

"They won't," he assured her. "You're getting excited for nothing," he added in a soothing voice. "You talked to Lester, he told you himself the core was acceptable, didn't he? And you saw the reports of the grout take. The only reason I'm telling you now is so there won't be any secrets between us. This company needs its top people working together and pulling in the same direction. We can't do that if someone feels they're being excluded from information."

Kate nodded. Had she felt a little bolder and had her tongue been a little sharper today, she would have asked Frank about the after-hours meeting in his office. That was a matter that had been kept from her. Perhaps, she considered, Frank had noticed she had become more reserved toward him after that discussion with the other men. He might even suspect she knew about it and that was why he was now sharing information. Another thought occurred to her. Maybe a decision had been made *not* to fire her, and now he was free to tell her things he could not talk about before. Of course, it was also possible Frank believed she had come to her own conclusion about what the missing core was like and he wanted to set the record straight before she put too much emphasis on the matter.

He smiled. "How about it? You seem to be furrowing your brow as if you think we buried sticks of dynamite in those core holes and plan to blow up the dam. This was not a matter of sabotage, it was simply a case of discretion being the better part of valor. You know how Ian Nigel is, he would have made an enormous issue of any little thing that wasn't perfect."

That might be true, Kate considered. Although Ian had not put much weight on her suspicions, it was hard to say how he might have reacted. Besides, Kate understood that further drilling would hold up work on the dam. Her eyes moved over Frank quickly. She didn't think he was lying to her; he wouldn't be in here telling her anything if he were going to feed her a pack of lies, would he? He would simply continue to keep the matter secret from her. When she had joined Amalacorp, one of the unwritten rules had been that she uphold the integrity of the company and have faith in it. Amalacorp had been in the engineering business a long time before she ever joined the ranks, and she didn't doubt they would continue without her. Businesses didn't survive and have the reputation Amalacorp enjoyed without doing things right. Besides, this wasn't any company, it was *her* company. She wasn't going to undermine it by not having complete confidence in the men who ran it.

"I'm sorry if I sound wary, Frank," she said with an apologetic smile. "Disregard my attitude until I have a day or two to readjust to work-life again. I'm afraid I've become spoiled during my week in England."

He stood with a grin. "I think you'll settle right in." He glanced over her desk. "From the looks of all the work you have to do, you'll have to."

She watched him walk from the room, his step proud and self-assured. He was the kind of man who inspired trust, Kate could not deny that. And the bottom line was that she believed him. After all, he had not come to her office to assure her that the cores had been lost. He had confessed that they had been destroyed. Why, then, would he have told her anything less than the truth about what the cores had revealed? She had let her pride get in the way before, Kate realized. She had overheard remarks about herself and she had reacted by distrusting anyone who had been part of that conference. That was childish. Surely every person in the company had come under discussion at one time or another.

Besides, she had discussed the facts of the missing rock samples with Ian and he had not seemed alarmed. Since she was the only one showing concern, that indicated how much she was overreacting.

Now that the subject had been settled in Kate's mind, she could turn her full attention back to the other matters awaiting consideration. She had a meeting with one of her project engineers in less than ten minutes, and she needed to contact the vice president of Rossel, a company Amalacorp was negotiating a subcontract with. Her schedule was far too busy to spend time dwelling on one subject.

Chapter 25

Elliot called Kate later that afternoon. "So you're finally back?" he began. "How has the place run without you?"

"Badly," she assured him.

"Busy tonight?"

"What did you have in mind?"

"I thought we could pick up a couple of six packs and sit out on the strip in my Chevy. You know, we'll whistle at the girls who go by and make lewd suggestions."

"Sounds lovely. I'll clear my calendar to make it."

"Fine, I'll pick you up at seven-thirty. See you then." Elliot hung up and Kate shook her head with a smile.

She was dressed in a pair of white slacks and a yellow camisole top when he arrived at 7:30. The heat from August was lingering on into September, she noted as she decided against taking a sweater with her and followed Elliot out to his car. Instead of the low-slung Porsche, he was driving a silver Mercedes.

"You traded cars?" she asked in surprise. "I thought you liked the Porsche so well."

"I kept it, I just got another—more respectable—one," he explained as he opened the door for her.

Kate watched him walk around the front of the car to the driver's side. There was something subtly different about Elliot tonight, but she couldn't quite put her finger on it. He looked the same, with the same deep red hair and green eyes. He was dressed in his usual style in chino pants and his print shirt was casually unbuttoned at the neck. Still, something was not quite the same.

"I thought we'd go to Houlihan's, unless you had your heart set on something else," he said as he started the car. "Go ahead and tell me about your trip but I think I know most of it, at least the glamorous portions. Jessica has done nothing but talk about Clariss, her house and her friends since she got back to Dallas."

"What a gracious invitation to share my travels with you," Kate said with a smile. "Actually, after one day in the office, I feel as if England were a million years behind me. English country houses are nice, but sifting through the work stacked on my desk and wrangling with employees and contractors is much more up my alley."

"I think Jessica was glad to be back too, even though she does still talk about the posh clothes everyone wore. Ask me what Lady Curl.E.Que was wearing at the big party. Go ahead, I'll bet I can tell you. Jessica's told me what everyone was wearing at least twelve times."

Kate laughed. "I'm sure you're exaggerating."

"Maybe just eleven and a half times," he conceded. "I stopped her before she got completely through the whole guest list again."

Elliot pulled into the parking lot of the restaurant and they walked inside to a room with Tiffany-style glass everywhere. It glowed red and golden from the windows and the lampshades that hung over the tables.

The rest of the decor was a jungle of potted plants and raw wood.

They were seated in a booth near the front. Elliot ordered quiche for both of them, a strawberry daiquiri for Kate and a beer for himself. Kate pushed back a lock of her hair and watched Elliot. No, she had not been mistaken, there was definitely a new exuberance to him, a certain sparkle that she had never seen in his eyes before and a jauntiness to his manner that proclaimed he felt capable of conquering the world.

"How have things been with you for the last two weeks?" she asked.

"Good. We got the contract for a set of condos on the North side. That's a boon for us and it's looking as if we may even get additional work from these same people."

"Congratulations." But Kate did not think a business transaction was at the root of Elliot's good humor. She was more inclined to believe his enthusiasm was caused by something in his personal life. That could only be a woman who was really special, Kate decided. A slow smile crept over her face as she resolved to explore the root of his new happiness. "Mind if I pry?" she asked sweetly.

"Depends on what it's about," he returned practically. "I'll lie if you get into something I don't want to discuss," he warned her.

"I'm just curious why you seem so lighthearted. Could there be a lady fair somewhere?"

Elliot took a drink of his beer and studied the foam as if it were a crystal ball. "Yes. There is a woman," he replied.

"Special?" she pursued with growing interest.

"Very."

Kate became suddenly serious. "Perhaps it wasn't a good idea for you and me to go out tonight. If she found out, she might be jealous. After all, this woman might not understand we're only friends."

"I can handle her," he said with a smug self-assurance.

"That sounds like the 'Me Tarzan' school of thought," Kate noted. "I ought to warn you it isn't very widely embraced by the more sophisticated women today."

He laughed. "Enough of my affairs," he said. "Were you swamped with work back at old Amalacorp?"

"Quite a bit had piled up," she confessed. "Duane and Frank took over my conferences and meetings and the really important paperwork while I was gone, but two weeks is still a long time to let other things stack up. I'll probably go to the office this weekend to catch up."

The waiter arrived with their food. As Kate dipped into her quiche, she considered the talk she had had with Frank today. She had already resolved that she believed him, but she suddenly wanted Elliot's reassurance that she had made the right decision. After all, Elliot had once worked for Burke and had been close enough to the top to know what really went on inside Amalacorp. He would tell her if she should still be suspicious. "Elliot, I'd like to ask you something. I promise I will keep any information you reveal strictly confidential."

"Size 11D," he answered promptly.

"I don't want to know your shoe size." Honestly, sometimes Elliot's refusal to be serious was exasperating, Kate thought as she pressed her question. "When you worked for Amalacorp, did you ever see anything that you would characterize as—" She looked around and lowered her voice further, "As a cover-up?"

He swallowed a bite of quiche before answering slowly. "That's a rather broad question. Are you referring to something specific?"

She suppressed a sigh of impatience. "A cover-up is a cover-up. Did anyone ever do anything that you thought was irregular or unethical? Even if there was a perfectly good reason for it, did you ever see anyone destroying material or information?"

Elliot studied her face for a moment. "Kate, Amalacorp is a big corporation. Sometimes it's necessary for a large company to sweep a few facts under the rug. Every big firm does that. If your question is did I ever see an executive do anything dishonest, I would have to say it all depends on how you define dishonesty. All big engineering companies have Cost Plus contracts, and everyone knows those can be a license to steal. Then, of course, it never hurts to scratch a few backs."

His vagueness was exasperating. "You're avoiding the question," she accused. "If you don't want to answer, just say so. I'm not going to a government regulatory agency or blowing the whistle on anyone, I just want to know for my own peace of mind."

"What if knowing wouldn't bring you peace of mind?" Elliot countered.

That gave her a moment's pause before she answered slowly, "Then I am working for the wrong company and I would start looking for a job with one I can have faith in."

Elliot regarded her with a lazy smile. "Very stirring speech. But the truth is that you're being naïve. Any other company you could go to work for is doing the same thing as Amalacorp. If you don't find out about it that simply means they cover their tracks better. I'm not saying Amalacorp is doing anything wrong, they're simply in that shady area of gray."

"Be specific," she said tersely.

"Okay. There was a little matter of a bribe in the state office a few years back in return for a nice, fat contract. As it happened, we were the only company in the state qualified to do the work anyway. I can't even say for certain any money changed hands. Maybe Amalacorp got the job because there is a strong 'old boy' network in operation. As it happened, the senator instrumental in getting the funding was an old family friend of someone highly placed in the company."

"A bribe!" she repeated, stunned.

"I'm not saying one was paid," he cautioned. "But I will say we came in under everyone else's bid and we got the job. In the long run the taxpayers were saved a great deal of money. That's gray, Kate, it's not black or white. It's economics dictating policy, and if the two men making the deal happened to be friends, that's beside the point."

Kate took a long sip of her daiquiri. "Do I try too hard to insulate myself from the realities of how business is conducted?" she asked, more of herself than of Elliot.

"Yes," he answered firmly, "and that's exactly what you should do. It's not important to you how Amalacorp gets the jobs, only that they build the best projects they can. You're in charge of foundations; are you trying to screw anyone by building a shoddy foundation?"

"Of course not!" she denied with feeling. "Everyone who works for me is very conscientious."

"There you are." He sat back in his chair with a smile of satisfaction. "The projects Amalacorp constructs are good. That's all you need to know. If someone else has a matter on their conscience, then it will have to be taken up with a higher authority someday outside the pearly gates. But that's their concern."

Kate nodded, but she was not quite convinced. "Suppose someone were actually tampering with construction work and hiding facts? The result could be the construction of an inferior project."

"Are you talking about a specific site?" Elliot asked.

She hesitated and then said slowly, "Denham dam."

"I thought so," he said with a nod of his head. "Jessica tells me the guy you are seeing is their chairman of the board. Has he put some ideas in your head that Amalacorp is up to something fishy? You ought to know that all big companies distrust each other. I'm sure your boyfriend is no exception."

Kate felt herself becoming defensive. "I assure you Ian Nigel did not plant the seed of my doubts," she said frostily.

"Hey, don't get mad!" Elliot said with a grin. "I'm your friend. I'm trying to help you by telling you you're worrying over nothing. Take my word for it, Amalacorp is as honest as any other big company."

Kate gave him a reluctant smile. "Somehow, instead of convincing me to have more faith in Amalacorp, you have succeeded in undermining my trust in all the other engineering firms."

"Don't stop there," he exhorted gaily. "Don't trust any organization, alliance, cooperative or corporation at all."

"Who does that leave that I can believe in?" she challenged in amusement.

"Lovable guys who wear size 11D shoes."

Kate didn't see Jessica until that weekend, although she talked to her a time or two on the phone. After work on Friday, they met to jog together. Jessica wore a peach-colored top and shorts with white satin stripes on the side. Her blonde hair had been recut and feathered back from her face in a new and flattering style.

Kate thought she had never looked better and said so. Jessica beamed.

"So how did it end between you and Matthew in England?" Kate asked as they started off at a slow pace.

"With a whimper, not a bang," Jessica told her. "I can't think what I ever saw in Matthew. He asked me if he could come to Dallas to visit; I told him I didn't think that would be a good idea."

Kate glanced at Jessica as they jogged past a park bench where another couple was resting. "You certainly seem to be in a good mood today," she commented. "That's why I thought you and Matthew might have gotten together after all."

Jessica shook her head as she continued running. "No, but I *am* in a good mood."

"Want to tell me why?"

"Yes," Jessica panted, "but I'm too short of breath to give you the full story now. Wait until we stop for a rest." Jessica moved in front of Kate to allow room for another group to pass them on the narrow jogging trail.

It wasn't until later when they were both slumped on a green bench that Jessica began to speak again. "There is someone really special in my life right now."

Kate looked at her curiously. "You sound just like Elliot. He's—" She broke off with a startled expression as the full significance of her own statement dawned on her. "Jessica, you're seeing Elliot again?"

Her companion threw back her head. "Yes! He came to my apartment after I got back from England last week. We talked for a while and—" she laughed coyly. "One thing led to another, and pretty soon it was just like old times."

Kate didn't have to ask what that meant. "Are you two going to get back together?"

Jessica's smile faded. "I really don't know."

Kate took the rubber band from her hair and shook her head so that her hair fluffed out around her. "I don't know all the details of what went wrong between you and Elliot, but I do know I've never seen either of you happier. Surely that accounts for something," Kate pointed out.

Jessica shrugged, and they started down the path again in silence.

After a few minutes Jessica resumed the conversation. "What about you?" she asked with a sideways glance at Kate. "You've been seeing a lot of Ian Nigel? Where do you now stand?"

"I really like him," Kate said casually, "but Ian and I have different problems than you and Elliot."

"Such as he's afraid of involvement," Jessica said shrewdly.

Kate gave her a look of surprise that relaxed into a smile. "I hate perceptive people," she mumbled.

Jessica grinned. "Okay. Let's talk about something neutral to keep from depressing each other. Do you think there really is a Loch Ness monster?"

For the next month Kate was so busy at work that she did not leave Dallas once. Ian came to visit her for two days and she was constantly in touch with him through letters and the phone. She tried not to dwell on the fact that seeing or hearing from Ian gave her as much pain as pleasure. The thought was always present that the few precious minutes she could have with Ian on the phone were so little compared to the long weekends she would spend alone.

As Kate settled back into her job, she felt the old rapport between herself and Frank being re-established, although she still kept her guard up around Duane and Burke. Work at Denham continued on schedule without further problems. She began to attribute her former fears to temporary paranoia, and yet an unacknowledged uneasiness lingered on. Kate hoped for the best—the worst could cost her everything.

Chapter 26

Kate looked out the upstairs window onto the ever-green laden with crusty white snow. Even in her bedroom, her mother had placed a small Christmas tree. The antique sled sitting in the front yard atop the white blanket of snow and surrounded by small pines gave the whole scene a peaceful Currier and Ives look. She let the chintz curtain fall and crossed to the oak dresser to brush her hair. She was happy—more so than she had been in a long time. Ian would be arriving shortly to spend the holidays with her. She had not seen him for over a month, and she was hungry just for the sight of him.

Walking out of her room, Kate traversed the length of the hall to the bedroom Ian would occupy. Granted this house was not comparable to his own mansion in Cornwall, but the two-story colonial was in one of the poshest suburbs of Cleveland, Ohio, and her mother had gone all out preparing for his visit. A basket of pinecones set atop the maple dresser and a rust-colored spread on the four poster bed blended nicely with the light beige of the walls. Curtains of yellow, orange and rust plaid were pulled back to reveal the winter scene outside.

Kate glanced at her watch. Four o'clock. Ian would be arriving in two hours. It was too soon to leave for the airport, of course, but she felt so excited she wanted to be doing something. She walked down the steps through a small foyer decorated with mistletoe and holly and continued into the dining room. Her mother was carefully arranging a centerpiece of pinecones and shiny red apples around an antique silver punch bowl. She looked up when Kate entered.

"Does it look too overdone?" she asked, stepping back to survey her handiwork critically.

"It looks perfect, Mom," Kate assured her absently, but she was studying her mother instead of the centerpiece. At fifty-two, Agatha was a slender woman with salt and pepper hair and a face softened, not ravaged, by age. Her mother was an attractive woman, Kate thought proudly.

Agatha adjusted an apple fractionally. "I have some walnuts too, but that might be a bit much, don't you think?"

"Suit yourself." Kate glanced out the bay window. "Did you hear that it's supposed to snow again?" she asked while her mother removed two apples and carefully inserted some English walnuts.

"Is it? I didn't hear that," Agatha murmured. "I hope it doesn't delay your friend's arrival." She stepped back. "Now, what do you think?"

Kate looked at the centerpiece. "Lovely," she pronounced, although she couldn't really detect any change in it. With a grin, she noted, "Honestly, Mother, you go out and sell houses like there's no tomorrow. You push them on people who probably don't want them and have no need for them, but you're so persuasive you can win them over. But when it comes to a small matter of Christmas decorations, you crumble."

"I don't crumble," her mother contradicted in a starched tone. "It's just that Ian is coming from a long way away to visit you and I want things to be nice for him."

"I'm sure he'll appreciate it," Kate assured her. In truth, she doubted Ian would give more than a passing glance to the centerpiece her mother was laboring over so assiduously.

Kate strolled out of the dining room across the hall to the living room. "The tree is beautiful," she called back to Agatha.

The live pine tree nearly touched the top of the nine-foot ceilings and was covered with strings of softly glowing lights and glittering ornaments. It stood in the corner of the room beside a walnut mantel with a fire burning cheerily in the grate below. The walls of the rectangular room were papered in a blue and white flock pattern. A thick white rug covered the center of the room, and a sofa and chairs were upholstered in deep blue, harmonizing with the dark walnut and mahogany tables in an eclectic combination of modern and antique.

Agatha followed Kate into the room and stood beside her. "It looks a little bare with so few presents under the tree, but I'll take care of that when you go to pick up Ian. I still have quite a bit of wrapping to do, and I'm sure he'll bring gifts too."

Kate thought of the navy cashmere sweater she had wrapped so carefully and placed under the tree for Ian. Beside it was a silver money clip and a monogrammed set of Irish linen handkerchiefs. Nothing very original, she admitted, but what did one give to a person who had everything? She had deliberately selected gifts that were not *too* personal. She didn't want to look foolish by giving him something intimate in case his present to her turned out to be a polite little trinket. But what if he gave her something very special? More than once visions of a diamond ring had flitted across her mind.

Her heart almost leaped into her throat at the

thought before she brought herself firmly back to reality. There had been no talk of marriage; she would do well to forget any images of diamonds for the moment.

Kate looked up from her reverie when she heard the thumping of her grandmother's cane hitting the tiled floor of the hall. It was blunted by the soft white carpet when she stepped into the living room. "There you are. Well, where's the young man?"

"He isn't here yet, Grandmother," Kate told her.

"Why not?" the old woman demanded. "I thought he bought a special plane just to fly over here to see you."

"He chartered a plane, he didn't buy one. His company owns planes, of course, but he doesn't like to use them for personal purposes; and his own plane is a small one that he doesn't like to fly across the ocean," Kate explained.

"Well, I hope he comes. You've got a stack of presents that will go to waste if he doesn't."

Kate smiled at her grandmother's teasing. "I think he'll come," she said with quiet assurance. She and Ian had talked over the holidays at length, running up an enormous long-distance bill. He had wanted to know what sort of gifts to bring her mother and grandmother and what colors they liked.

"You don't have to bring them anything," she had insisted.

"What?" he had countered in mock horror. "And spend all day Christmas watching them root under the tree for presents from me that aren't there? I should say not. Just give me their sizes and I'm sure I'll come up with something suitable."

"Are you expecting a certain something in a small jeweler's box?" Kate's grandmother pressed with a sly smile.

"Mother!" Agatha objected.

"Why not?" the old woman argued. "Didn't she say she's been seeing him for months? And she's not a spring chicken anymore, either. No sense turning her nose up if a nice young man makes an offer."

Kate flashed a surreptitious grin at her mother. Granny had always been blunt, and she still spoke of the ways of life she understood—women marrying and raising families. Agatha's own preoccupation with her real estate work was beyond the old woman's comprehension. "In my day women stayed home where they belonged," she had informed Kate and her mother countless times. Granny believed if Agatha had "put her mind to it," she could have "landed another man" after she became a widow.

Kate glanced at her watch. It was 4:30. It was still an hour and a half before Ian would arrive, but she wanted to be there in plenty of time. "I'm leaving for the airport now," she announced.

"Don't drive wild, the streets are slick in places," her grandmother warned.

"I'll be careful," she said dutifully.

Inside her mother's claret-colored El Dorado, she turned on the radio as she started for the airport and then immediately switched it off again. She was too keyed up to listen to music. Ian would be here soon! He would stay for over a week. She had a curious expectancy about this visit; she almost sensed that something was going to happen between them. Surely it would be a change for the better from the present uncertainty of their relationship.

By the time she drove into the airport parking lot, she was humming Christmas carols to herself and planning the next days with Ian, even down to what they would say to one another.

Kate had not answered her grandmother's question about what she expected Ian to say about their future, but she felt certain she knew what he would say. There had been tenderness and almost a promise in his words the last time they had parted. Something very special was going to happen to her in the next few days; she was almost certain Ian was going to propose. She had thought the question over carefully and she knew her answer. Of course, she could not abandon her career, but she was willing to take a job with another firm in London. Bechtel—indeed all the major American companies—had offices in London. Since it was impossible for Ian to move, she was willing to do so. Being with him was more important than remaining in Dallas. As long as she could have both her career and Ian on the other side of the Atlantic, she was anxious to make the move.

Christmas eve was perfect. After a dinner of turkey, ham, sweet potato pie, homemade rolls and cranberry sauce, Ian, Kate, her mother and grandmother adjourned to the living room to open the stack of presents under the tree. Granny and Agatha were already dressed in long gowns for the party they would be attending later. Ian and Kate had decided not to go. They had been to a party last night and would be going to more throughout the following week. Tonight they wanted to be alone with each other.

Kate distributed the presents and then watched while Ian opened his. He smiled when he unwrapped the money clip with a crisp new dollar bill folded in it.

Her grandmother unwrapped a robe and a pair of houseslippers from Ian. She exclaimed over the pretty color of the deep jade robe. "I hope you didn't pay too much for it," she added as she moved on to her next package.

"You're not unwrapping your gifts," Agatha accused Kate.

Kate looked at her little stack of gaily-wrapped presents with a glow of excitement. She wanted to wait, to savor the moment when she opened them until she had enjoyed her anticipation to the fullest. She could tell by feel that her mother's gift was a book; granny had dropped enough hints for her to know her present was a handknit scarf and hat. It was the small box bearing Ian's name that intrigued her; she was almost certain it was a jewelry box.

She unwrapped her mother's gift first. It was a handsome art book with richly-colored photographs. Her grandmother's present was a lilac-colored scarf and a hat to match. Kate tried to act surprised at them. "How lovely, Granny," she told her. Her grandmother beamed from the sofa beside Kate.

Kate watched Ian extract a set like Kate's that was knitted in a chocolate-brown wool. She caught his eye and gave him a secret smile as she picked up her remaining package. She moved it to the center of her lap and turned it over carefully before she began untying the little red bow and taking off the silver paper.

"I hope you like it," Ian said.

She took the small gray box from the wrapping paper and pulled the lid off gently. Inside, on a bed of green velvet, rested a gold chain with a diamond on it. It was a beautiful pear-shaped diamond, but it was a necklace —not a ring. Disappointment welled up inside her, but she summoned a smile quickly and looked up. "Thank you, Ian, it's very lovely."

Her mother's voice broke in cheerfully. "Come here, everyone, and stand by the fireplace. I want to take some pictures before Granny and I leave for the party."

Kate laid the necklace aside and walked to the fireplace, smiling as she stood beside her grandmother, who was dressed in a long red velvet gown. Agatha snapped the picture. Then Ian took a picture of her mother, in a blue silk gown, standing beside Kate and her grandmother. Finally Kate took one of the others. Agatha and Granny left in a flurry of goodbyes.

By the time Kate and Ian were alone, she had recovered her footing again. It had been presumptuous of her to have expected Ian to bring an engagement ring. After all, they had no definite plans for a wedding.

Tonight, while they turned the lights out and sat before the low-burning fire, they would talk of their future. That was the time to begin anticipating diamond rings, Kate told herself as she turned to Ian with a smile.

"Well, we're alone."

"At last."

"You don't like my family," she accused playfully.

He turned the hall light out and drew her toward him. "I love them and I'm glad as hell they're gone. I want to be alone with you."

Through the door of the living room Kate could see the red and green lights shining on the tree and the fire sending out warm red flames. "Everything is perfect," she murmured against his chest. "It's a holiday, I'm home, I'm with you—I wish this could go on forever."

"It can, you know. Us being together, I mean."

She hardly dared breathe as she looked at him. She studied his face in the soft light coming from the other room. He had never looked more handsome than now, she thought. His eyes were a soft blue and his face was etched in shadows and light. This was the moment she had been waiting for. Ian had said they would be together.

"I want you to come to England," he continued. "I don't want us to live an ocean apart any more. It's tearing me up inside to listen to your voice on the telephone and not be able to hold you."

Kate held herself perfectly still, straining to hear him say the words she knew were coming. And then he spoke them, softly and sincerely. "I love you, Kate. I don't want to be without you."

Warmth flowed through her and a flush of joy stained her cheeks. "I don't want to be without you either," she whispered. They clung to each other in a fierce embrace.

"Let's go upstairs," he whispered, and they walked up hand in hand. Kate had never felt so suffused with happiness as she did at that moment. She felt the glow inside her would put all the Christmas trees in the world to shame. They were no longer a man and woman who would come together for brief interludes, they were going to be together always. Tonight was the beginning of forever!

That idea flowed out of her mind and through her whole body as they lay down on the bed in her room. Other moments of pleasure with Ian flashed through her mind, but they were only photographs. From now on her life with Ian would be more than a series of still shots. It would be like the continuous movement of a motion picture—something that developed from one scene to the next into something grander and finer than anything that could be built on a few scattered pictures.

They discarded their clothes like so many useless encumbrances and stretched out beside each other on the yielding mattress. His lips grazed her breasts and his hand stroked firmly across her back before moving deftly around to the front and tracing the contours of her breasts and lingering on the peaks. Then his mouth replaced his fingers. Kate threw her head back and arched her body upward.

She felt a rapture spreading through her that contained a curious innocence. Hers was the joy of a child to whom a candy store has been thrown open. While her present passions cried out to be satiated, she was already strangely replete with the knowledge they were going to be together from this moment on.

There was a sweetness to this beginning that Kate hoped she could always retain. She felt they had never been this intimate; the moment of their coming together had never been so powerful as it was tonight. And when they moved, it was in unison, like two people who swam stroke for stroke together. Tonight when he whispered that he loved her the words were clear, and there was no doubt in her mind of what he said, nor that he meant the words.

She didn't close her eyes once for fear that she would miss something of the magic taking place in her life. Hands touched her and excited her and lips moved tantalizingly against her mouth and her throat and her breasts. Her own hands moved with intimate knowledge of him. For the first time she felt they were in total possession of each other. Memories of his laughter came back to her and she could see the way he looked when he was serious and his eyes were a deep gray. Everything that Ian was was now going to be a part of her. Not for a short while, but forever.

Chapter 27

It was almost midnight when Kate looked at the clock. She had heard her mother and grandmother arrive home an hour before, and Ian had long since gone to his own bed. She rolled over and savored the happy feeling that lay over her like a warm and downy blanket. She was far too excited to sleep. Ian loved her! Everything would be totally perfect if he were still lying here with her, but it was enough to know that he was very close.

Soon they would be together for more than just a few stolen moments. In a short while they would be with each other permanently. Kate turned her bedside lamp on quietly and picked up the necklace lying in its box on the stand. With a smile of pride, she watched the diamond twinkle in the lamp's glow. For long moments she gazed at it and tried to recapture the elusive moment when she had first known she loved Ian. They had shared painful times too, of course, but she would not think of them now. They had no place in her happy present.

Kate looked up in surprise when the door opened and her mother walked in. She had a pink silk robe wrapped around her nightgown. "Can't you sleep, dear?" she asked in concern.

"No," Kate answered with a radiant smile. Her mother sat down on the side of the bed. "I'm just like I was when I was a child. I still stay up late to look at my presents."

Her mother glanced at the necklace. "That's only *one* present," her mother teased, and then became serious. "He's pretty special, isn't he?"

Kate felt she would burst with happiness. "Yes," she said, and continued in a rush of words, "I'm going to move to London to be with him."

Agatha looked startled before she said quietly, "Do you mean you're going to marry him, or just live with him?"

"We didn't exactly discuss that," Kate replied steadily. "A piece of paper isn't that important to me, as long as we both understand what our intentions are."

Her mother was silent, looking at Kate in concern before she said briskly, "I'd better be getting back to bed. It's going to be a big day tomorrow."

"Mother!" Kate called. "Is it important to you that we be married?" She was puzzled because Agatha had never set a great deal of emphasis on whether or not couples were married if they lived together. Of course, it had never been her daughter before.

Agatha halted in the doorway and turned. "What's important to me is that you not be disappointed, Kate. I like Ian, but you're my daughter and I love you. Is he offering you enough for you to leave everything that you have worked so hard to build here?"

"The job isn't a major obstacle," Kate explained. "Of course, I wouldn't give up being an engineer; I'll simply switch to another firm in London."

The older woman looked unconvinced. "You would be moving to another country in the hope that your relationship with Ian would be permanent. Isn't that true?" When Kate nodded, she continued, "But what if it isn't? What if you spend two very happy years with Ian and then discover it wasn't meant to be? You'd end up moving back to the States and maybe in a lower position than you have now. Jobs like yours don't come vacant often."

"On the other hand, we could be married for two years and then find out it's over," Kate noted practically.

"That's true, but at the outset of a marriage both parties *think* it's going to be forever. When two people just move to the same town to live with one another, they're not offering the same commitment. Don't get me wrong, I'm not condemning that lifestyle. I'm trying to point out that I think you'd be giving more to this relationship than you might end up getting out of it." She pulled her robe tighter around her. "It's chilly, isn't it? I think I'll go turn the heat up a little. Goodnight, honey."

"Goodnight." Kate turned out the bedside light, still holding the necklace clasped in her hands. Her father had told her once, when she was very young, that it was okay to hold onto dreams and to try to reach goals, but not to wish so hard that she was blinded by reality. Was she being blinded now?

Kate turned over on the bed. She loved Ian and he had told her he loved her. She had wanted that to be enough. She had wanted it so badly that she had refused to think everything else through. But there was no denying the truth of what her mother had said. Kate was going to give up a management position to go to London to live with Ian. She would probably not be hired in a job equal to what she now had. What was Ian sacrificing to make their relationship work? The sad truth was he did not seem to be putting anything on the line—not his job or even his freedom. The bottom line was that she wanted more than simply sharing her nights with him; she wanted a long-range commitment that they intended to share their lives together.

It was not until three days after Christmas, when Kate's mother and grandmother went to the after-Christmas sales, that Kate and Ian had the house to themselves again. She was playing Scrabble with him at the kitchen table when she broached the subject. "I don't know if I'm going to move to England," she said casually.

His head jerked up. "What?"

"I said I may not be moving to England," she repeated as she carefully rearranged her tiles on her rack.

"What brought this up?" he demanded.

She shrugged. "I've thought it over, and I've decided you're not offering me what I want." The words sounded cool and demanding, but Kate could think of no other way to present them.

He looked at her in disbelief. "Just what do you want?" His tone had acquired a cutting edge.

Kate's eyes met and held his. "All right, I'll lay it on the line. I want to know if I give up my position and my life here that I am giving it up for something that has a better base than a 'let's see how it works' attitude." She sighed. "That's not how I want to say this," she said wearily. "What I mean is that I care a great deal for you. But don't you see that I would be giving up all I have worked for? It just doesn't seem that the same demands are being made on you."

"What do you want?" he asked quietly, but there was a nervous twitch in his jaw that revealed his emotions were tightly controlled.

Kate couldn't answer that question, not with the truth. For her to say she would accept nothing less than marriage was to issue an ultimatum, and she didn't want to do that. To say anything else wouldn't be the full truth.

"Never mind, I know what it is," Ian said tersely. "You already have a career and I wouldn't be offering you anything more than moving your career to a different location. I told you that I love you, Kate, but I can't ask you to marry me."

"Well, that's that." She pushed her chair back as tears began to crowd into her eyes. She would not let herself cry in front of him, she vowed silently. Ian reached out a hand and took hers.

"I'm sorry, Kate. It doesn't have anything to do with the way I feel about you. It's the fear I have of marriage. In the beginning I was devoted to my wife. Our life together started beautifully and died quickly— long before she was thrown from a horse. I don't know if I can make a good marriage, and it isn't something I want to experiment with."

"Oh, but you're sure you can have a good live-in relationship," Kate said icily. "So you have no qualms about experimenting with that." She hated herself for putting it on such an emotional basis. She was a sophisticated woman; she knew how unfair it was to say, "If you love me you'll do this for me." But somehow that was all she could think as she choked back a sob. If he loved her, really loved her, he would put aside his stupid prejudice against marriage.

"You're getting yourself worked up for nothing."

His calmness fueled her misery to anger. "Why don't you give up being chairman of the board and move to Dallas?" she challenged.

"You know I can't do that," he said coolly.

"No, of course not! But I can throw my job over on a whim."

He stood abruptly and threw the tiles into the Scrabble box. "You're not being logical. If you're going to get all emotional about this, then we can hardly iron it out."

"I'm sorry," she snapped. "It's a terrible flaw I have, not to be able to see this as a business relationship. Yes, I am getting emotional! I thought emotions and feelings were involved between us. They are for me, even if they aren't for you."

Ian drew in an audible breath and said curtly, "I don't understand what brought this on. You were perfectly happy when we discussed this on Christmas eve."

"That was because I hadn't given it serious thought." She pushed back her own chair and stood.

He walked out of the room and up the stairs. Kate stood beside the table, clutching her hands into fists at her side and feeling pain and rage trembling inside her. She had handled it all very badly, she admitted, but if this was the way he felt then she was glad they had it in the open. All those words of love from both of them meant nothing when compared to the idea of him giving up his freedom. Well, let him keep it! She was not going to sit around waiting at his beck and call.

Her sense of rebellion drained from her as quickly as it had come. Oh God, she thought weakly, how had they gotten themselves into this mess? She brought her hand to her temple and rubbed it absently, as if she could thus erase the memory of their discussion. She heard Ian come back down the steps and into the kitchen, but she did not look up.

"I've called the airport and made reservations to leave," he informed her. "It would be uncomfortable for both of us if I stayed here with this disagreement hanging between us. It appears we have both taken a firm stand. All that we can do now is to reconsider if that's what we want." His voice softened and he crossed the room. Putting his hands on her shoulders, he continued, "Kate, this is crazy. We don't need an ocean between us. I want to be with you all the time, and I know you want to be with me."

"Then why am I the one who has to compromise everything?" she asked morosely. "I want my relationship with you to be a two-way street."

"It would be," he told her. "I won't make demands on you. Just say you'll come to London."

For a moment she felt herself weakening, but she steeled herself quickly. Nothing had changed except his tone of voice. That wasn't enough. "I don't think that will be possible."

"Kate, I loved my wife and we destroyed each other. I wouldn't want the same thing to happen to us. Can't you understand that?" He lifted a curl from her shoulder and let it slide through his fingers.

"Yes," she told him. His touch unnerved her, but when she answered her voice was as level as she could keep it and still stifle a sob. "But that doesn't alter how I feel. I'm willing to move to London, give up my job and take another one there, possibly even at less money, if I know we are planning a future. But I can't do it this way. We don't have to get married," she said bravely. She was even willing to let that dream slide by if he would only offer her the promise that he would look on their life together as something permanent. "Just tell me we're going to do more than set up housekeeping with each other. Tell me this will be forever."

"I can't do that, Kate," Ian said regretfully.

She stepped back. "All right. I guess that explains where we both stand."

She saw his jaw harden and his mouth tighten into a firm line. "You're being stubborn. You wouldn't ask this if you knew what I'd been through." He glanced at his watch. "I'm going to have to leave shortly. Tell your mother I enjoyed myself and was called away on unexpected business. I'll call you as soon as I get back to England. We'll take it from there and figure out when we can see each other again."

Kate studied him in disbelief. "What do you mean?" she asked faintly.

"Just because we can't agree on whether or not you will move to London doesn't mean we have to stop seeing each other totally," he replied. "Feeling the way we both do about each other, of course we'll continue to be in touch just as we have been."

She shook her head firmly. "No."

"Kate, why are you being so stubborn?" he asked in exasperation.

"I won't see you again socially; I am not going to allow our relationship to drag on the way it has been. It's already become too painful, and it would only be more so now. If you leave today, you leave for good." She clenched her hands behind her back to conceal the fact they were shaking. Part of this was a gamble and she knew it. She hoped she won. Surely Ian wouldn't leave if he knew it would be over between them? Surely that would jar him into a realization of how deeply she felt about them making a commitment to each other? It had to! She didn't know what she would do if he walked out the door. She didn't think she could let him go.

He drew himself up straight. "It sounds as if you have everything pretty well thought out, Kate," he said crisply.

"I'm just telling you how I feel," she replied in a voice that wavered.

"Well, this is how I feel. I love you, but I will not be manipulated by you or anyone else. If you want to make our parting final, that's entirely up to you. And once I leave, I won't call you except at your office for purely business reasons. You know how to contact me if you change your mind. If I don't hear from you, then I can only assume that you don't want to see me."

Kate felt her knees begin to give way, but she forced herself to stand straight as she said proudly, "I know how to contact you, Ian, but I won't try to." Was she mad, she asked herself in silent panic. She should give him the whole world if that's what it took to hold him. But she stood rigidly and did not give an inch.

He nodded and turned to walk from the room. "I have to pack. I'll be leaving soon. I'm sorry it's ending this way."

She heard his footsteps in the hall as she sank into the chair. Dear God, what had she done? The temptation to run up the steps and throw herself in front of his

door was unbearably strong. She would agree to everything just the way he wanted and they would go back to
having each other whenever they could. Wasn't that
better than nothing? Wasn't anything better than never
seeing him again, she asked herself in desolation.

But she knew that it wasn't. What would she have if
she gave in and agreed to do things Ian's way? She
would have a few days a year with him and a terrible
loss of pride. How would she think of herself then? She
had worked so hard to get where she was. Her respect
for herself would crumble if she allowed herself to
crawl. Losing Ian would be painful, she wasn't going to
try to kid herself, but she would survive.

Kate was still sitting in front of the kitchen table
when Ian appeared again. He was dressed in a tweed
jacket and flannel trousers and was carrying his bag.
"Goodbye, Kate."

"Have a nice trip." She did not turn to look at him.
She waited for the front door to close before she laid
her head down on the table, unheeding as Scrabble tiles
scattered over to the floor. Her tears broke and her
sobs were cries of despair. Even when they subsided,
her sense of desolation was not diminished.

Chapter 28

The gown Kate chose for the Valentine's day party was a strapless creation of soft white batiste that followed the lines of her body gracefully. It had red ribbon across the top of the bodice and around the tiers of flounces at the hem. A red rose was tucked above her ear. She studied herself in the bathroom mirror and then added another touch of blush-on. Since Christmas she had lost weight, and her cheeks were beginning to look positively hollow, she noted indifferently. Laying the blush-on aside, she picked up a black mascara brush and added a little to each eyelash. Her eyes seemed so dull and lifeless, but she did not really think it was something makeup could correct. Finally she stroked the lipstick brush across her lips again, bringing out the dewy fullness of them to a deep ruby color.

The overall effect, she decided as she studied herself again, was of a beautiful and empty mannequin. Jessica had told her as much not two days ago. "This whole thing with Ian has brought out a haunting and tragic beauty in you. Unfortunately, most men prefer a more flesh-and-blood woman." The words had been sharp, calculated to jolt Kate back to a reality of what she was doing to herself. But Kate had merely shrugged and turned back to the report she had brought home from work to review. A few moments later she heard Jessica slam out of the house in exasperation.

The doorbell rang and Kate started down the steps. Tonight she would enjoy herself, she told herself sternly. Jessica was right. No man wanted to spend an evening with a woman who sat in a corner and pined away for someone else. She had accepted Craig Greenfield's invitation to go to the Valentine party with him, and she was damn sure going to have a good time.

She opened the door with a smile. "Craig, you're right on time. Just let me get my wrap." In the living room she took the finely-knit red shawl from the sofa and picked up her purse. "The flowers you sent are lovely," she told him as she walked back to the door. "Roses are my favorite."

"I'm glad you liked them," Craig answered.

He was tall and suave. Tonight he was dressed in a tux and black tie that did justice to his blond good looks. He was a highly-placed official in one of the state's largest banks and absolutely everything a woman could want—but he was not Ian.

Craig held the door of his dark blue Bentley open for her. It looked almost exactly like Ian's Rolls, Kate noted as she slid in.

"Stop it," she murmured aloud as Craig walked around to get in on the driver's side. Ian was out of her life. Her date tonight was with Craig, and she was going to have a good time with him.

"I'm afraid there's going to be a real crush tonight," Craig told her as he started the car. "Everyone I know is going."

"Really?" Kate searched for something witty and conversational to say, but nothing came to mind. Over the last few weeks it seemed as if she had even lost the art of making small talk. The only place she seemed to function normally was at work. Perhaps that was why she was staying late so frequently and going in often on weekends.

When Kate had first returned from Ohio to Dallas, she had waited by the phone, praying that it would ring and willing Ian to call. He had said he would not, but she refused to believe that. He would call; she knew it! After apologizing and insisting she had been right, Ian would beg her to come to England and marry him.

But when the phone did ring, it was never Ian. Slowly, painfully, she had come to the realization that he was not going to call. He was gone for good unless she was willing to compromise. And she was not. Pride had warred against pain and she had tried to look at her situation from every possible angle. In the end the easiest course of dealing with her loneliness and heartache had been to try to live through it mindlessly, to wait for time to pass in the hope that it would carry away with it the memory of all that she had lost. For the present she felt like an automaton.

"We're here." Craig stopped the car and helped her out. "From the looks of all these cars, so is everyone else." He glanced down the line of cars in front of the Fairmont as a uniformed parking attendant drove his car away.

"The more the merrier." Original, Kate thought dryly. But perhaps Craig was just happy to hear her say anything. She hadn't exactly been a fountain of conversation so far this evening.

Inside the spacious lobby, they took the elevator to the top floor where a penthouse suite had been rented for the party. Kate stepped into the room and looked around. Standing by a silver champagne cooler was Beatrice Marshall, an advertising executive Kate knew slightly. She was dressed in a gold lamé gown that showed generous cleavage. Beside her was a handsome younger man. Kate had heard Beatrice's penchant was for young and beautiful males. Nearby was Angela Rotsby, a television anchorwoman who looked sensational in a deep rose silk gown. Kate noted dispassionately that Angela looked happy on the arm of her third husband. Loretta Moyer, Frank's oldest daughter, was present with the doctor she was currently seeing. And yes, there was Jessica, looking smashing with her blonde hair threaded through with a white satin ribbon that matched her figure-revealing white satin gown. She had a glow on her face that Kate had noticed often of late. Elliot stood beside Jessica, elegant and at ease in black tie. He held both of their drinks while Jessica told a story, using her slender hands expressively.

"Let me take your wrap," Craig offered. His hands brushed across her bare shoulder as he helped her remove the red shawl. Then he disappeared into a smaller room and returned moments later.

He put a hand around her waist and led her into the room. They were stopped and engaged in conversation with an older couple. Kate noted the way the man kept his arm possessively around his wife's waist. Well, it was Valentine's day, she told herself with a pang. It stood to reason those present would be lovers. This was a party to celebrate that emotion. She only wished her own heart didn't feel so heavy.

A white-coated waiter took their orders for drinks. He returned a moment later with Kate's gin and tonic and she sipped it slowly as she and Craig continued to mingle among the guests.

Elliot and Jessica joined them, holding hands and smiling happily. "Don't let Craig try to talk you into a game of handball, Kate," Elliot warned her. "He's murder on the courts."

"I'll bear that in mind." Kate took another sip of her drink and studied Craig from beneath her long lashes. He had the blond good looks of a West Coast surfer and the body of one as well, she thought. She knew he was divorced and was considered very eligible. If she were seriously looking for a man, he might appeal to her. The problem was that she was not looking for a man. She was not yet ready to become involved with anyone else. And the truth was, she knew, that she had not given up the hope that she and Ian would be reconciled.

Jessica turned to Elliot and handed him her glass. "Hold this, darling, I'm going to powder my nose. Kate, do you want to come along?"

Kate trailed after her, smiling at people she knew as Jessica marched toward the women's room.

"Having a good time?" Jessica asked.

"Okay," Kate replied disinterestedly. "You and Elliot seem to be enjoying yourselves," she commented. She moved to the mirror and readjusted the flower in her hair. It was odd that her words to Jessica had sounded amost bitter; she hadn't meant them to. She knew Jessica and Elliot had been seeing more and more of each other and were getting along very well. Kate wasn't jealous; she was really very happy for them. "I'm sorry, Jessica, I didn't mean for that to sound bitchy."

Jessica put the top back on the tube of lipstick and rubbed her lips together. "I understand. When Elliot and I first got divorced, I think I hated every woman who looked happy with a man. I'd worry more about you if you didn't show any resentment."

Kate followed Jessica back to where Elliot and Craig stood by a window. They had been joined by three other people and the subject was the best restaurants in town.

"I can only judge a good French restaurant by how much the waiter condescends to me," Craig said with a smile. He moved a step closer to Kate. "The orchestra is playing. Shall we?" he said as he drew her away from the others and onto the edge of a cleared space in the center of the large room.

It was a slow dance. Around them couples moved in slow time to the sweet strains of the music. Craig drew Kate close against him and put his arm firmly around her waist. His chin brushed the top of her hair. "Your hair smells like lilacs," he whispered. "Nice."

"Thank you." Craig was an excellent dancer; she felt

almost as if she were floating with him. She was tempted to close her eyes and lean closer against him, but she did not allow herself to do so. It was a trap, she knew—a trap she was setting for herself. With her eyes closed she could pretend that this handsome man with the strong arms was Ian. He was not Ian, she reminded herself grimly. She must keep both eyes open and remain constantly aware of the fact she was with Craig. It wouldn't be fair to anyone for her to try to play tricks in her own mind and substitute Ian for Craig.

"Your boss didn't stay long," Craig commented.

"Burke was here?" Kate looked up at Craig and saw that he was regarding her steadily. His lips were only inches from hers and she could feel his breath on her cheek. She was strangely unmoved by the proximity of this attractive and virile man.

"Only for a short time. He talked with Foster Michaels and another man and then left."

"Oh." Foster Michaels was the president of Craig's bank, Kate knew. She wondered briefly if Burke had had a business discussion with Mr. Michaels and had left after he learned some disappointing news. Kate pushed those thoughts from her mind. She was doing it again, she chided herself. She was letting her imagination run wild when she didn't have any evidence to make evaluations. Just because Burke had talked with a banker didn't mean he was seeking financial assistance. "Burke isn't much of a partygoer," she noted to Craig. "He probably just came to put in an appearance."

"We've been hearing some rumors over at the bank that Amalacorp is financially troubled."

Kate felt a quiver of anxiety, but she responded lightly, "I can't comment on that, Craig, but I can say that paychecks have been coming through regularly and there have certainly been no cutbacks in employment." But Amalacorp had not been awarded the huge suspension bridge contract, and she knew that it had been a blow to lose it. Although no one in the company voiced any worries about Amalacorp's money situation, Kate

could sense an undercurrent of unease. Duane's face
had looked drawn of late, and Burke was in a perpetu-
ally short and unpleasant mood. Other things could
have caused both of those symptoms, Kate knew, but
she did not think they had. Whatever Amalacorp's
position, Kate was not going to express any doubt or
disloyalty to anyone on the outside, including her date.

"I've heard Burke has approached another large
engineering firm or two to discuss a merger," Craig
pursued.

"I don't know anything about that."

The music ended and they walked toward a window
that looked out onto the deep purple sky and the lights
of the other highrises. Kate was glad when they were
intercepted by another couple and engaged in conversation. She didn't care to answer Craig's question about
a merger. That was another rumor that had made its
way around the Amalacorp halls, but no one had ever
discussed it with her, and as far as she was concerned,
there was not yet any possibility of one.

She was yanked out of her reflections when a woman
in a full-skirted lime gown stopped beside her with a
smile. "Didn't I meet you in England?" the woman
asked with a smile. "Yes! Of course, you were visiting
Clariss at her house in Kent."

Kate smiled brightly although she didn't remember
the woman. But there had been so many people at the
party she could not have recalled all of them.

"I'm Augusta Ferber," the woman continued. "I
introduced you to Lady Davina. Kate, isn't it?"

"Yes." Kate only dimly remembered Lady Augusta,
but the other name the woman had spoken brought a
very clear image to mind. Lady Davina was the lovely
blonde Ian had once dated. Suddenly Kate wanted to
find out whatever she could about Ian and what he was
doing now. She glanced at Craig and saw he was talking
to two men beside her. "Tell me," Kate said, turning
back to Lady Augusta, "do you remember that handsome man Lady Davina used to date?"

"Lord Stymore?"

"No, this man was a chairman of some board," Kate continued with deliberate vagueness.

"Oh, you mean Ian Nigel."

Kate hoped her face didn't betray how intense her interest was. "Yes, I believe that was his name."

"They're seeing a bit of each other again, off and on, I understand," Lady Augusta supplied. "I don't know how serious they are. Everyone says Ian will never marry, so I daresay he is as serious about Lady Davina as he has ever been about any woman."

"No doubt," Kate murmured.

"If you will excuse me, I see someone else I know." With a smile, Lady Augusta disengaged herself and was soon lost in the crowd.

Kate looked up as Craig placed a glass of champagne in her hand. "Are you having a good time?"

She nodded with a smile; she did not trust herself to speak. So that was that. Ian was back with Lady Davina and she was here at a very classy party in Dallas. It had not taken Ian long to find another woman, Kate reflected as she took another sip of champagne to dull the gnawing pain inside her. Of late she had thought of calling him a time or two, but that seemed rather pointless now. Lady Davina was really a charming woman. Kate wondered if Ian were as happy with her as she had been with him.

Chapter 29

Even though it was the middle of May, Kate was packing wool slacks and heavy sweaters. She knew England would not be as warm as Dallas. Jessica picked up a hunter-green sweater from the bed and folded it. "Are you nervous?" she asked.

"A little." Kate had been trying not to think of the man she might see on the other side of the Atlantic. She had not seen Ian since December. In many ways she thought she was over him; she had not cried about him in the still privacy of her bedroom for over a month. But she still wasn't sure what the sight of him would do to her.

"Did you have a good time last night with Alex Dryer?" Jessica asked.

"So-so," Kate replied absently.

Jessica sighed. "Honestly, Kate, you've been out with some of the most elusive and eligible men in the city, and you act as if you're dating the dregs of mankind. Alex Dryer owns enough oil wells to keep your car running for a very long time."

"Maybe that was why his hands felt a little greasy," Kate quipped, and was immediately contrite. "I'm sorry, Jessica. I'm not making fun of him. Really, we had a wonderful time. We went to the opera and had a lovely dinner at the Venetian Room."

"I get the point. Alex was wonderful, his family is wonderful, his houseboy is wonderful, and you don't ever want to go out with him again."

Kate didn't answer. Instead, she walked to the closet and took out a dark plaid pleated skirt and navy blazer. "I've already packed two suits," she commented as she carried the clothes back to the bed. "I suppose three will be enough, since I'm only going to be there a week."

"I'm getting the impression that you don't want to talk about last night," Jessica capitulated. "All right. Let's talk about what you're going to do when you see Ian again."

Kate felt her pulse race faster at the thought, but her reply was deliberately nonchalant. "I'll act toward him like I would any man from my past; I'll be polite but distant."

Jessica rolled her eyes toward the ceiling. "He's *not* just a man from your past, Kate. You're still crazy about the guy, and you know it."

Kate looked up at her friend with a smile. "You've become a romantic, do you know that? I think I can trace the exact date it happened. It was about three days ago, when Elliot appeared at your apartment with that little jeweler's box, and the pair of you decided you were insane to live apart."

With a dreamy smile, Jessica looked down at the square-cut diamond on her finger. "Isn't it ridiculous for me to have an engagement ring and to plan a large reception just like I was getting married for the first time? My mother thinks I'm going off the deep end, although his parents are ecstatic."

"They should be," Kate said firmly. "They're getting a wonderful daughter-in-law."

"You're prejudiced," Jessica said amiably. "I just wish you could be as happy as I am. I wish the whole world could be!"

"Well, I have a date with Mark Stow next week, so who knows, maybe he and I will hit it off in a big way."

"Kate, when are you going to be honest with yourself? You aren't going to hit it off with any of these guys you're seeing. You're still in love with Ian. If you could just get over being so stubborn and consider what you're missing without him—" Jessica broke off with a rueful smile. "Listen to me. I have all the answers for someone else. It didn't come easy for me to recognize that I was being too unbending with Elliot."

Kate nodded agreement and continued packing. Even though she had admitted to herself that it was over between herself and Ian, that did not make the thought of seeing him again any the less nerve-racking. But she had no choice about going to England. The dam had been completed and an unseasonal rash of rains was already filling the reservoir. Frank had been there in March and Burke himself had gone in April. Now she knew she should go. After all, the foundation work on the project had been done under her direction. She should be there to ascertain there were no problems with it during initial filling. That was the most critical test of the design of the earth embankment.

"Okay, I get the hint, you don't want to talk about Ian," Jessica said. "Fine. Let's talk about Elliot. Have you noticed how handsome he looks when he's serious?"

"I've never seen him serious," Kate countered mildly.

"And his hair looks so terrific now that he's let it grow," Jessica continued enthusiastically. "I think he's the most attractive man in the world," she concluded happily.

"Mmmm," Kate murmured. "I wonder if I need to take a heavy coat, or if a thick cardigan sweater will be enough?" She had better take the coat, she decided.

She would have to keep herself warm; she would not have a man to do it for her like Jessica had in Elliot.

Kate checked into the inn and was given the same room she had occupied the last time she had been there. She changed from the plum-colored linen suit she had worn on the plane into a pair of brown velour jeans and a brown and white print blouse. On her way out the door, she stopped to look at herself in the mirror. The possibility of meeting Ian was remote, but not to be overlooked. She wanted to look her best when she did see him.

Her hair had been cut just last week and styled so it framed her face in loose curls. Small bangs swept back away from her face from a part in the middle. She looked different, and for some reason that new look gave her confidence. She knew she was not the same woman she had been last year when Ian had first met her. She did not look the same and she would not act the same with him.

She walked down the narrow stairs and outside, slipping into her rented car and tossing her briefcase onto the seat beside her. It was strange how everything looked so familiar, yet somehow different. She started the car and drove through the green Cotswold Valley to the dam site.

When she arrived at the cluster of buildings that housed Amalacorp's office and labs, she could see signs of bustling activity. Men were loading core boxes onto a truck. Inside the office, Doris looked up with a smile when Kate entered. "Hi, Kate. You just missed Stan. The mess and confusion were too much for him, so he went down to look at the embankment."

"I'm going to drive down there myself in a minute," Kate replied as she crossed to a window. Below her, where only a few months back she had seen dirt and earthmovers, there now stretched a majestic blue lake held back by a neat wall of dam. Kate could see carefully-tended green grass that made the whole downstream face of the dam look like an elongated football field tilted at an angle. Across the top of the dam was a two-lane strip of blacktop road. "It certainly looks different, doesn't it?" Kate commented, more to herself than to the secretary.

"It does," the other woman agreed. "And it's filling so fast! Already the water at the dam is over sixty-five feet deep." She stopped and regarded Kate with a worried expression. "It's not filling *too* fast, is it?"

Kate laughed. "No. We built this dam to hold water, and the more we have coming in the better. I'm going down to look at the toe. I'm not expecting any calls, but if there are any, I'll be back."

Kate got into a company pickup and started toward the downstream side of the embankment. She reached the end of the dam and made a sharp turn down a road marked, "Private, do not enter." The road descended sharply to the bottom of the dam and wound around along the bottom, providing a route for employees to use when monitoring the toe drains and piezometers and relief wells. Ahead of her, she saw Stan's truck; she pulled up beside it and got out.

"That's a beautiful lake you have up there," she greeted him cheerfully.

"Like it? For the right amount of money, I can build one just like it for you."

"I'm afraid I don't have fifty million dollars to sink into a dam, but thanks just the same. How is everything looking down here?" she asked, becoming serious.

"Good," he told her as he leaned back against his truck. "I've just checked the relief wells, and they all seem to be working."

"That's what we want to hear." She looked up. The height of the dam made her feel small and insignificant.

"We'll be moving to Spain now," Stan continued conversationally.

She smiled. "The job there is going to be interesting," she remarked. And badly needed, Kate knew. There had been a great many rumors circulating about how direly Amalacorp needed that job before the contract had been awarded. Now Kate could see a new confidence in Amalacorp's executives. Burke was strutting around like a rooster that wanted to crow.

"I've got to get back to the office and straighten out some of the things on my desk," Stan continued. "The movers are coming next week."

Kate watched Stan drive away before she began walking slowly toward the right abutment. Her feet sank a little now and then when she stepped on a particularly soggy area. Water seeping through the dam made the ground wet, Kate knew, but that caused her no concern. Water coming through the embankment was perfectly natural. In fact, the dam had been designed to accomodate it.

Kate stopped abruptly and looked at a stream of water flowing through the grass. The water was coming from just above the toe of the dam; it was not coming through the filter and going out the path that had been created for it. This was uncontrolled seepage. Kate knew it would have to be monitored carefully. Bending, she felt around in the wet grass until she touched the spot where the water seeped out from the ground. She let the water flow across her hand for a moment and then straightened, rubbing her fingers together carefully. She did not feel any silt or clay. It was evidently clear water. That was a relief.

At the project office she went directly to Stan's office. "Did you notice the area near this abutment where there is seepage coming out at more than five gallons per minute?" she asked.

He glanced up from his task of emptying the top drawer of his desk. "I noticed a little seepage," he replied, "but I don't think it was five gallons per minute."

"That was just an estimate, of course," she agreed. "But it was above the toe," she continued, "so it is uncontrolled. I think we need to have a weir put up to monitor the flow. Of course, this is a new dam and seepage paths are still developing, but we want to have a good handle on what's going on down there. It's possible we'll have to put more relief wells in around it."

"I'll send a man down now," Stan said.

Kate started to leave and then turned back to him. "This is probably a coincidence, but I think the water is coming out near where we drilled a couple of holes." She watched him closely as she continued, "They were the core holes whose rock samples were destroyed."

He looked blank. "I wouldn't think there would be a connection. We grouted those holes, you know."

She nodded. "Well, keep an eye on it. I've had a long flight and I just drove out for a brief look around. I'm going back to Chipping Down now. Let me know if there's any change in the amount of flow."

"Sure thing."

The seepage was nothing major, Kate thought as she left, and the worst that could happen was that they might have to put in more relief wells. Still, it was a source of irritation to her. If she did see Ian, she would like to tell him everything was absolutely perfect at the dam.

Kate drove back into the village, stopping in front of the inn. The ruddy-cheeked innkeeper greeted her with a smile and a folded piece of paper. "A man called," he explained.

Kate took the paper with a look of calm that belied the emotion she felt. It would be from Ian, she felt certain. She carried the note up to her room before she opened it. The message was from Ian, just as she had suspected, and the note was brief. "I want to see you," it read. "Please call me." That was all, except for the number where he could be reached.

She sat down on the bed and folded the paper neatly. Ian might want to see her about the dam, she warned herself sternly. She brushed that thought aside. He *might* want to talk about them. Kate unfolded the note and read it again. Finally she was going to see Ian again. After nearly six months of silence they would be face to face and would talk, even if they only exchanged the most mundane commonplaces.

She felt nervous. She wanted to see Ian, and yet she was afraid. What if he felt nothing for her now? What if he spoke to her only in clipped, business tones? That would destroy a little island of hope she had preserved so carefully. Now she was coming to the moment of truth. She would know if she had deceived herself by keeping even the smallest flame of hope alive. Suddenly she wasn't sure she wanted to know the answer to that question.

Chapter 30

It took Kate half an hour before she felt calm and in control enough to call Ian. His voice on the phone was brisk and efficient. "I'm at my cottage. Is it agreeable with you if I come to the inn to discuss a few matters with you?"

"Fine." She was gripping the phone so tightly her knuckles were turning white.

"I'll see you then," he replied.

Kate put the receiver down slowly. She felt a stab of regret; Ian certainly had not sounded anxious to be reunited with her. Not that she had expected him to, but somehow she had hoped—Kate did not allow herself to finish that thought.

She showered quickly and changed into a gray jersey dress with a scooped neck and a little white jacket that matched the wide white belt at her waist. She ran a brush through her hair and put the brush on the dresser. She was nervous and rapidly becoming more so. She, a woman who spoke in front of large groups without a quaver in her voice, a woman who had to face irate executives, needling contractors and insistent staff members, and who did so coolly, was coming completely unraveled at the knowledge that she would soon be with Ian again. She was not made any more comfortable by the way he had spoken on the phone.

By the time Ian arrived in front of the inn, Kate had recovered some of her poise. It was lucky that she had. Otherwise, the first sight of him as he stepped out of his car would have reduced her to anxiety. As she watched him from her window, she experienced a pang in her chest. He looked older, with deep lines under his eyes and a careworn look on his face. No boyish enthusiasm showed in his step as he walked toward the inn. She drew a deep breath to steel herself and walked down to meet him.

Kate stopped at the bottom of the stairs and he halted halfway across the stone entryway. Both of them looked at each other a moment in silence.

Ian spoke first. "Hello, Kate."

His voice was cold. More so than she had anticipated. "Hello," she said stiffly. She would not tell him he looked well; he didn't. Besides, he had not said as much to her. But it was obvious he didn't think she looked well either. She had caught the brief look of surprise that had registered in his eyes before they had become carefully gray and blank again.

"I don't think there is anyone in the parlor if you'd like to use it," Kate said, leading the way as she spoke.

Inside the oak-paneled room she sat in a chintz-covered armchair while he paced to the fireplace. He studied the coat of arms emblazoned on the stone. "I suppose you've been to the dam," he began.

"Yes," She rested one hand atop the other to keep them from fidgeting.

"I was there yesterday," he continued.

"I see." She waited for him to speak again. She didn't really think the dam was what was uppermost in his mind, but she could not say for sure. This new Ian, so distant and cool, was hard to read. Perhaps it was easier for Kate that he was maintaining such an aloof attitude. It certainly kept her from melting from the sheer force of being near him.

"I had thought you would call me," he said, turning to look at her directly.

"I told you I wouldn't," she responded. She met his eyes in an unwavering look. Oh, how she had longed to call him, but stubborn pride had prevented her.

"Yes, I suppose you did," he said vaguely, and looked back at the fireplace.

Kate noticed with concern that he didn't stand as straight as he had when she had seen him last. Something about the way he held himself in rigid control made her want to run across the room and throw her arms around him.

"I've missed you, Kate." He spoke the words just above a whisper. Suddenly he whirled and faced her again. "I don't know why I'm saying these things. It isn't at all what I intended to talk to you about."

"What did you want to say?" she asked, and held her breath waiting for him to reply.

"I came to discuss the dam, of course." For the first time Ian gave something that resembled a smile. "All right, the dam was an excuse; I think I just wanted to see you again, if that makes any sense at all."

It made a great deal of sense to Kate, but she said nothing. What was there to say? She and Ian were two people who obviously still had a great attraction for each other; they were both fighting that feeling as hard as they could. Kate knew he had not changed his mind since Christmas, and she had not changed hers either. It seemed they were both waiting for the circumstances around them to alter and resolve their problems.

"You got your hair cut," Ian remarked, looking at her with an expression that softened the hard lines of his face.

"Do you like it?"

"It makes you look different," was his reply.

"I felt I was ready for a change." Kate paused and looked at the floor. This was a ridiculously stilted conversation for two people who had been lovers. Still, what did she say to a man she had been intimate with? The subject of how close they had once been was, of course, taboo, and so was any discussion of what the future might hold. That left only the banalities of the present—the weather, the crops and her hair.

"Is everything going well for you in Dallas?" Ian asked.

"Perfect."

"I daresay you are busy all the time."

"Yes, I keep quite active." Kate was certain Ian was not referring to work. She did date a lot, even though she rarely went out with the same man more than a time or two. She had heard he wasn't doing so badly himself. She had seen pictures of him in Jennifer's column of *Harper's and Queen* showing him at some of the more trendy parties in and around London.

"That's good." His words were stilted and he started for the door abruptly. "I guess I'll be seeing you at the dam tomorrow, so I won't keep you any longer now."

Kate walked to the door with him. For a moment, when he turned and took her hand, she was certain he was going to draw her into an embrace. Then he checked himself and shook her hand formally before walking out of the inn and back to his car. Kate watched him go with tears welling up in her eyes. She knew the moment had been as emotional for him as it had for her, but that didn't change the fact that he was leaving. Nothing had altered between them. She blinked back tears and returned to her room.

Now she had more things to sort out—more inflections in his voice to weigh and to try to determine if there were an underlying meaning to his words or his tone. Did he still love her? And if he did, could they overcome the difficulties that separated them? She was forced to concede that it did not look likely. Although he had admitted he had missed her, he had left without a tender word to her.

Kate was at the dam early the next morning. As she walked along the toe on the downstream side, her thoughts were more concentrated on Ian than they were on the huge bank of soil beside her that held back a wall of water 70 feet deep and almost a mile long. She was barely conscious of anything about the dam until she reached the little wooden weir that she had ordered constructed. Where she had noticed the uncontrolled seepage, a piece of galvanized aluminum had been inserted into the V section to give a knife-edge to the weir. She stopped and stared at the weir, all thought of Ian gone for the moment.

Water was flowing rapidly over the small wooden weir at double the flow it had been yesterday. But what alarmed her was that the water was a muddy brown color, indicating material from the dam itself was being eroded from the interior and washed away.

Kate walked back to her truck and drove directly up the hill to the office. Stan was just unlocking the door. "I think you had better come down here right away," she said tersely.

"What's wrong?"

"The flow at the weir has doubled, and the water is carrying fines out with it."

Stan gave her a startled look. "One of the men set the weir up last night and he stayed to monitor it a while. He didn't report any material coming through the dam then." Stan stepped into the building and turned to her. He was clearly disconcerted.

"Maybe it wasn't then, but it is definitely carrying suspended matter now," Kate replied. "We'll have to do something about it."

"There's always the possibility of a concrete diaphragm wall."

She shook her head. "It takes too long to build one. The one they put in at Wolf Creek took two years of tedious and sophisticated drilling. We may not have that long to correct the problem." She walked to the window and looked out on the dam below. "Tell me something, Stan. Do you think the water is piping through cavities in the limestone? After all, it's coming out below an area where we did some additional foundation work and further drilling."

"I don't know," he said wearily. "It's possible we didn't get enough grout in to fill all the cavities."

Kate threw diplomacy to the winds and voiced her fears. "Is it possible the grout reports weren't accurate? Do they really reflect how much grout was put into the holes?" She was under a strain and her impatience was showing. "For godsake, Stan, what I'm asking is did Amalacorp falsify information about those core holes to avoid further drilling and grouting?"

"Let's not get carried away!" he snapped. "First we need to correct what's wrong. Then we can go back and point fingers."

"All right," she replied rationally. Stan was right. The thing to do now was to solve their immediate problem. "The only possible thing I can see is to put a sand and gravel filter over where the water is coming out. That would stop the flow of fines and prevent us from losing any more of the embankment than what is already gone. But we'll need sand and gravel."

"We can call a truck and it should be here by this afternoon."

"Okay. I'm going back down to the weir. Tell the man it's an emergency, and ask him if it can possibly be delivered any sooner than this afternoon. Another thing, I think we should open the tainter gates and release all the water we can."

The sense of unease that had been born yesterday when Kate had seen the uncontrolled seepage flowing from the dam had intensified this morning when she had realized the water had turned from clear to brown. Now she felt a growing knot in her stomach as she absorbed the full implications of the situation. Perhaps the seepage was not a minor problem which could be corrected with a filter. It was possible there had already been major damage done beneath the dam, and that would require costly repairs.

Stan's voice broke into her unpleasant thoughts as he hung up the phone. "I've called for filter material. Let's go down to the weir and see what's happening there. It's possible it could have plugged itself closed with sediment."

"Let's hope so." She followed him out the door and drove down after him, parking beside his truck as they both walked toward the seepage area. The folding ruler that had been set up behind the weir to gauge the flow had water rushing swiftly past it. Kate read a mark on it and calculated rapidly. "That's thirty-five gallons per minute." And the water was undeniably a crusty-looking brown. Both she and Stan bent to feel the material in the water. It was a grit that left a filmy residue on her hands.

She stood quickly. "I hope a filter will solve our problems."

"Ought to," Stan replied confidently. "The sand will keep the fines from piping out and the gravel will hold the sand down. Never seen one fail."

She nodded. "I'm going to walk along the toe and see if water is coming out anywhere else."

It was an hour and a half later before Kate arrived back at the project office. "I didn't find any other seepage areas," she told Stan as she walked back into his office.

He was standing by the window looking out. There was something about his look that sent a shiver of fear through her even before she turned to look out the window. What she saw below her intensified that feeling a thousand times. In the center of the lake a huge whirlpool was spinning to a vortex. "Oh, my God!" she whispered. The water was funneling downward—draining, she knew, either beneath the lake or through the dam.

"I've been with this company seventeen years," Stan said dully. His words were formed with obvious difficulty, as if he were in a state of shock.

Kate stared for another moment, held immobile by the awesome sight before her. Then she swept into action. "We've got to get some dozers out there to try to release some of the water before the whole dam goes. If we can get enough pressure off the embankment, maybe we can drain it slowly and it won't fail."

Stan had also come out of the grip of paralyzing fear. "There are still some large dozers on the site. I'll get a couple of DC8's or a 9 with a ripper down there immediately." He picked up the phone.

Kate walked into the outer office. Doris had taken the day off, so Kate sat down at her desk. Her hands were trembling so much that it was difficult for her to pick up the phone. But she bit her teeth hard against her bottom lip, and put a call through to Dallas.

Burke Walters' secretary came on the line. "This is Kate Justin, I need to speak to Mr. Walters immediately."

"I'm sorry, he's in a meeting right now."

Kate's mind went blank for a moment and she could not think what to say. "In his office?" she finally mumbled.

"Well, yes—"

"Then get him out," she said in a stronger voice.

"He specifically asked not to be disturbed," the secretary said calmly.

Kate exploded. "I'm disturbing him! Now get him!"

"One moment, please." Burke came on the line a minute later.

"What is it?" he asked gruffly.

Her mind was becoming clearer now. She spoke in concise sentences. "We are having a severe problem at the dam. The decision has been made to breach it."

"Who the hell decided that?" he thundered.

"I did."

"You just undecide it. We don't build dams so we can go back and tear them down."

Her temper was rising, but she forced herself to say smoothly, "Any damage we do to the dam by breaching it will be very small and certainly easily repaired. If there is a complete failure, the damage will not be so small, and it will be a great deal more costly to rebuild."

She could hear him draw in a sharp breath. "Hold the line," he grated. Then, without covering the mouthpiece, he barked, "The meeting is over. You men wait outside. I'll call you when I'm through with this." Kate heard papers begin to rustle. "Leave them!" A moment later there was a shuffling of feet and then the door closed.

"All right, let's have it slow and clear now. What is the problem?"

She swallowed. "Water is seeping at an ever-increasing rate in an uncontrolled area above the toe. It is brown and contains silt and clay. A short time ago we spotted a vortex forming in the middle of the lake. It's draining itself, possibly through the dam. At any time there is a possibility of complete failure. In addition to breaching it, we are going to have to notify the authorities downstream of the lake that evacuation should be considered."

"You listen to me," he said in a voice of steel. "If you have to alert authorities, then do it with a minimum of information and don't talk to any damn newspeople. Give them the name of Denham or the subcontractor. Keep Amalacorp's name out of this!"

"I scarcely think that will be possible," Kate responded impatiently. They were talking about a potential disaster—what difference did it make if their name was known? Amalacorp was responsible.

"I'm not paying you to *think*. I'm paying you to do what I say. Just smile pretty for the camera and pat everyone's hand, but don't give them any concrete information and don't you *dare* mention the missing cores!"

Burke hung up without another word, leaving Kate staring down at the phone with a growing sense of horror. It had all been true. Amalacorp had built a dam with major foundation flaws—had done so willfully and as part of a deliberate cover-up.

Chapter 31

Kate felt as if she were watching a movie as she stood at the office window and watched the dozers working on the dam. First they had dug down about 55 feet on the downstream slope to control the erosion. Then they had moved up to the top of the dam and begun digging a trench, ripping through the blacktop road and down toward the water level.

Kate was so intent on watching the work that she didn't even notice when someone came to stand beside her.

"I don't know exactly what's going on, but I know it's bad," Ian said in a tightly-controlled voice.

She turned to face him reluctantly. "There's a stability problem with the dam, so we're breaching it. Right now we're trying to get the level of the lake down as quickly as we can. The outlet works alone wouldn't release water fast enough."

"There's nothing that can be done to correct the problem except this?" he demanded.

She shook her head. "No. For a while we thought we

could put a filter on the problem area, but it's too late for that. Even if it weren't dangerous to go downstream of the dam, it would be like putting a band-aid on a severe headwound."

They both glanced up as a helicopter flew by. It was probably another group of newscasters. News of the possibility of the dam collapsing had been on the radio and television, and people downstream had been directed to evacuate their homes.

She continued calmly, to reassure herself as well as him. "There are no houses between here and the confluence with a much larger stream. If we can draw the lake level down—say, to a head of forty feet—even if the dam failed the valley would be flooded below us, but once the water reached the larger stream it could probably be contained within the banks or with a minimum of flooding. Certainly there would be little property loss." That was one of the more optimistic things that could happen, but Kate did not stress that to Ian. He looked as if he were already operating under enough strain.

"Why are the men jumping off the dozers?" he asked in alarm.

"It's all right," she said. "They've reached the water level. They can't get the dozers out, but they'll be safe. See, the water is going through the trench they created. It will erode downward at a slow enough rate that it won't cause any great pressure on the dam or take any large sections of the embankment with it." She recalled pictures she had seen in a magazine of a man jumping off a dozer before Teton dam had failed. The idea of the embankment actually giving way and a 50-foot wall of water rushing out made Kate feel slightly nauseated.

"Have you ever seen a dam fail?" Ian's voice was edged with steel.

"No." She looked up in surprise as her hand was taken in a warm clasp.

"You look pale as death, you'd better sit down," Ian said. There was concern in his voice.

She nodded dumbly and allowed him to lead her to a chair in the outer office. He left and returned a moment later with a cup of coffee. "Drink this," he commanded.

"I really don't think I can," she murmured.

He pushed the cup more firmly into her hands. "Oh yes you can." His voice indicated he would brook no arguments.

She obediently took a sip. For a wild moment Kate had to control the impulse to laugh hysterically. What difference did it make if she were pale? Her own health seemed terribly insignificant when she considered there was a dam outside containing 44,000 acre-feet of water that could go completely out of everyone's control at any moment.

"I guess Stan is still out directing the men," he said wearily.

She nodded. They settled into a silence that lasted for over an hour. Occasionally one or the other would walk to the window and look out. The whirlpool still raged, its area increased from what it had been when Kate had first seen it.

She finally finished the cold dregs of the coffee and cleared her throat. She would have to tell Ian what she knew about the dam. Bravely, she began, "I talked to Burke earlier to tell him we were going to breach the dam."

He turned from the window and regarded her in cold silence, waiting for her to continue.

"You may as well know I'm sure there was a plot concerning the dam." She lowered her lashes and continued, "I don't think when the bid for the dam was let Amalacorp had any intention of conspiring to build an incompetent dam, but money problems got worse and worse and—" She broke off and rose. "I guess motives aren't important, are they? Amalacorp willfully and deliberately concealed the fact that the foundation needed a lot more work before an embankment should ever have been placed. They gambled, Ian."

She looked at his hard face and concluded, "They hoped the foundation would be capable of supporting the dam without additional work."

"Why are you telling me this?"

She shrugged weakly. "Even if the dam doesn't fail, you'd have to know that a lot more work would be needed before water could ever be impounded behind it again. Besides," her voice dropped to almost a whisper, "I want you to know that I had no idea about this conspiracy. I'm telling you in case the worst happens and the dam fails. You probably wouldn't ever want to have anything to do with an Amalacorp employee again."

He nodded curtly and looked back out the window. Kate watched him in dejection. Did he believe she had not been a party to the cover-up? It was true she had once talked to him about her suspicions, but there had been a six-month silence between herself and Ian since then. He was not likely to be charitable in his thoughts about her. Kate felt despair wash through her; she had lost him.

All the love she felt for him would surely account for very little if the dam collapsed. It was a structure she had been indirectly in charge of, and one Ian Nigel's corporation had spent millions of dollars to build. The fact men were working desperately to save it would mean nothing if it failed. That would be the final rift that divided Ian from her. Kate felt anguish rush through her, and she put a clenched fist to her mouth to stifle a sob. Ian did not hear, or if he heard he did not care, for he did not turn from his position at the window.

Kate sat morosely, staring at her hands. Well, she thought with self-recrimination, she had done exactly what she had set out to do. She had put her professional life ahead of all other considerations, and where had it gotten her? Company officials had lied to her and put her in the impossible position of being in charge of a dam about which she did not have all the information.

What was more, she would not even have her job much longer; she would surely be fired.

At that thought another idea occurred to her. When she had heard Frank and Duane and Burke talk about firing her, it had been in connection with the dam. She suddenly realized they had not been disappointed in her work, but worried she would discover the truth. Kate straightened in the chair as she recalled that she had also wondered why she had been sent to reassure Ian that the dam was competent. At the time she had wondered at Frank's motives, but Frank was not the head of Amalacorp. Of course! Burke must have known that Ian had a personal interest in her and hoped she could use her feminine charms to divert him from probing too deeply. She grimaced as she realized what a willing dupe she had been. She had been so anxious to believe the best of her company, she thought bitterly.

She lifted her eyes to look at Ian; he was still standing with his back to her. What would he think of her if the dam failed? She accepted with despair the fact that losing the dam would simply be one more nail in her coffin. She had lost on all counts—the man she loved, her job and her professional integrity. Her only chance for redeeming herself to Ian was to pray that the dam didn't give way. If she could talk to him after this was all over, perhaps she could convince him that she had been a fool to leave him and that she was willing to take any compromise. With a wry smile, she realized that it would look to Ian as if she were willing to concede because she had nothing left to lose.

"Come here!" he snapped.

Kate stood quickly and rushed to the window. A large sink hole was developing on the downstream slope of the dam. She gasped and Ian looked at her.

"What does it mean?"

"The material beneath it has been eroded away, it's falling into a huge cavity below." Kate's eyes moved from the sink to the water level. How high was it now?

Was it low enough that the downstream tributary could handle the volume? She hoped so, because she knew with dreadful certainty that the dam was perilously close to collapse.

"Oh, no!" Ian whispered thickly.

Kate stared in disbelief at the spectacle unfolding before her. The abutment where the seepage had been discovered was being devoured, and tons of sand and gravel were tumbling downward as water roared out of the reservoir and jetted in thunderheads of spray into the valley below.

"It really failed," she murmured as she watched the billion-pound wall of water tumble out into the valley, knocking off trees in its path as if they were toothpicks.

Kate continued to gaze outward in dry-mouthed anguish. This manmade structure, which had been so carefully designed to hold back the force of the water, had been knocked aside by a ferocious liquid torrent. Where once there had stood a dam a mile long, there was now only a lashing, foaming sea rushing headlong through the valley, intent on reaching the ocean.

Ian's face was ashen. He did not speak at all as he turned and walked out of the office. Kate watched him go with a heavy heart. It was not the overwhelming knowledge that the dam had failed which left her so utterly bereft; it was the realization that she had lost Ian forever.

Kate was up late that evening. She had heard the final reports about the dam failure. No lives had been lost and very little damage had been done—not counting the dam, of course. The large stream below the dam had been able to contain the flow with a minimum of spilling outside its banks. Only the scarred valley below the dam had known the full ravages of the water. It would take a while to heal and for trees to grow in it again. But that was small, indeed, compared to what could have happened if the dam had not been breached and water released from it before the failure.

Kate paced restlessly around her room. She had talked to Burke and told him of the catastrophe. Then she had told him tersely that she was resigning; she had been surprised when he had protested, but she had stood firm. Knowing what she now knew about Amalacorp, it would have been impossible for her to have continued to work for them.

She had enough money saved so that she did not need to find another job immediately; she would go back to Ohio until the furor over the dam died down. After that she didn't know what she would do, and she was too dejected to try to sort that out now.

Kate glanced up listlessly when the telephone rang, but she did not answer it. She knew it would be another reporter, and she had no more stories to give.

Wearily, she stretched out on the bed. She would not sleep, she told herself, she was far too nervous for that. She closed her eyes and thought of Ian. If she had had everything to do over again with him, would she have done it differently? No, she decided with the calm clarity born of fatigue. She could not have given Ian what he wanted. She could not have given up her life to accommodate him. But, oh, how she wished that decision had never had to be made! Why couldn't she and Ian had been in the same city to start with? Her thoughts blurred together as she felt herself slipping away into the refuge of sleep.

It was deep in the night when she stirred. Her hand touched the pillow and then rested against her other hand. It was odd, she thought sleepily, that she could not feel one hand on the other. Then she realized that the bottom hand was not hers. It had the firm, sinewy feel of Ian's skin. No, impossible. But then an arm came around her and banished the night air.

Kate sat up straight in bed, instantly awake. "Ian?"

"Yes," he said softly. "I didn't mean to frighten you. Lie down again." He pulled her back into his arms.

"But—I don't understand. What are you doing here?"

"I had to come." She could hear a lazy humor in his voice. "You weren't answering your phone, and you were so sound asleep that you didn't hear me knocking at the door." Apologetically, he added, "I borrowed a key from the innkeeper while he wasn't looking. Are you mad?"

"No," she said tentatively. She wished she could study his face. Suddenly she was conscious that her clothes had been removed and she was lying in her undergarments. Ian must have done that while she was sleeping.

He brushed a hand through her hair. "There's going to be a lawsuit, of course, you realize."

"Yes."

"I won't have any trouble proving fraud," he continued.

"I know," she assented. She felt confused. Ian was lying in her bed, but he was talking business. Perhaps this was just a dream after all; her mind was becoming hazy and she forced herself into wakefulness.

"I've resigned from Amalacorp," she told him. "I'm ashamed to have been associated with anything so dishonest."

"Oh, Kate," he said softly. "I never doubted your innocence, believe me." He paused, and then continued, "Kate, I know this isn't the time to discuss us with everything else going on, but it's very important to me. When I left you in December, I was determined I wasn't going to marry anyone." He laughed shortly. "I sound pompous just talking about it, especially because of the way I've felt since then. On any one of those sleepless and lonely nights, I would have given my right arm to have had you beside me."

"You never called," she breathed.

"No, I didn't," he said slowly. "It didn't seem like something we could discuss over the phone. I did go to Dallas once to see you, but you were out of town. After that I decided to wait until you came to England. The truth was, Kate—" he paused and then continued slowly, "I was scared. As more time passed, I decided you were no longer interested in me. And when I came to the inn yesterday, you seemed so aloof I was convinced you no longer cared."

"I was frightened about seeing you," Kate replied quickly.

He stroked a hand gently back and forth across her cheek. "I want to marry you, Kate. I won't ask you to move to England; I'll move to the States, wherever you decide to relocate. I'll allocate the management of some of the business here and handle the rest of it from an office in America."

"Oh, Ian," she murmured, choked with emotion. They were the words she had waited so long to hear. He wanted to marry her! And he was willing to arrange his whole life around hers; she knew how much that concession had cost him. Tears spilled forth and washed down her cheeks.

"What's wrong?" he asked quickly. His arms tightened around her.

"You don't have to do all that."

"It's all right," he assured her. "You're more important to me than anything in the world."

Her voice was husky when she said, "I thought when the dam failed that you would never want to see me again."

"I don't care if the world comes to an end," he said emphatically. "I'll always want you. We'll be married by special license. No," he contradicted himself, "we'll go to Ohio, that way your mother and grandmother can be there."

She wrapped her arms around his neck. "If that was a proposal, I accept. By the way," she added with a light kiss on his lips, "I'm sure I can get a good engineering position in London. I appreciate your sacrifice, but it isn't necessary. Besides, I like England. Really."

"I'll try to be a good husband," he told her solemnly.

"I don't mind telling you that it still scares me to contemplate marriage, but it scares me a hell of a lot more to think of living without you."

"It's okay. We'll have some problems, but I know we can resolve them." Her fingers moved lightly over the back of his neck. "By the way, did you take my clothes off?" she asked provocatively.

"Yes, why?" he countered.

"Then I think you'd better finish what you started," she whispered as their lips joined.